Affliction

ACCRUE'S END : BOOK ONE

AFFLICTION

E.R. SMO

Dark Tempest Press, LLC.

Copyright © 2023 by E.R.Smo

All rights reserved

ISBN: 979-8-9871898-0-1

This is a work of fiction. Any resemblance to actual

persons, living or dead, businesses,

or events are entirely coincidental.

Cover by J Caleb Design

Instagram: @jcalebdesign

To Ann and Leah,

I wouldn't have gotten this far without you.

Chapter 1

A secret of considerable power lay hidden nearby, and Kyo intended to find it. The details escaped him—vague mentions overheard outside the chancellor's office was all he had to go on. But it was enough for Kyo to wake up and leave the house before the sun peeked over the horizon. A handful of mornings within the past several weeks had been spent searching various and often restricted locations around town with nothing to show for it.

Hopefully today would be different.

The excitement didn't prevent him from yawning for the fifth time in ten minutes but losing sleep hardly mattered. A light breeze brought the scent of the island's salty sea air as he trudged the dirt trail to his destination, stopping to overlook his home from above. Mist covered much of the town, hiding the streets and lower levels of the mostly two-story buildings. Beyond Mistwell, the moon reflected in the calm ocean waters. Despite the chill air, he removed his gray hoodie and tied the sleeves around his waist, continuing along the path before venturing into the trees.

If Kyo found what he sought, it could help him protect those who couldn't protect themselves—help him be like his parents. Why would the chancellor hide something supposedly useful instead of using it to begin with? Probably some old geezer mentality of it's too dangerous.' Kyo may have been too young to join the town's enforcers or the fabled Aurora who protected the world without regional borders, but maybe they'd make an exception if what he found was as helpful as he hoped.

Pushing tree branches aside, he arrived at a large well wide enough for multiple adults to lounge in. Surrounding the white stone well was a rope, a mere suggestion to keep away.

"Oh no, a rope. I guess I'd better turn around," Kyo muttered as he disrobed down to his undershorts, hanging his clothes on the nearest branch.

He stepped over the rope and placed his hands on the well, peering into the clear water.

A red crystal coin sat upon a brick jutting out further from the rest. The idea of giving offerings to the pantheon had never sat well with him. Regardless of how they felt about humanity, they could only enter the human world when called by a summoner. While the Altruists aided and protected the summoner, a Relinquished — like the one this well had been built for — usually went on a rampage destroying everything in its path. A few coins or other valuables tossed into a well wouldn't change that. Stupid.

Kyo dipped his head beneath the water, seeing nothing but mossy stone. He pulled back and ran his fingers through his silver hair to keep the water out of his face. "Time for a swim."

Covering his mouth with his right hand, he pulled on the magical energy within himself, dragging it down his arm and to his palm. The energy emerged as air that circulated over his mouth as he dunked his head back into the water. A bubble formed over his lips then spread to cover his entire head.

AFFLICTION

The air inside wouldn't last long, but he was hardly going deep-sea diving.

Allowing the rest of his body to sink into the water, he floated unmoving, save for the shiver that ran through him from head to toe. If he wasn't fully awake before, the icy chill of the water certainly did it. He swam down, already noting the well ran deeper than expected. As he descended, he rotated his body to get a clear look at his surroundings, hoping to notice something unusual. So far, nothing but the walls of the well.

He placed his hands on the walls and pushed himself down faster. When his feet hit the ground, he looked around and noticed a tunnel more than wide enough to swim through. Did this well travel all the way through town and to the ocean? A grin crept upon his lips, delighted at the idea of finding a hidden passage of sorts. And if something were to be hidden, this seemed a likely place. An image of him fighting off some powerful mage or striking down a dragon flashed in his mind, and his grin grew to a wide smile.

Kyo used the naturally rocky walls to push himself along, looking above, below, yet found nothing of interest. For the first time since deciding to come down here, he considered it might take more than one trip to find what he wanted. Several minutes passed with no luck, his only discoveries being the tunnel and a few varieties of underwater flora. At least the glowing fungi growing on the walls helped in his search.

Stifling a curse, he turned around, swimming toward the wall and upward before air ran out.

When he surfaced, he wiped his hand across his mouth, removing the spell and inhaling fresh air that didn't reek of morning breath. He wrung water from his short, low ponytail which rested along his upper back, and slicked the front of his hair back and out of his face.

"Enjoy your swim?"

Kyo looked up to find a young man and woman staring down at him. They wore the hooded robes of Mistwell's enforcers. Light blue with white trim, each had an emblem on their breast of a mist covering part of a house.

Of all people, it had to be these two — the twins, Ruby and Ren. With their raven-black hair and similar facial features, most notably their aquiline noses, no one could confuse them for anything but siblings. They were constantly a thorn in his side and liked to keep an annoyingly close eye on him.

"Want to join me? The water's a bit chilly, but it's nice," Kyo said with a smirk, resting his arms on the edge of the well.

"Counteroffer." Ren squinted, a smirk on his lips and pointing up, a glowing golden ring of magical energy circling around his finger. "Come with us without a fuss, and we won't have to bind you like last time."

Kyo's lips tightened. He'd gotten into a harmless little scuffle with another boy a couple months back. Ren and Ruby had thought it appropriate — and funny — to bind his wrist and ankles, carrying him off like a hog ready for roasting. Even if it was too early for anyone to see it, he'd rather not let it happen again.

"You drive a hard bargain." Sighing, Kyo pushed himself from the well.

Palms facing down, he pulled out his magic again, air blasting up from around his feet for several seconds, long enough to get his skin mostly dry.

After putting his clothes back on, he followed Ren down the trail with Ruby walking at his side. Along the way, she stumbled a few times and nearly faceplanted on one occasion. Kyo stifled a chuckle. Even though he'd been caught, he could at least feel pleased that they'd had to mess up their sleep schedule to make it happen.

As they escorted him through the streets, the only souls they passed were the early risers: a woman spraying water from her fingertips onto the flowers in her garden, a man he recognized as the owner of a nearby restaurant on his way to open for the day. Kyo was doubly glad they didn't hogtie him.

They turned a corner, and Ruby stumbled into him.

"Come on," Kyo said. "If you can't even walk, go take a nap or something."

Ren slowed, reaching for his sister's hand. "Are you all right?"

Clenching her eyes and exhaling heavily, Ruby said nothing but motioned for him to keep going.

Kyo eyed her for a few lingering seconds. Even he, who had a habit of sleeping in, didn't fare that badly from waking up well before the sun. A mere nap might not cut it for her.

Making a right turn at the next intersection, he realized they weren't leading him to the enforcer's station but the chancellor's office, a three-story building with a large wooden carving of the town's symbol on the roof. And who should be standing outside the main doors but Chancellor Demaskus himself, leader of Mistwell and its world representative.

"Good morning, everyone," the elderly man said, stroking the long white beard that reached down to his navel. As many aging spots as wrinkles covered his face, and the bald spot on his head surrounded by gray hair couldn't be missed. A bit of his red sleeping top peeked out from behind his light blue robes. His focus turned to Kyo. "Enjoy your morning, dear boy?"

"Hey, old man Chancellor. Even you're up early, huh?" Kyo asked.

Ren slapped the back of Kyo's head. "Show him some respect, will you?"

Kyo narrowed his eyes at Ren then turned to the chancellor. "Do we really need to do this? I get it, the well is important to *some* people. They want to look good for Aquarivus despite it being a Relinquished. But swimming in it isn't exactly a crime, right? So technically, I didn't do anything to warrant" — he motioned to the three standing around him — "this."

"Mm, your words aren't without merit. However, sneaking around the roof of my office and eavesdropping on private conversations may very well be a crime." The chancellor narrowed his eyes and grinned. "Don't you think?"

Kyo glanced away. He couldn't argue with that. It could probably be considered espionage on a technical level.

"Mischief like that is one trait of your parents you shouldn't aspire to." Taking a few steps forward, the chancellor gently placed a hand on Kyo's head. "Allow me to guess. You believe there to be something down there that could give you power closer to what they had, correct?"

Kyo crossed his arms over his chest. "I won't apologize for trying to be like them. They were heroes."

It didn't matter that they'd left home for weeks or more at a time. Whenever they'd left, he'd run around his house pretending to be them, thwarting monsters and evil mages, saving the world. He may have been a kid back then, but his opinion of them never changed.

"Oh, indeed they were," the chancellor said. "I won't dispute this. But I wonder, would you truly be satisfied being like them, only because you rely on borrowed power?"

Borrowed power. Even if he'd found whatever lay hidden in the well, could using it be considered cheating? It might not be fair to compare himself to his parents when it wasn't his own magic he'd built up and used to protect others. Still, the realization did little to calm his curiosity about what the chancellor was hiding there.

"Please think on that, will you? Also, do not bother to try it again. Assuming there was something in that well, at this point, it would only make sense to move it elsewhere." Turning with his hands resting against his lower back, the chancellor strolled toward the doors to his office. "And I will not tolerate finding you on my roof again. Consider this your one and only warning. Ruby, Ren, thank you for your assistance. You are free to continue your patrols."

"Actually, sir," Ruby said, her voice wavering. "If I may, I would like to request time to rest today. I don't feel ill, just… I don't know how to explain it."

The chancellor turned to look at her. "Oh? This is unlike you. Very well. Go rest and do what you must to recover."

"Thank you, sir." She wandered off, Ren's focus entirely on her.

"So, I guess I'll just head home then." Kyo took several steps backward then yelped as his hair was yanked.

"Yeah, you're not getting off that easily."

Kyo winced, turning to find his godfather with his arms crossed over his chest. His spiked, bright red hair reflected the anger on his face.

"Hey, Alden," Kyo said. "Um…good morning. Did you sleep okay? Want to get breakfast?"

"Yeah, we'll get breakfast. Then you can spend the day helping me with my work. I have a few enchantment jobs lined up." Alden guided him by the back of his head, maintaining a tight grip. "And we'll talk about what you tried to pull today."

Great, a whole day being his little helper.

While giving unusual properties to inanimate objects was interesting, Alden didn't need an assistant.

'Helping' meant keeping Kyo where he could see him and giving lectures at every opportunity.

As the day dragged on, Kyo followed Alden around town, performing various jobs, including enchanting a young girl's toy crown to produce snowflakes that would gently fall around her, a gift from her father. Between each customer, Alden reprimanded him on his behavior and insisted he take the future more seriously. This continued even as the sun began to set.

"It's not like I don't understand. Your parents dedicated themselves to protecting others. And it says a lot about you that you'd want to be like them. But it takes more than power. It takes common sense and a solid understanding of the world around you," Alden said, keeping his eyes on the small notebook in his hand as he jotted down notes. "How do you expect to join the Aurora when you do stupid things like you did this morning, which could get you locked up? You're lucky Chancellor Demaskus is more understanding than most. You have to start thinking beyond the capacity of a dullfish."

Always with that same comparison, a fish with great magical potential but not the intelligence or instinct to utilize it. Kyo grumbled under his breath, wanting to argue, but kept his mouth shut. He couldn't bring himself to give Alden the attitude he often gave others. The man was there when he'd come into this world and for every birthfete afterwards. He was there when Kyo's parents had died — were murdered — and each day since, taking up the mantle of guardian alongside being his best friend. So, Kyo busied himself tightening the hoodie around his waist.

"If nothing else, you at least are the spitting image of those two," Alden said. "I'm sure you can do great things, but please try to stay out of trouble until then. For both our sakes."

Glancing at his own reflection as he passed a shop window, Kyo admitted that no one would deny he looked like his father at least. They shared the same narrow eyes, a trait found halfway across Feracael on the mainland. Wanting a similarity to his mother, he'd had his natural black hair magically colored silver, just as she'd done.

"People really need to take the sticks out of their butts," Kyo said. When Alden glared at him, Kyo rushed to continue. "But yeah, I'll try. Just because you can't handle trouble like I can." He lightly punched Alden's arm.

Alden slapped his hand away, and Kyo slapped his back. They tried punching and poking while blocking the other's attempts, Alden wielding his pen at a weapon. The game ended with Alden poking his fingers into Kyo's side, with a few curious onlookers staring, a giggle emitting from one.

"You still can't beat me, brat," Alden said.

"That won't last long. Your movements are getting slow, geezer." With the evening upon them, the scent of freshly cooked cockatrice meat from a nearby restaurant filled his nostrils, making Kyo's stomach rumble. "What are we eating tonight?"

"Good question. We should go shop for ingredients and figure it out."

Kyo grabbed Alden's wrist to stop him. "Then let's go this way. It'll be quicker."

He slipped through an alley between two shops and noticed someone loitering. They turned to look at him, and he froze. A cloak covered their body, and they did their best to have the hood hide their face…or part of it. Half their face was covered in a shadowy aura, eye glowing with a golden hue. He'd never seen anything like it and struggled to look away.

"Ruby?" he asked. Though only half her face remained revealed, he couldn't mistake those features.

Eyes wide with fear, she turned and dashed into the opposite street. What could have happened to her? She may have often been a thorn in his side, but her look of terror and fresh tears streaking down her cheeks was enough for him to ignore it and give chase.

"You go shopping." Kyo ignored Alden's cry to come back as he raced after her. "I'll catch up later."

The roads were crowded with people doing their evening errands. He thought he caught a glimpse of the tan cloak she wore and weaved through anyone in his path. A woman yelled at him as she dropped her bag of groceries when he bumped into her, but he didn't stop.

Did Ren know something was wrong with her? She did her best not to be recognized, so he guessed she hadn't told anyone.

Once off the main commercial thoroughfare, there were far fewer people to navigate around. Ruby ducked into another alley. Chasing her this way became old quick. Crouching, Kyo launched himself into the air with wind blasting from his feet, landing upon the triangular roof of a home. Looking down both directions of the next road, he saw no sign of her. She must have dashed between the homes on the other side. Taking a breath, he jumped the distance over the road, his feet barely managing to land on the next house. He slipped, faceplanting onto the dark walnut-colored shingles, but dug his boots into the rain gutter to keep from sliding off.

Righting himself, he saw a few people outside a home on the next street. While none appeared to be Ruby, one had the same dark veil around half their body, an elderly woman. Standing before her, another wore a black robe with hood up and hiding their face. Since robes were mostly used as uniforms, he wondered what group or organization this person belonged to. He couldn't recall one that wore all black.

They put their hand against the old woman's chest. Translucent blue and violet energy seeped from her body and down the cloaked figure's hand. Unlike the rainbow of colors found in the raw natural magic of nature and feral creatures, a human's magic maintained the two varying hues.

It was her magic being pulled from her. Kyo's eyes widened in shock.

But how was that possible? Using magic to affect someone's body, he understood, but it shouldn't be possible to manipulate another person's magic. The more energy the figure drained from the woman, the more the shadowy aura dissipated, until it vanished completely. The old lady slumped forward, caught by the cloaked person.

Kyo jumped down from the roof and approached them. "Hey. What was that?"

His focus remained on the old woman long enough to see her chest rise and fall. Questions rushed through his mind, and he hoped they'd be willing to answer them.

"That was the corruption, little boy." A woman who had been leaning against the exterior of the home stepped forward. This was a woman who stuck out like a fire blob in the arctic. She wore a black-and-red dress down to her knees. A corset kept the torso tight, while the bottom half had layers of frills. Combined with high white socks and black shoes, she looked like a living doll. "I don't expect most people from this secluded, backwater town in the corner of a small island to know about it yet."

How friendly. Kyo clenched his jaw to keep from saying something offensive. Otherwise, he might not learn anything. "Is she okay? What's the corruption?"

The woman brushed some of her long, wavy red hair behind her ear. "The granny is fine, just tired. She'll need to sleep it off. As for the corruption…" A wicked grin spread across her lips as she drew closer. "An infection of the magic. And if left unattended, it'll turn someone into a shadowy beast that'll viciously attack anyone and everyone around them. Until…" She used her fingers to slide across her throat and tilted her head, sticking her tongue out like a child playing dead. "They're put down."

"What? There's no way that's true." It couldn't be. Something so insane, they would have heard about it for sure. Then again, she wasn't wrong about Mistwell being isolated. There were three towns on Kattelink Island, and a mountain with a tunnel carved through it separated Mistwell from the other two. Despite having a few farms on their side of the mountain farther inland, they rely heavily on supplies delivered by caravan or ship.

"Believe whatever you wish. Lucky for your little town, we're the only ones capable of curing the corruption." She turned to her companion. "Blanq, bring her inside, would you?" Blanq nodded and, being no taller than the old woman, had to practically drag her into the home. The woman turned back to Kyo. "'Why so curious? Do you know someone who needs our services?"

"I'm not sure if I do…uh…?" Something about her presence sent a chill down his spine. The way she spoke almost admirably about what would happen to someone who succumbed to the corruption and her eagerness to find others. She was no cleric; he didn't get the feeling she was out to help others.

The woman straightened her back and placed a dainty hand over her chest. "Sybilla. A pleasure."

"Right. Well, I thought I saw someone else, but I'm not sure where—"

"Kyo!" Alden jogged toward them. Panting, he placed his hands on his knees. "I told you…to wait."

Kyo forced him upright by his shoulder. "Sorry. I was chasing down Ruby. I think something is wrong with her."

Alden's eyes met Sybilla's for a moment before focusing on Kyo. "Wrong how?"

Recounting what he saw and what he'd learned from Sybilla was like confirming his fears to himself. By the time he finished, it seemed more like a horrifying truth than a possible lie. As much of a pain as Ruby could be, he didn't want her to turn into some monster and be killed. He mentally kicked himself for losing track of her.

"Well, that sounds like even more reason for you to stay away from this. It's too dangerous. Let the enforcers handle it." Alden placed his hand on Kyo's back to guide him away from Sybilla. "Why don't you do the shopping and head home? I can speak to the chancellor, and he can get the other enforcers to look for Ruby."

That didn't sound like a bad idea. They'd be far more effective than Kyo searching alone. Alden stumbled as a man bumped into him and continued without a word.

"Geez, rude." Kyo's eyes narrowed at the man's back, resisting the urge to yank on his long black hair as punishment. "Fine, I guess I'll do the shopping, just tell me what to get then."

"Right." Alden stopped, bringing his hand to his face. Grunts and pants left his lips as he hunched over. "I don't feel well. Kyo, you should—"

Dark energy burst from the right half of Alden's body, flicking like a living ember.

Kyo gulped, his heart pounding. Sybilla's words rushed back to his mind, each feeling like a stab to his heart. Monster. Vicious. Put down. His own breathing became erratic as he rushed to look at Alden's face.

This couldn't be happening, not to the only family he had left. "Alden!"

Chapter 2

Kyo's shaky hand gripped his godfather's uncorrupted shoulder to keep him upright. How could this happen? Would it spread to him too if he remained close? It didn't matter. Though they may not be blood, Alden was all he had left.

No. Not Alden.

His chest tightened at the thought of having no one.

"My, what an unfortunate situation," Sybilla said as she approached. Cupping Alden's chin, she examined his face and shook her head. "Or a fortunate one, as it happened right on our doorstep."

"You can cure him, right? I just saw you do it for the old lady." Kyo's words came as quickly as his heartbeat. If it cost more cryst than he had to spend, he'd work to pay it off.

Grabbing Alden's hand, Sybilla yanked him away. "Yes, we can cure him. But it's not an instant process. Preparations need to be made. Draining someone's magic completely can be a traumatic experience for the body if done so suddenly."

Kyo noticed a look he couldn't decipher cross her face before she turned to examine Alden again, raising his arm, focused more on the shadowy energy cloaking him than his actual body. A tiny ember of shadow whipped at Sybilla's finger. She retracted it quickly and brought the tip to her lips.

"You…saw them…do it?" Alden asked.

"Yeah, before you showed up. They'll have you back to your old self again, promise." Kyo fought back tears, keeping his jaw clenched. He couldn't show any hint of doubt, not wanting to give Alden reason to worry.

Sybilla pointed a finger at Kyo without looking in his direction. "You will be a distraction. So, I suggest you go home, little boy. Eat, sleep, play with dolls, whatever children do. You can come back around midday tomorrow. He should be fine by then."

"You expect me to just leave?" Kyo asked, stomping his foot. "There's no way I can leave him behind like that."

"You can come back," she repeated, the annoyance in her voice clear. "Around midday tomorrow."

"Hey. It's worth it…if she can fix me, right?" Alden asked, struggling to get the words out. The slight twitches in his face gave away the discomfort he attempted to hold back. He turned his attention to Sybilla. "I'm guessing this isn't something a cleric can deal with?"

"Afraid not. You'll only waste your time seeking help from them. And time is of the essence. How long it takes each person to fully shift into a shade varies, so it's best not to delay." Sybilla pulled Alden toward the same nondescript home Blanq had taken the old woman.

"Be strong. I'll see you tomorrow," Alden said before the door closed behind him.

Kyo stood alone, his body unwilling to move. He'd seen them, or at least Blanq, cure the corruption himself, so he had no logical reason to doubt Alden would be okay. Even so, he couldn't help but fear the worst. A part of him wanted to barge in and refuse to leave, but with so much he didn't understand, maybe he *would* be a distraction. He opened his hand, drawing on his magic and forming a ball of swirling air.

"Dammit!" he cried as he hurled it at a nearby home's fence, shattering the painted wood.

* * *

Despite it nearing midnight, Kyo's leg shook, and fingers erratically tapped on his black shorts with excess energy. He'd spent the last hour on the roof. Stargazing usually helped him relax when something bothered him. It brought back memories of good times. He stared up and imagined his father on his left and mother on his right like when he was young. It was a Sonata family tradition, pointing out constellations of the pantheon like Tutelvus, the protector, or Florlantvus, representing fertility and growth. He'd always enjoyed learning hands-on over reading from a book.

After his parents' murder, Alden had taken over stargazing with him. Kyo shook his head, not wanting to think of continuing this tradition on his own.

How could he think of becoming an Aurora when he couldn't even protect Alden? Aurora were supposed to be able to protect everyone—almost everyone. Even they weren't perfect.

He'd seen that himself when he was much younger, something he'd never forget. His parents took him to Oasis. Fun in the sun, the desert city's beach…each day there was like a dream at that age. He'd befriended a young boy whose family stayed at the bungalow next to his, and they played together day after day. Out of nowhere, a massive scorpion dug through the sand, towering over everyone. Such events weren't unheard of, all manner of creatures big and small roamed the expanses between towns and cities. Under normal circumstances, the enforcers would have arrived to handle it, but Kyo's parents were already on the scene when the feral appeared. They were quick to dispatch it.

But not quick enough.

And not as swift as they were to pick Kyo up to keep him from seeing what'd happened. But he'd caught a glimpse of his new friend's mangled, blood-covered body on the sand and heard the wails of his parents. It took hours of consoling from his parents to stop the tears. At first, he thought they'd failed, asking why they didn't save his friend. But when individuals and families thanked his parents for hours on end, he realized they *had* saved many people.

No one could save everyone, not even them.

He sighed, letting his vision lose focus as he stared at the roof shingles, mind wandering. Sometimes, he wondered what that boy would have been like years later if he'd survived. The tragedy that had befallen that boy, the heartbreak of his parents; these were the situations he wanted to prevent so people could peacefully go about their lives.

Ruby, the old woman the hooded person cured, Alden…this felt like a tragedy in the making, and here Kyo sat on his rooftop, doing nothing. Pulling the last juicy fruit ball from the bulla core in his hand, he popped it into his mouth. With a frustrated shout, he launched the fruit core into the air with a burst of wind from his hand, not caring where it landed.

He couldn't sit idle anymore. If he wanted to prevent a disaster, he had to listen to his gut. And his gut told him something was off about those two.

Kyo jumped from the roof, wind from his feet slowing his descent to the ground. He ran down various roads, guided by the flickering fire of streetlamps, until he reached the house used by Sybilla and Blanq. While the lower level remained dark, a light shone from one of the second-story rooms. Though he could just walk inside, he decided against it. They'd likely send him away again. He'd be satisfied with watching from a distance so long as he saw proof of Alden's wellbeing.

An overhang roof between the first and second story would allow him to walk up to the window. Kyo launched himself and landed as quietly as possible then remained still until the lack of commotion inside assured him he hadn't attracted attention. He tiptoed across the roof and to the side of the house until he reached the window and peeked inside.

Six beds sat in the room, three along parallel walls, and each held an occupant covered up to the neck with a blanket. Sybilla did say the process was exhausting, and the old woman from earlier couldn't stand on her own after Blanq drained her magic. At least they were given a soft place to rest. At each end of the room sat a bedside table with a dome-shaped light, a common magic-tech light that illuminated with the most minute administering of magical energy. Even a toddler could light them for a while.

As he glanced over the patients, his heart dropped. He'd have been able to spot Alden— with his bright red hair—without trying, yet none of them were him.

Calm down.

Sybilla had said it took preparation. Maybe they hadn't gotten to that point yet.

Sitting against the exterior wall, Kyo ran a hand over his face and sighed.

A loud bang made him jump. It felt like his heart would burst from his chest. The sound came again, from the front of the house. Remaining crouched, he moved far enough to peek down to the lower level, finding someone knocking on the front door. An exterior light turned on, illuminating Ren's face, and the door opened.

"Hello, Mr. Enforcer." It was Sybilla's voice. "What can I do for you?"

Ren stiffened, arms at his sides, but his fingers twiddled nervously. "I know it's late, but I've been informed of your operation by the chancellor. My sister has been missing all day, and I've heard a few reports of her running through town, attempting to hide her appearance. Most of the townspeople don't know of the corruption yet, but we both know what it could mean, so I thought perhaps she's found her way here."

"Is that so?" Sybilla's voice held a kinder tone than when she'd spoken to Kyo earlier. "Anyone who has come to us, or who we have approached, is currently upstairs resting. You're welcome to come inside and see if your sister is among them."

Ren stepped inside, and the door closed. Kyo silently crept to the far side of the window, peering inside. A moment later, Sybilla opened the door. Ren walked inside, examining the room while Blanq entered behind him.

"We'll have to ask you remain quiet. They all need plenty of rest before returning home," Sybilla said.

Ren nodded. "I've heard about how this goes. It still feels unreal that you can forcibly drain someone's magic."

Kyo shivered at the memory of the old woman having her magic pulled from her. While he agreed it'd be worth it to remove the corruption, there was something wrong about it.

Sybilla scoffed. "It sounds so aggressive when you word it that way."

While Ren moved between the beds looking over each occupant, a thought occurred to Kyo. If both Blanq and Sybilla were here, where was Alden? Could he be in another room or maybe downstairs? He hoped they had another room with beds, since all the ones here were taken.

Ren sighed. "She's not here. I'd only heard about you earlier today, so I suppose she hadn't at all before wandering off." Bending over a middle-aged man, Ren examined his face. "They're okay, right?" he asked in a hushed voice. "They seem…off." He rounded the bed and placed his hand on the man's back.

Blanq's eyes glowed a deep blue as their hand raised discreetly at their side, fingers twiddling. As if in response, the sleeping man's arm rose, swatting Ren away gently. A faint blue glow came through the man's closed eyelids. Kyo's body trembled, and he had to grip the windowsill for balance. Ren's words about something being off was an understatement.

"I'll have to remind you not to disturb them. We should leave them be," Sybilla said, turning but glancing over her shoulder to ensure Ren followed.

After a second's hesitation, he did.

"I'm sorry your sister wasn't here," she said. "But we'll be glad to help search tomorrow."

"I appreciate that." Ren closed the door behind him.

Kyo wasted no time pressing his hands against the window and pushing up. Thankfully, they'd left it unlocked. He slipped inside and turned to the nearest bed, crouching before the man whose eyes had glowed blue a moment before.

"Hey, you okay?" he asked.

Using his thumb, he raised the man's eyelid to find no glow underneath. It must have been a response to Blanq's spell. But even then, the man didn't stir.

Kyo's gaze fell to the man's neck. Reaching a shaky hand out, he positioned two fingers to feel for a pulse. A pulse that wasn't there. His own heart pounding, he scanned the room. He took a slow, deep breath and checked each patient. Not a pulse to be found.

Sympathy for the victims turned to anger toward Sybilla then himself. He'd known something felt wrong, that her demeanor was suspicious, and he'd still left

Alden with her. But what choice did he have? Could clerics fix this with their healing magic, or did she tell the truth about the two of them being the only ones able to cure the corruption? It had to be possible for them to remove the corruption without killing the afflicted. A person using their magic until it was drained didn't kill a person, so why should this?

Someone had to tell the enforcers, the chancellor, anyone who could put a stop to this. But not before he found Alden. Kyo couldn't leave him with these murderers a second longer.

Footsteps sounded from the other side of the door.

Good, let them come in and he'll force the answers out of them.

He approached the door, and in his right hand appeared a short sword with a wide, black blade. As soon as the door opened, he thrust his blade forward and halted right before Sybilla's throat. Her wide eyes gave him grim satisfaction.

"Where's Alden?" he asked in as commanding a tone as he could muster.

Her eyes softened, and a grin spread across her face. "I'm sorry, who?"

Kyo clenched his teeth. He pulled his hand back then thrust his sword toward Sybilla's gut. She swatted his blade away like an annoying insect, her arm coated in grainy rock from elbow to fingertips. An alteration mage.

He retreated to put some distance between them before she could try anything else. "Don't act as stupid as you look. I'll find him, no matter what I have to do."

Sybilla shook her head. "I did tell you to stay home, little boy. It was for your own safety." Blanq peered from behind Sybilla but otherwise did nothing. "But I suppose I'll have to teach you what happens to children who don't listen."

"What, you going to kill me like you did them?" Kyo shouted, motioning to the six corpses in the beds. "Just try it. If Alden is still alive, I'll save him. And if he isn't…I'll make sure you regret it."

He charged forward, swinging his blade toward her head. Sybilla blocked it with her stone arm, but he materialized a second blade within his left hand, thrusting it at her chest. It didn't hit soft flesh, but through the slice in her dress, he could see more gray stone in place of skin.

"Oh-ho, a dual-wielder? I must admit I didn't expect that. I almost didn't manage to protect myself. Not that it would have mattered." Sybilla snatched both blades from his hands and tossed them over his head and across the room.

They vanished and reappeared in his hands before they hit the floor.

Kyo thrust at her neck, then her stomach. He tried slicing her thigh, with no effect. Her entire body wasn't covered in stone, but her spellcasting was so precise and quick, she covered what areas she needed to protect herself for those brief seconds and nothing more.

"You wouldn't be having such trouble if you weren't so weak," she said. "But my magic is leagues above yours. You could never hope to hurt me. I, on the other hand…" Sybilla rotated her body to avoid his next stab then thrust her stony fist against his stomach.

Kyo hunched over, the air forced from his lungs. While all he could do was cough, she punched him in the chest, knocking him on his back. Pain radiated through his torso—he barely managed to crawl back as she tried to jump onto him. He scrambled to his feet, each deep breath making his chest tighten.

The swords vanished, and he turned his right palm up, air circulating around it. Swords didn't do well against stone anyway, unless a lot of magic was behind the attacks. But the fact that she could injure him easily with so few strikes gave credibility to her claim. With little effort, she was able to bypass the natural protection his magic offered his body.

Air rotated faster above his palm, the excess whipping the curtains about and shifting the bed sheets off the bodies. He'd practiced this spell plenty of times but never got it to work quite right. When he was young, his father demonstrated it to him, and it had stuck in his mind ever since. The air current formed the shape of a spinning drill in his hand.

"You think you have what it takes? Go on then, let's see," Sybilla said with a taunting smile. She puffed out her chest, daring him to strike.

"You're too confident." Kyo quickly closed the distance between them and thrust the wind drill into her chest.

Instead of keeping its form, it dissipated upon impact.

His eyes widened, and he tensed.

Before he could back away, Sybilla grabbed him by the throat and slammed him into the wooden floor. His vision blurred. Choking against her hand, he gripped her wrist and tried pointlessly to pull her off. When he attempted kicking her, she sat on his legs, keeping them pinned. Tears leaked from his eyes as he struggled to breathe.

"I suppose adding one more wouldn't hurt." With her free hand, she reached into a brown leather pouch at her side and pulled out a grainy yet translucent orb.

Inside, blue and violet energy swirled calmly in random directions.

Kyo tensed as similarly colored energy leaked from his body, down her arm then across to the orb in her opposite hand.

She was draining him of his magic.

Already his body sagged with fatigue. The strength in his arms failed, tugging at her hand with no more power than a tired child.

"Just relax and let this happen. Maybe we'll let you join the others," Sybilla taunted.

He was going to die here. Another corpse for that hooded weirdo to control for who knew what reason. How could he die here? What would happen to Alden? If only his body moved as wildly as his mind.

Through his fading vision, he made out the shape of Blanq placing a hand on Sybilla's shoulder.

She looked back at Blanq, the draining process pausing. After a few seconds of silence, Sybilla sighed. She gritted her teeth and removed her hand from Kyo's throat, but not before punching him hard in the face with her rocky hand. "Right...fine."

The room spun, and all he could do was lie there, taking deep breaths and releasing the occasional cough. So utterly defeated, and he didn't learn anything about Alden. He was such a failure. Aside from Alden's fate, another question burned in his mind. Why did she stop?

"I guess we're done with Mistwell anyway. Blanq, gather your things. It's time to go," she said in a firm, annoyed tone.

Footsteps stomped toward the door. A faint, blue glow pierced Kyo's blurred vision. Then feet shambled through the room all around him. One even made it a point to step over him. Blanq must have been controlling them again. How could they do that, and why?

His head throbbed when he thought too hard. Curling up on his side, he clenched his eyes shut, trying to will the pain and exhaustion away.

Feet trudged across the room, down the stairs. Then silence.

Kyo didn't know how long he lay there attempting to recover from what should have been his end. So much didn't make sense. But he could wallow in self anger and run questions through his mind later.

Gripping the nearest bed, he struggled to pull himself to his feet. His legs wobbled, and he nearly fell forward. He'd been low on magic before, pushing himself too hard in training on occasion. Having it forcibly pulled from him had left him in a far worse state. Magic was like an extra set of muscles in the body that didn't take up physical space. Having it forced from him so quickly and forcefully, it felt like he hadn't slept in days. Moving his body became a laborious chore.

"Damn you," Kyo grumbled as he took slow, deliberate steps to the next bed then the door to the room, leaning against the doorframe. He could only guess how many times he'd collapse once he left the house. But he had no choice. If he was going to get Alden back or find out what happened to him, he'd need help.

Chapter 3

Kyo braced himself against a lamp post and clenched his eyes to stop the world from spinning. At least his vision was no longer blurred, but it still took more effort to move than it should.

Among the questions and tasks floating in his mind, the image of that orb Sybilla held kept coming back to him. It didn't take a genius to figure out it stored whatever magic she drained, but how much and why?

One thing at a time.

Finding an enforcer had to come first, and it must have been nearly an hour since Sybilla and Blanq had left. Even at this time of night, a couple enforcers usually patrolled the town. He didn't have the energy or coordination to go on a lengthy search, but maybe he could get someone to come to him.

Casting any spell would hurt him in the long run. From what he could feel of the energy flowing within him by subtly controlling it, he guessed Sybilla left him with around a quarter of his magic.

Taking in his surroundings, he spied a wooden crate outside a restaurant. He stumbled over to it and, seeing no lid and nothing inside, pushed it toward the middle of the street. In his weakened state, the task took too long and as much effort as if it were full, but he managed.

Kyo panted, his arms shaking. "I really hate this. I'll pay her back."

The lamp posts around Mistwell weren't powered by magic-tech like in other towns but climbing one wouldn't be happening. Instead, he approached a nearby shop with a lit sconce next to the front door. He opened the window of the sconce, removed the candle, and held the flame to the wood of the crate. After more time than he would've liked, the crate blazed in the middle of the road, leaving him to do nothing but sit and wait.

Minutes later, footsteps hurriedly approached before a torrent of water doused the crate. "What do you think you're doing? This is extreme even for you. Desperate for attention?"

Kyo had never been so happy to see Ren, easily ignoring his annoyed tone. "I need your help." He stumbled in his attempt to stand but managed to recover. "Those two… They killed people—they took Alden. We need to find them."

"What are you talking about? Don't tell me this is because you had a bad dream." Ren approached, and Kyo placed a hand on Ren's shoulder to keep his balance, which thankfully came a bit easier after his moments of sitting and waiting.

Kyo shook his head, then gathered his thoughts before speaking again. "I know you were with Sybilla and Blanq, looking for Ruby. I was outside the window, and I saw everything."

"So soon after what the chancellor told you about eavesdropping?" Ren squinted. "Never mind that for now. What happened to your face?"

"Does it look bad?" Reaching to feel around his right eye and cheek, he pulled his hand back with flakes of dry blood. "Actually, forget it and listen. Sybilla did this. I left Alden with them earlier because he'd become corrupted. I went back to check on him and was on the roof when you showed up. The people in those beds were dead."

"That's impossible. I saw them myself. One waved me off."

"I think Blanq can control them even when they're dead. I saw their eyes glow blue, same with the man you were checking." Kyo recounted what happened after Ren left, sparing no details. "Now they're gone, and they must still have Alden."

"This doesn't…" Ren's eyes shifted wildly. "Come with me." He began walking, but when Kyo stumbled again, Ren backtracked to support him by the waist.

"I saw Ruby." Kyo's eyes remained down, watching his footwork to keep himself steady. "I lost her, but that's how I found Sybilla and Blanq. Though I don't think she was there."

There was a brief pause before Ren spoke. "It's fine. Thank you."

Kyo didn't know where they were headed, didn't even know which streets they traveled, whether the buildings around them were businesses or homes. As they continued, enough strength returned that he didn't need to rely on Ren's support. But before he looked up, Kyo heard a knock. They were at someone's home.

Ren knocked again, louder this time. The sound of footsteps came from the other side. Then the door swung open.

Chancellor Demaskus stood before them in a red nightgown and matching sleeping cap. He glanced between the two. "Come in, come in."

They stepped inside, and once the door closed, the chancellor placed his hand upon the base of a lamp on a small table, the light illuminating the space around them. A couch, a bookshelf with a variety of books and tomes so thick Kyo would never think to try reading them—a pretty standard set up.

The chancellor didn't have the chance to ask what happened before Kyo started recounting events. Ren added his side of things when appropriate, and they finished with them arriving at the chancellor's door.

"Those two are dangerous," Kyo said. "We have to find them, quickly. And make sure Alden is okay."

Pacing around the room, the chancellor stroked his beard. "I was suspicious to begin with, but clearly, I did not give those two enough attention. This is a failing on my part."

"You were already suspicious of them?" Kyo asked.

The chancellor nodded. "When a pair comes around claiming to cure something like the corruption, it's certain to raise eyebrows. They met with me in my office to explain what they could do, and their desire to set up shop. With reports from the mainland, then a case in Calmarock, I knew it'd be a matter of time before we had our own cases here. So I agreed, on the condition they let us be the ones to spread the word, which I'd planned to do tomorrow. It's true Ren went to them to seek out Ruby, but he also did so at my request, to get a closer look at their operation."

"I'm sorry, sir." Ren's eyes drifted to the floor. "I utterly failed at both. I was right there but couldn't see what was really happening." His fists tightened by his side.

"No, do not blame yourself, my boy. I highly underestimated them and their intentions. The fact that Alden Somera is now missing makes this a far more dire situation." The chancellor headed toward the front door but paused when an elderly woman descended the stairs.

"Is everything all right, dear?" she asked.

"I aim to find out. But don't wait for me. I have to see something for myself." Chancellor Demaskus shared a brief kiss with her before opening the front door. "Come with me you two, quickly."

They followed the chancellor outside. Despite his advanced age, he hustled down the street with the speed of someone half his age. Though still a bit sluggish, Kyo kept up with some effort. They turned onto a dirt trail and climbed a hill and soon found themselves back at the well. The chancellor raised his hands, the water parting to one side and rising well above the well.

"Remain here." He leaped into the well, an *'oof'* echoing from within seconds later.

"Don't break those legs, old man," Kyo called after him. He must have made the right choice when searching for whatever the chancellor hid. Which meant he'd missed it somehow. Of course it wouldn't be left out in the open, but he may have found it if Ruby and Ren hadn't arrived when they did. He turned to Ren. "Do you know what he hid here?"

Ren shook his head. "Not in any detail." His eyes drifted to the town below, shifting anxiously on his feet. "But I know it's important."

Several minutes passed before the chancellor emerged again, rising on a pillar of water and stepping onto solid ground. "As I thought. It's gone. The connections were obvious, but I still hoped for a better outcome."

"So, what exactly did you hide down there?" Kyo asked.

"According to your tale, you have already seen it, but I will not give you more details than that. Know that, in the wrong hands, it could be catastrophic." Chancellor Demaskus sighed, tapping his foot.

He'd seen it already? Kyo ran the events of the past day through his mind, starting from the well, accompanying Alden, to his confrontation with Sybilla and…

The orb.

But what was so special about it? Storing magic in a single object happened all the time with magic-tech, from lights and food boxes to the engines that propelled airships.

"Ren, I know you are lacking in sleep," the chancellor said, "but I suspect with Ruby missing, you wouldn't retire to your home even if asked."

Ren nodded in response.

"Then I would have you assist me. You must inform the enforcers of the current situation. I, meanwhile, will attempt to contact Chancellor Ambers in Aquarin Port and have their enforcers keep an eye out for our three criminals as well. And your sister, of course."

Ren nodded again and ran off down the trail.

"Sorry, did you say *three* criminals?" Kyo's brow rose. "Sybilla, Blanq—don't even try telling me you're considering Alden in that statement."

"Please, my boy, don't take it personally. Given the gravity of the situation, we must assume the worst, yet we can hope for the best. The fact of the matter is it was Alden who I had enchant the item in question to keep it from curious parties so they might pass it by without realizing." His gaze narrowed accusingly. "This also means he is one of the few who knew what it is and its location. While I find it hard to believe his corruption affliction could be more than chance, it is suspicious that the item and he would go missing at the same time."

"There's no way he'd steal it though." No wonder Kyo couldn't find anything in the well. He would have had to touch or move every brick and rock down there in hopes of finding it, and even then, Alden's enchantment could have kept it hidden. Damn Alden being so good at what he did. Though a spark of hope did light from the chancellor's words. When Kyo had left, Alden had trouble walking on his own, hunched over in pain. If he had in fact taken what was hidden in the well, did that mean Sybilla or Blanq had cured him first? "And even if you were right, he could have been blackmailed or something."

"That falls under the idea of hoping for the best. I have known Alden for many years, and while I am not against giving him the benefit of the doubt, he must first be found. We will ensure all comes to light after that." Chancellor Demaskus placed a hand on Kyo's shoulder. "You should be lectured for going against my advice about eavesdropping so soon, but truth be told, I am grateful you did. Thanks to you, we may be able to deal with this before anything terrible happens. While I expect the same stubbornness as Ren, between not sleeping for nearly a day and having your magic forced from you, I suggest you go home and rest."

Kyo hesitated then nodded. "Yeah, I could use some sleep. Please make sure Alden is found though. And Ruby too."

He turned and made his way down the trail. Truthfully, he didn't feel tired. Weak, yes, but with every passing minute his strength returned. Having his magic drained and the subsequent recovery taught him Sybilla's claims of needing lengthy preparation and ample recovery time were a load of bovine crap.

The enforcers should be enough to find them, but what if they weren't? Was he expected to sit at home and twiddle his thumbs, let every minute be an agonizing wait?

Kyo refused to be helpless. His pace quickened as the full scope of the situation dawned on him. If his parents were alive, they'd have been asked to help with this sort of situation. If he intended to be like them, he couldn't let this chance slip away.

Dashing through his front door, he ran upstairs and opened his closet, pulled out a sleeping bag and spare pillow, and shoved them into the small pouch kept at his side. Like Alden's, it shouldn't physically be able to fit them. Enchanted pouches weren't uncommon among travelers and living with an enchanter meant even he had one. He rushed to gather what he might need for the trip—food that wouldn't spoil quickly, glass bottles of water he wrapped up in towels, spare clothes, anything he could think of in his frantic mindset.

Mistwell had boats, but they were no more than fishing vessels—none that he'd seen had magic-tech engines. If Sybilla and Blanq were looking to leave Kattelink Island, they had to be heading west toward Aquarin Port. He could make it by tomorrow afternoon, assuming he didn't stop to rest.

He gathered any stashed cryst, the multicolored crystal coins used as currency, from Alden's room, and headed downstairs. Pausing, he glanced at a small, wooden shrine against the far living room wall. He took a breath to steady himself then went to kneel before it, opening the cabinet doors. Two small candles sat on either side, next to two incense burners. Against the back was a painting of a black, serpent-like dragon. Duxvita, the Prime Altruist and the one responsible for creating humans, so they said. Kyo's eyes focused on the two lifelike hand drawings of a man with narrow eyes like his own and a woman with long, silver hair. Below each picture sat a plaque with the names Kei Sonata and Iris Sonata engraved on them.

Kyo cleared his throat. "Um…hey, Mom…Dad. I'm going to be gone for a bit. Alden got himself into trouble, and I have to find him and bring him home." He smirked. "He was always more childish than you, but you two were the troublemakers. I guess you rubbed off on him, huh?" Exhaling hard, he clenched the edge of his shorts. "So, don't worry about me. I'm sure I'll be fine. I might even have a head or two to bash, just like you did back in the day. Who knows, maybe this is my trial run before joining the Aurora. You know, follow in your footsteps and all."

A pang of guilt hit him in the gut. It'd been months since he spoke to them like this, maybe over a year at this point. Every time he saw those drawings of them, the tears welled up.

"So, yeah. First time leaving Mistwell since you took me to Oasis way back when. But I'm sixteen now, so time I get out in the world, right?" He closed his eyes, knowing he didn't have time to waste. "I'll let you know when we're home. Love you."

Kyo closed the doors and stood. Some suppressed heartache emerged but also a wave of confidence. He made sure to turn off every light, opened the front door, and stepped outside. Best to leave before the enforcers began their own search. They'd try to keep him home and out of the way, but he wasn't a kid anymore. Besides, how could he justify letting them find Sybilla before he had a chance to pay her back? He'd get his punches in before she and Blanq were sent off to Spellnix Hold and he brought Alden home.

Chapter 4

Aside from boat or airship, Solitude Pass—the path long ago carved through the mountain—remained the sole way to get anywhere from Mistwell. Kyo's head throbbed from Sybilla's strike, and fatigue racked his body. It had been about half a day since Kyo left Mistwell, but at least this should be the last tunnel before he made it to the other side.

Behind him lay the corpse of the creature he hated most in this world, an eight-legged feral about shin height. Big ones, small ones, it didn't matter—he hated them all, and the thought of one of any size crawling on him made his arms flail on their own in hopes of swatting it off.

The tunnels connecting the massive, dome-shaped rooms were so dark he couldn't see his hand in front of his face, which made the fact he was able to slay the skitter nothing less than a miracle. Kyo held his sword out before him, shifting it back and forth, trying not to hit the hard surface of the tunnel walls and floor but checking for any more hidden dangers. The further he traversed through the tunnel, the more light shone through from the other end. He stepped into the final massive room, the mouth of the pass opening to cloudy skies, but at least he could see.

"Thank goodness," he said to himself. Dismissing his sword, he examined every bit of the walls, floor, and ceiling one last time.

His eyes widened when he found something but not a skitter. Huddled in the corner of the room, arms around her knees, sat a person beneath a tan cloak. A woman with a sharp nose and half her body covered in shadow.

Ruby. This was where she'd gone. But why?

As soon as the question came to mind, his shoulders slumped. Assuming clerics couldn't heal the corruption, around other people would be the last place anyone would want to be before turning into a monster.

He tiptoed toward her, stopping a few steps away, yet she didn't react.

Kyo cleared his throat. "Um…hey, Ruby? Are you awake?"

Ruby shifted then raised her head, staring at him with half-lidded eyes.

Her eyes widened, and she scurried away from him, hiding behind a large rock. "Kyo? P-please. Just go. Leave me alone."

He thought about approaching, but her obvious fear had him consider otherwise. "What are you doing out here by yourself? Shouldn't you be finding help?"

At first, there was silence. If she truly wanted to be left alone, she may not answer at all. But then in a soft, whimpering voice, she responded. "There is no help for someone like me." Her arms wrapped around her stomach. "We enforcers were briefed on the corruption, and I know better than to hope."

Though it may cause him problems later, he reached into his pouch, pulling out a buttery loaf of bread wrapped in cloth and broke it in half. "You're probably hungry by now, right? I can at least give you this. It's not much, but it should help."

Still unsure how safe it was to be close to her, he placed the bread and cloth on the ground and backed away, taking a bite of his half. Ruby peered from behind the rock. After eyeing the bread for several seconds, she left her hiding place to grab it and took as big a bite as she could manage.

For a moment, her half-corrupted face became Alden's. Ruby had been corrupted for at least a day and still hadn't turned. How much time did she have? It couldn't be much less than Alden, becoming corrupted on the same day.

He thought of his parents and what they would do in this situation. The answer became obvious before he finished posing the question to himself. Even if she'd always been a pain in the ass, he didn't have the heart to leave her. "I'm heading to Aquarin Port. You can come with me if you want. I'm following two others. They're dangerous but might be the only way to get you back to normal."

Once the words left his lips, he mentally kicked himself. Sybilla had nearly killed him, and Blanq controlled dead bodies. They were not the type he should expect help from. Though if the alternative was Ruby turning into a monster that could harm others, what other choice was there?

"What are you talking about? Who?" Having finished the bread, Ruby gazed up at him from a kneeling position. The tinge of hope in her voice was unmistakable, and Kyo tried to hide his nervous cringe from giving her hope when there may be none.

The enforcers must have been briefed about them after she'd run off, so Kyo explained what had happened with Alden, Sybilla, and Blanq and emphasized the danger of approaching them. There would be no point in trying to ask Sybilla for help. His teeth clenched at the thought of her. Blanq, on the other hand, he knew nothing about. They had removed the corruption from the old woman, though he wasn't sure if she'd died then or after. On the other hand, their interference had kept Sybilla from killing him. He had no idea who or what resided under the hooded cloak, but they were Ruby's only hope.

Kyo shook his head. There were many questions, but they could wait.

"I did see a pair come through here several hours ago. A woman and another hooded figure?" she asked. When Kyo nodded, her breath hitched. "If they're that dangerous, I suppose I was right to stay away. But if they could cure me…"

"Well, we should find them in Aquarin, right?" he asked. He was helping her as much for his benefit as for hers. If he could bring her to Aquarin Port, and, by some miracle, convince Blanq to help without killing her, then there had to be hope for Alden as well. That, of course, relied on getting Alden's whereabouts from the two. Having to rely on them for help nearly made him sick to his stomach. The idea of beating the cooperation out of Sybilla, however, brought a grim smile to his face. "So, no sense in waiting around here. Stand up."

Ruby nodded and rose, using the jagged wall for support.

Though what she'd said concerned him. Sybilla and Blanq had passed through here several hours ago. He hadn't thought they were so far ahead. Multiple hours hadn't passed from the time they'd left to the time he'd done the same. They must have been moving faster than him, but it shouldn't matter so long as they stayed in Aquarin for a while.

Kyo remained several paces from Ruby as they left the tunnel into the late morning light. He squinted, his head throbbing from the increased brightness. In contrast to the green grass and flora on Mistwell's side of the mountain, the brush around them remained dry and barren, not having yet begun to regrow after the cold season. That may not last much longer though, as he noted darker clouds in the distance.

"Looks like a storm is coming. But we should get there before it hits." Kyo hoped some casual conversation might brighten her spirits.

Ruby gazed into the distance, barely lifting her head like a timid saber pup. "I like storms. The lightning is pretty. I'd watch it from the window with Ren. He used to be scared of it when we were young, so I told him the lightning and thunder were the pantheon playing games in their realm."

He picked up what she wasn't saying: the two of them had similar fears—never seeing their families again. Frowning, Kyo kept his eyes on the clouds. "Don't worry. You'll watch storms with him again soon enough. After we get you back to normal."

His gaze fell to her for a second, before a force from his left struck his arm, knocked him to the ground, and soaked his clothes. He cringed and grabbed his throbbing arm, and he caught sight of a blob, a gelatinous creature known for using elemental magic. Its blue color and his soaked clothes were enough indication of which element this one used.

"You little…" Kyo returned to his feet, standing between it and Ruby.

The blob's body rippled, free-floating eyes fixed on Kyo as another stream of water blasted from a hole that could be interpreted as its mouth. Kyo dashed to his right, and though not as swift, Ruby did the same.

"You have a problem, you liquid booger?" he said. "Don't make me eat you right here and now." A blob's flesh, if it could be called that, was perfectly edible. Though hardly a treat on its own, Kyo enjoyed the sugary, often fruity treats they could make, especially at festivals and parties.

"I'm sorry I can't help. I've had trouble using my magic ever since this happened to me. I'm sure even you can handle a blob, right?" Ruby asked.

"I *should*, yeah." If he were at one hundred percent strength, it would have been no problem. Though his magic had slowly returned since yesterday, he still judged himself to be at about half power at best.

The blob's body stretched, long tendrils whipping at Kyo. He summoned a sword in his right hand, deflecting the attacks while trying to ignore the pounding in his head.

"Get back further," he directed.

The shifting of dry brush told him without looking that she'd obeyed. Cursing, he ran again, keeping his distance while moving in a circle around the feral. A blob shouldn't be a problem. For mages like himself who practiced magic for battle, they were practically baby's first feral, the type a novice might practice combat skills on under supervision. But in his current condition, it became a more serious threat.

"Kyo, be careful," Ruby cried out.

"Easier said than done," he called back.

This blob was relentless, firing balls of water with dangerous force while still lashing with its tendrils. Kyo couldn't block them all, occasionally being whipped in the leg, the side, and once along his face, leaving a harsh sting behind. If it pissed him off further, he really might eat it out of spite.

The attacks ceased, but what Kyo saw made him pause. From the grass, brush, and even air around it, thin streams of energy in every conceivable color gathered toward the blob.

Oh, what luck, it could harness natural magic.

He didn't even know they could do that and wished humans were capable of the same. It meant the power of their spells weren't limited to the magic within them.

Its mouth opened, and water swirled like a vortex.

Kyo propelled himself to the side with wind from his feet, barely avoiding the torrent of water that tore up the ground wherever it touched, leaving a deep gash behind. As he rose, the tendrils reappeared. He had more than enough magic to deal with a lone blob. All he needed was an opening.

He threw his sword, and the creature parried and sent it to the ground. Kyo launched himself forward, closing the distance in a second. His right hand thrust through the blob's cool, sticky form—this alone would never cause a blob any harm—and the tendrils wrapped around Kyo's arm, torso, and neck, tightening by the second.

Air blasted from the hand inside the blob, its body bubbling and expanding. Its grip loosened, eyes darting around inside itself wildly.

It burst. Chunks of viscous flesh scattered everywhere.

Some reached Ruby, who shrank in on herself with a yelp to avoid them. Kyo wasn't so lucky. What a sight he must have been, half his body soaked, welts all over, a bruised face, and covered in gelatinous goo.

"I'm ready for today to be over." Starting back toward Ruby, he tried brushing away as much of the goo as he could from his skin and clothes.

Her shriek forced his eyes up. Three more blobs, one blue and two red, surrounded her.

"I'm coming," he yelled, running toward her. His right hand extended outward, the sword he'd thrown vanishing from its place on the dirt path and appearing in his hand. The shadowy essence around her expanded, and with a single swipe, sliced the three blobs into pieces.

Bits of what remained flew into the brush.

"I-I didn't try to do anything! It just happened on its own," Ruby cried in a shaky voice and hugged herself, head shaking. Her chest rose and fell rapidly, and the shadowy corruption around her twisted, as if ready to strike any who came close. "Just...leave me."

Kyo's mind spun. The corruption went beyond some weird illness, even beyond turning one into some monster. It appeared it had some sort of consciousness or at least instinct. Weak though blobs were, if it could swipe away multiple with minimal effort, he' would've hated to see what a fully transformed person could do. Especially to other humans.

"No." More than before, he intended to keep his distance, but he wouldn't abandon her. "We're going to Aquarin, and we'll try to get you cured."

"No, I shouldn't go near any town. I might hurt someone." As if in response to her emotions, the corruption lashed out toward Kyo, but its reach fell short.

"Ruby, look at me," he said. It took her a few seconds, but she glanced his way. "I haven't seen it myself, but from what I've heard, this corruption will eventually overtake you completely. If that happens, you might hurt people whether you want to or not."

She shuddered and lowered her head, staring at the ground.

"The only way to ensure you don't hurt anyone," he continued, "is to come with me and find those two so they can remove the corruption." With any luck, he could find Blanq without Sybilla by their side, though even that might prove pointless. "And it's the only chance you have of seeing your brother again."

At first, she didn't move. Her gaze remained fixed on her feet, but her breathing appeared to calm. Her arms loosened from around herself, and she turned toward him. "I do want to see him again. He must be beside himself."

"You have to do whatever you can, if for no other reason than for him." He took a few steps to lead and ensure a safe distance between them.

After a lengthy silence, Ruby muttered, "Thank you."

Each hour they trekked along the dirt path, the dark clouds grew closer. The temperature dropped, and the wind picked up. But not a drop of rain had fallen by the time they stepped foot in Aquarin Port.

Clean, white storefronts and homes with blue roofs, patterned stone roads, and from the southernmost end of town, a hill with a great view of the sea and the ships docked at port.

"Okay, we made it," Kyo said. "Now we just need to find them, right? I bet if we ask around, we might get some answers. Their outfits aren't exactly discreet."

The confidence in his words soon diminished as he noticed passersby keeping their distance, some rushing in whatever direction could get them far from Ruby.

"Oh, quit gawking," he said. "She just needs help. We're looking for a pair who would have come into town recently. A woman in a weird black-and-red dress and a shorter person in a black robe. Anyone seen them?"

No one responded, instead hurrying away in the opposite direction.

"What a bunch of cowards," he said.

"I don't think we'll find any help," Ruby said.

"Don't worry, maybe if we —"

"Stop right there," a voice called out from their right.

Two men in enforcer robes approached them atop white-and-black-striped sabers. The enormous cats growled, two thick canines jutting from their mouths to below their chins. Typically, they had friendly demeanors toward humans, though he wasn't about to pet one trained by enforcers.

"There we go," Kyo said. "They might know something." He approached the pair, but one grabbed his left wrist, pulling it behind his back. Body shaking from the pain of the jerky movement, he couldn't keep the enforcer from doing the same to the other wrist before clasping them both in metal cuffs. "Hey, what do you think you're doing?"

Ruby cried out as the other enforcer attempted to do the same to her.

"Be careful," the enforcer said, forcing Kyo onto the ground before helping his partner.

The pair worked together to avoid the lashing of the corrupted energies and cuff Ruby's wrists behind her back. Once the cuffs were on, the shadowy energies partially receded. Kyo could better make out the corrupted side of her body. But how?

"She hasn't done anything wrong. We're trying to get her help." Kyo clenched his teeth, trying to draw magic out of himself, but he couldn't. Nixium cuffs, made from a special mineral that suppressed magic. He wouldn't be able to fight back as long as they touched him.

An enforcer grabbed Kyo by the back of the neck, forcing him to his feet and guiding him down the road. "She is dangerous, and you have questions to answer, kid."

Kyo struggled but couldn't remove himself from the enforcer's grasp. Ruby had family to return to—he said he'd do his best to help her. At this rate, he would not only fail her but delay finding Sybilla and Blanq, which would put Alden at greater risk.

It couldn't end up like this.

Chapter 5

Grumbling under his breath, Kyo glared at the two enforcers, one sitting across the table and the other pacing. Renewed pain stabbed at his head—the man sitting before him was hardly gentle when cuffing him.

The interrogation room had nothing aside from a table with two chairs, slick metal walls, and a single light hanging from the center of the ceiling. It wasn't his first time in such a room. Ruby and Ren had broken up more than one fight back home, leaving Kyo to defend his actions in similar places.

His thoughts turned to Ruby, who they'd placed in a cell. He could hear her crying as they locked her in. He had given her hope, and these two took it away, earning them bared teeth.

"Please stop glaring at us like that. You haven't done anything illegal, so we won't be locking you up," the enforcer said not for the first time, staring at Kyo, golden eyes matching his blond hair.

"No, Karo, you're just locking up someone who is ill and needs help," Kyo said. "And I know who can help her. But by all means, keep her here until it's too late to remove the corruption—I'm sure that'll work out great for everyone. Why not go to the cleric temple and arrest anyone there in need of healing while you're at it?" Kyo said, followed by a powerful yawn. He shook his head, trying to clear his vision. Between not sleeping overnight and the cuffs suppressing his magic, fatigue was kicking his ass. But he couldn't let that slow him down.

"His name is Karu. And a broken arm or well-understood illness is not the same as…whatever that corruption is," the other enforcer snapped. "We've been given strict instructions by Chancellor Ambers to detain anyone exhibiting signs of corruption. They are a danger to themselves and the townsfolk, and until we understand more about it, we need to keep them away from others." He adjusted his glasses and huffed.

Karu waved his hand as a signal for his partner to relax. "Easy, Milo." He turned back to Kyo. "We're not keeping her here because she's in trouble or has done something wrong. But from what we understand, even clerics can't cure such people, and this is the only place secure enough to ensure the safety of others." He picked up several papers, tapping them on the table to line them up. "Still, going back to your story, it is a bit odd. Despite the claims you made about" —he took a few seconds to read over his notes— "Sybilla and Blanq, you're now seeking their aid. And you think they'll help you?"

"It's not like there's any other choice. They can remove the corruption. I've seen them do it. It's either that or we let Ruby and my godfather turn into monsters. And between the two, Blanq hasn't actively tried to kill me yet." Kyo rose and kicked the chair back against the wall then leaned over the table, glaring at Karu. "Which is why I was trying to find them so they could help her, until you two geniuses decided to arrest us. And time is just a bit of a factor in this situation."

Chancellor Demaskus had said he'd alert Aquarin's chancellor about the situation. Apparently, that hadn't reached the ears of the enforcers yet, or Kyo wouldn't have had to waste time explaining everything.

Milo stomped toward Kyo, but Karu held out his arm to stop him. Grunting, Milo kept his eyes narrowed. "I get it. I'm not going to pretend I wouldn't be desperate if I had a loved one in the same situation." Rising, he placed a hand on the back of Kyo's neck and the other on the cuffs, guiding him out of the room. "But we can't let her leave that cell so long as she is corrupted."

"Then how am I supposed to help her? I won't leave her here," Kyo shouted, his fists clenched and eager to throw a punch.

They brought him to the main lobby of the enforcer station, dark clouds gathered outside the window dotted by a few drops of rain. Karu unlocked the cuffs. Kyo rubbed his right wrist and flexed his magical energy within himself, smiling as he could freely control it again. He disliked the stiff feeling when the cuffs were on, as if a vital part of himself had gone missing and his body knew it. As soon as his magic flowed unimpeded again, his body lost some of its sluggishness. It took some control not to cast a spell or punch something that would hurt his fist. He settled for twisting his upper body and stretching his arms across his chest but hesitated to move too quickly. A sickly feeling settled in his stomach, unsure if it came from lack of sleep or not eating enough since leaving home. Probably both.

"Then find that person and bring them here," Milo said, aggravated. "If they really can do what you say, we won't arrest them until the job is done."

Kyo opened his mouth to respond then closed it.

Ruby would stay in one place, people wouldn't avoid him, and there would be no risk of her attacking him or anyone else. Of course, convincing Blanq to walk into an enforcer station after what they'd done may not be possible. Thanks to Milo and Karu, the situation had become even more hopeless.

"Fine," Kyo said. "I'll be back, so you'd better be ready to bring me to her."

Milo glared. "You don't get to order us around, kid. We—"

"We need to work on your people skills, Milo," Karu finished then turned to Kyo. "And we'll open a missing person's case for your godfather while we're at it. Especially if he's corrupted, it'll be important to find him."

Milo released an annoyed huff then stepped aside as the door opened. An old man and a boy with sun-kissed skin and messy, dirty-blond hair about Kyo's age entered the station. The white robes with gold trim easily identified them as clerics.

"Thank you for coming, Cleric Micha."

The elder man nodded. "Of course. From what I've heard, other clerics have had no luck in helping the victims of corruption. But I will see for myself and do what I'm able."

"And who is this with you?" Karu asked.

Cleric Micha placed a hand on the boy's shoulder. "This is Marsh. He's new to the clerical practice but has a particular interest in the corruption. So, I thought he should come along, merely to observe. I hope that's okay."

Karu smiled. "Of course, I have no objections."

"I agree, now can we get on with it? You all talk too much," Milo said, waving his hand for them to follow. Karu frowned and mouthed an apology to the clerics.

Kyo stood motionless for several seconds then followed the group, keeping his footsteps light and a gap between himself and them. Could the clerics help Ruby? If they could, then helping Alden would be easier than he'd thought—once he found him. Even if they couldn't, having one of these two heal his throbbing head could save time. The group walked through metal double doors, and Kyo slipped through before they closed. His heart pounded, hope rising.

They walked through another set of metal double doors toward the back of the building. Both sides of the long, dim hallway were lined with prison cells, most of them empty. In the fifth cell on the right sat Ruby on the provided cot. Steel walls and a window too small for a grown woman to fit through ensured she had nowhere to go. Though not in legal trouble, it was hard to tell from looking at her accommodations.

"How are you feeling, Ruby?" Karu asked.

She glanced up but said nothing until her eyes fell on Kyo. "You're okay. Did you find those two that can help me?"

All eyes turned to Kyo.

"What are you doing here?" Milo asked, glaring. "You were supposed to leave."

"I came to check on Ruby. And also, for the clerics." Kyo waved his hand dismissively at Milo, stifling a yawn and focusing on the clerics. "Do you think you can help her?"

Cleric Micha turned to Ruby. "I'm uncertain. I can try, but I've heard of no success from others in this regard." He stepped toward the cell door, which Karu opened then closed behind him.

"For the safety of others," Karu said.

"I understand." Cleric Micha stepped cautiously toward Ruby. "Hello, young lady. Ruby, correct?" She nodded. "I wanted to examine you if I could. See if there is anything I can do about this corruption."

Ruby looked up at the older man, tears trickling down her cheeks. "Please, help me."

"Cleric Micha, I haven't heard of the corruption being transferred by touch, but I still advise caution," Karu said.

Kyo wasn't sure if Cleric Micha heard Karu or not, giving no response. The older man gently took Ruby's shadowy hand, still cuffed behind her back, in his as she turned. The dark aura around half her body twitched in response, but otherwise did nothing. Kyo thought back to when it had slayed three blobs at once. Ruby was stressed and in danger then. The energy clung to her body as if resting, both events hinting that the corruption, at least to some degree, reacted to her emotions.

"You can do it," Marsh whispered.

Kyo's attention turned briefly to Marsh, who gripped the cell bars and watched with intensity through the strands of shaggy blond hair hanging over his green eyes. Fists shaking and breathing deep, Marsh appeared more nervous about the outcome than Kyo was.

"Why so interested in the corruption?" Kyo asked.

Marsh jolted, as if the words broke some sort of trance. Their eyes met for a moment before Marsh turned back to Cleric Micha, whose hands glowed green against Ruby's. "I…want to help people. To be useful." His words came slow and deliberate, revealing a proper manner of speech. "Traditional healing is fine, but if I can learn to cure this corruption, there is much suffering I could help end." He stared at the floor for a moment. "I have seen cases in Oasis. It was heartbreaking being unable to help."

Kyo turned his attention back to Cleric Micha. For the moment, the idea of having his head healed faded into the back of his mind. Green magical energy trailed up Ruby's arm but got as far as her elbow before it struggled to go any further. The shadowy aura pushed against the healing magic, the two energies vying for dominance.

The corruption overtook the healing spell. Beads of green energy burst into the air from her arm then vanished.

"Well, that didn't work," Kyo muttered. Of course it wouldn't be so easy, but he had still hoped.

Marsh sighed and shook his head. "What is this corruption?"

"It's a damn problem, that's what. All we know is, if it's not cured after a while, the person becomes some sort of monster and rampages," Milo said. He stumbled when Karu nudged him and glared. "What? No use sugar-coating it."

"Perhaps I should take a better look inside. Ruby, try and relax for me, okay? Close your eyes and try to calm yourself," Cleric Micha instructed.

Ruby exhaled and shut her eyes. The cleric did the same.

Several seconds passed with no change.

"Well, this is exciting," Kyo said, turning back to Marsh. "While we're waiting, can you heal my head?"

Marsh raised a brow.

"It's been throbbing since yesterday. Smashed with a rock, hence my face." Kyo figured there'd be no point in telling him the whole story.

"I am quite new to being a cleric. It may be best to have Cleric Micha do it when he is finished," Marsh said, struggling to maintain eye contact.

Kyo slapped Marsh's chest with the back of his hand. "You're a cleric, right? Come on, heal up. I don't want to waste any time after seeing if he can help her or not. I have things to do." When Marsh made no move, Kyo sighed. "If you can't, I'll get him to do it. But just try, okay?"

He glanced at the two in the cell, his right leg shaking in anticipation and impatience.

Finally, Marsh placed his hands on either side of Kyo's head, fingers gently rubbing against the skin. "No bone fractures. Quite a bit of bruising though. Especially around the eye. Damaged muscles. I…should be able to help."

Like his superior, Marsh's hands glowed a pale green. The pain lessened instantly. But the hands gripping Kyo's head shook as Marsh stared into his eyes. Maybe waiting for Cleric Micha would have been better after all.

"Hey, take it easy. You're not mixing a potion. You really are new to this, huh?" Not that Kyo had doubted Marsh's earlier words, but he hadn't expected the cleric to be so nervous over a simple injury.

"Apologies. I did warn you. Perhaps we should wait until—"

"You're doing fine. It's starting to feel better. Keep doing what you're doing," Kyo said. Yawning again, he blinked hard.

Marsh shifted his hands so one went over Kyo's eye then continued healing. The two enforcers had their own whispered conversation, and there'd been no change from the two in the cell.

After another minute passed, Marsh pulled his hands away. Kyo rotated his neck and ran his fingers over his eye, feeling only a slight bump, giving a satisfied grin. Minuscule pain lingered, but that was normal. Clerics never healed an injury to its fullest unless absolutely necessary, not wanting to risk the body becoming dependent on the healing spells.

"Thank Tutelvus, that's so much better." If it came to a fight with Sybilla, Kyo no longer had an injury to restrict him. Sending her tumbling across the ground with a wind-powered punch would make his day.

Cleric Micha gasped and pulled away from Ruby, causing everyone outside the cell to jump.

Karu opened the door and helped the cleric to his feet. "Are you all right?"

The cleric released a heavy breath and nodded. "I am, yes. The corruption actively fought my probing into Ruby. As if it belonged and I did not." He and Ruby stared at one another. "But it felt like more than a mere instinctual reaction. I can't explain it, but it seemed there was more to it than what you'd see in a virus or traditional illness invading the body."

"What does that mean for her though?" Kyo asked.

Karu attempted to pull Cleric Micha from the cell, but he didn't budge.

"The only thing I know is that I am incapable of helping her." The cleric placed a hand on her uncorrupted shoulder. "I am so sorry."

Ruby said nothing, staring at the ground, quietly sobbing.

"Damn it." Kyo slammed the side of his fist against the cell bars. "Well, I guess that means the old plan is still the current one. I need to go. Now."

As Kyo turned to leave, Marsh grasped his arm. "Wait. What is this old current plan of yours?"

"Yes, I would like to know as well," Cleric Micha said.

Kyo told them about the events of Mistwell and meeting Ruby on the way to Aquarin Port, though he spoke as quickly as possible.

Cleric Micha rubbed his chin. "Dead bodies moving? I've heard of such spells. Old and banished long before I was born. Disturbing details. As for the individuals themselves, a black robe and an odd red-and-black dress. I'm certain I saw a pair matching that description earlier today."

Kyo rushed to stand right in front of the elder cleric. "You did? Where? What were they doing?"

"They looked to be leaving town, heading south. To Calmarock, I'd assume. I tried to offer them shelter for the coming storm." His eyes shifted to the ceiling. For the first time, Kyo registered the sound of rain battering against the roof. "Well, the storm that is here now. But they refused."

Kyo gripped his hair and groaned. "Calmarock? I don't have time to chase them all over the island." He stumbled and leaned against the cell bars, vision blurring. "Or the energy."

Cleric Micha raised Kyo's head by his chin. "Are you all right, my boy?"

"Just tired. Didn't sleep last night."

The elder cleric cupped Kyo's cheeks. "This is not something I normally do. However, seeing as the situation is a dire one, I will make an exception."

His hands glowed with a white light, spreading and overtaking Kyo's body. The weight lifted from Kyo's eyes, his vision clearing and even his thoughts coming more clearly. Seconds later, the cleric pulled his hands away.

In this condition, Kyo could run all the way to Calmarock, or at least he thought so. "What did you do?"

"You can consider it like healing your body's stamina. It should nullify your lack of sleep. It can, however, be quite addicting to your mind and body, so I will not be doing it again. And before you ask, Marsh has not learned this skill as far as I am aware. You *must* sleep properly this evening."

Kyo jumped in place several times then raised his fists near his face. He punched, a burst of air escaping and harmlessly hitting a nearby wall. "This is great! Thanks."

"Do not cast spells like that in the station," Milo shouted.

"If you wish to thank me, would you consider taking Marsh with you?" Cleric Micha asked. Both Kyo and Marsh turned to him, Marsh's mouth hanging open.

"He did wish to learn more about this corruption and how to heal it. I think this would be good for him."

"But I do not have enough skill or experience to—"

"Sure, why not," Kyo interrupted. "I could use my own pocket healer. But we need to leave now." He grasped Marsh's arm and looked back at him. "Come on, bedhead."

Kyo wouldn't let Marsh argue. Sybilla deserved payback for what she'd done, but if she ended up being more difficult than he anticipated, he might need Marsh's healing abilities. So what if a storm was coming? What harm could a bit of water do? And he dealt with heavy winds on a daily basis.

Puffing his chest, Kyo mentally dared the storm to try and stop them

Chapter 6

Rain fell sideways in the heavy winds, Kyo and Marsh's clothes drenched after the first minute of the storm. A little water never hurt anyone, but a torrential downpour was another thing. Kyo's shirt clung to him like a second skin even under his hoodie. Walking with soaked shoes along a muddy path felt like someone had cast a gravity spell on him. And Calmarock was still several hours away.

"I know it is important to reach Calmarock quickly, but it might be a good idea to seek shelter," Marsh shouted through the howling winds.

"We'll be fine. There isn't even any lightning. And it's not like we can get wetter than we already are." Aside from helping Alden and Ruby, who knew what might happen to the people of Calmarock if they didn't hurry. Though hopefully Chancellor Demaskus should have warned Calmarock's chancellor by now. Maybe they'd arrive to find Sybilla and Blanq already in custody.

A tree leaned his way, and Kyo jumped but then swung upright again as the ground beneath it rose.

No, not the ground. The tree grew on the back of an enormous tortoise. Releasing a low groan, it adjusted itself in the hole beneath it, before falling back in with a thud.

"Yeah, me too, buddy." Kyo groaned too, mimicking the tortoise's.

"Do you see that? Up ahead, on the trail," Marsh said, pointing forward.

"I can barely see the next few steps I'll be taking." As far as Kyo could tell, the rain created a whiteout. How could Marsh see through it?

Marsh grabbed his wrist and pulled him along. Eventually, Kyo did see something—some*one*. A burly, older man with graying hair and thick, full beard sat against a turned over wagon, a wide assortment of goods scattered across the ground. His chest heaved, which at least indicated he was alive.

Kyo crouched next to the man and patted his cheek a few times, hoping he'd open his eyes. The man gave a pained moan in response. "He sure is out of it." He gave the man a once over and saw no signs of physical injury. "I guess it's your time to shine, bedhead."

Marsh gave a worried glance before turning his attention to his patient. He raised the man's left eyelid then checked his pulse. Leaning forward, Marsh trailed his fingers over the veins along the man's neck, which were not only bulging but had a green tint to them. "What is this?"

He placed his hands on the man's chest, and they glowed white.

"I don't know, but I wish I hadn't seen it." While his new partner worked, Kyo stood and grabbed the wagon's bonnet, pulling hard. Whatever happened here had damaged it enough that he was able to tug it free and drag it across the mud. Even with holes in it, placing it over Marsh and the sick man would be better than nothing.

"There is some sort of poison in his lungs, and it is spreading," Marsh said.

"Well then, time for you to do your thing, right?" The rain battered the bonnet above them, forcing them to raise their voices to be heard.

"I understand the principle. I have studied a spell that removes poison, but I have yet to put it into practice. What if I mess up? Make it worse?" Marsh's hands trembled as they rested against the man's chest.

"I shouldn't have to point this out, but I'm pretty sure he'll die if you don't do anything. You can't possibly make it worse." Kyo slapped Marsh's back. "Besides, you felt the same way about my head and face, but that turned out fine. Stop overthinking so much." He forced a smile, not wanting to show his concern.

The poor man released a barely audible groan. Was he conscious?

After taking several deep breaths, Marsh closed his eyes, and his hands glowed a pale purple. The man's body jolted then calmed. Kyo watched, careful to do nothing that might distract Marsh from his efforts. He understood the basic premise behind how a cleric's magic worked. In a way, they could see through their magical energy and understand what was happening within the body. The idea made him shudder. Examining the gross inner workings of someone's body was not for him.

Together, Marsh's hands trailed up his patient's chest with deliberate slowness, as if afraid he'd break something. The man jolted again, and Marsh's eyes shot open.

"Apologies! I promise I am doing my best. Bear with me." He got no response.

"It's okay. Take a breath and go again." Kyo didn't need to see inside the man's body to realize Marsh wasn't as careful as needed. He took the man's hand in his, wishing he could do more. Unfortunately, not everyone could be saved by fighting something. He clenched his teeth, hating how useless his skills were in this situation.

Marsh's hands moved again, starting where Kyo assumed the lungs were then rising to meet each other farther up. This time, there was no violent response. Marsh trailed his fingers up the chest and over the throat and, after a brief hesitation, became level with the man's lips. As he pulled his fingers toward himself, a green gelatinous substance escaped the man's mouth. Kyo took it upon himself to blast it away through a hole in the bonnet with his wind.

"See? You did it. I told you," Kyo said, gently nudging Marsh's side.

Shaking his head, Marsh returned his hands to their original positions. "There is still more."

"Oh." Kyo remained crouched as Marsh repeated his earlier efforts.

Marsh pulled droplets of the sludge from the man two more times then kept his green glowing hands on his chest and neck. "I must repair what damage I can. He should recover, assuming he gets looked at by a more experienced cleric soon."

His arms slumped a bit, and he released a sigh while he worked on his patient.

Each minute felt like an hour, Kyo's fingers twiddling the entire time. When the man groaned and his eyes fluttered open, the tension eased.

"Hey, look who's awake. Sleep well?" Kyo asked.

"Kyo, please." Marsh's hands rested on his knees. Though his body visibly trembled, he smiled at the man. "I am glad to have you back with us. How do you feel?"

Looking between the two, the man shifted, rotated his shoulders, and moved his legs slightly. "Horrible. Like one of them damn tortoises…kicked me in the chest." He took a deep breath and winced. "But I'll manage, I think." He grasped Marsh's hands. "Thank you, cleric."

Marsh nodded, a tear threatening to escape from his eye. "I am glad I could help you. What is your name? And can you tell us what happened?"

"The name's Donavi," he said, grabbing the side of the overturned wagon. Donavi tried to stand but hit his head on the bonnet. Rubbing his head, he peeked through one of the holes, as if realizing his surroundings for the first time. "We're traders. Just finished up in Calmarock and were heading back to Aquarin."

"We?" Marsh asked.

Donavi raised a brow. Then his eyes widened. He pinched the bridge of his nose. "Yes…we. There were three of us, before those two showed up."

"Let me guess. A woman with red hair and a weird dress and someone in a black robe?" Kyo asked, narrowing his eyes.

Donavi glared at Kyo. "You know them?"

"They're why we're heading to Calmarock. We were hoping to find them before they hurt anyone else." Kyo eyed the damaged wagon. "I guess they're giving up on the idea of subtlety. Did the poison come from the one with the black robe?" While Sybilla made effective use of her alteration spell, Blanq had yet to show any form of offensive magic.

"No, it came from the damned red-haired woman. She got all three of us with it. And I swear the psycho enjoyed it." Donavi slammed his thick fist against the side of the wagon. "She said I could die slower, probably because I called her a few unflattering names. I had to watch my partners suffer." He took a deep breath, cringing slightly. "One was barely into adulthood. Need to find a way to take their bodies back at least. The salasaurs pulling the wagon buggered off. Damn good-for-nothing lizards."

Marsh and Kyo exchanged glances.

"I am sorry," Marsh started, "but I do not recall seeing any others. Kyo, could you have a look?"

"Sure, I'm soaked to the bone anyway, so why not?" Kyo ducked under the bonnet.

The heavy rain and wind bombarded him. He searched all around the wagon but found nothing. For the sake of efficiency, he trekked through the nearby trees on either side of the trail, searching around them and through tall grass, unsure if he stepped on the backs of any more tortoises or not. Kyo didn't know why he agreed to come out here. He knew what must have happened to the bodies of the other two. From what he could gather, Sybilla ended people's lives, then Blanq raised them. He didn't want to think about why.

With water dripping off his hair and onto his face, he returned to the safety of the bonnet. "Sorry, they're not here."

Before Donavi could speak, Marsh beat him to it. "What is important now is to ensure you return to Aquarin Port safely. Do you need an escort?"

Donavi rotated his hips and shook out his legs. "No, I think I'll manage. Still hurts to breathe, but I'll check in with another cleric when I get there. You little yolks should keep going, maybe try to talk to the chancellor and warn him about those two. I'll do the same with Aquarin's chancellor. Maybe ask for a search party for what remains of my partners." He turned his head, as if gazing into a distance he couldn't see with the bonnet in the way. "Them people in Calmarock are a tough bunch, but they don't have an organized enforcer team. Hope they'll be all right."

"So, it sounds like nothing's changed," Kyo said. "We're still heading there to put a stop to those two." And in the process, save Alden and Ruby. Why did this fall to the two of them? If the Aurora were here, he bet this would have been resolved in less than a day.

"If you insist on returning alone, please be careful." Marsh raised the bonnet a bit, sighing as the rain fell upon his robes. "Do not overexert yourself. I have removed the poison and repaired some of the damage to your lungs, but there is still more work that could be done to improve your condition."

Donavi placed his hand over his heart and bowed his head. "I'm grateful to you, cleric. I'll be sure to show my thanks by making it to Aquarin in one piece. And if you do find those two, rain the fury of the pantheon upon them."

He ducked under the bonnet and stumbled into the storm, pulling his brown leather jacket over his head.

"I guess it's our turn to get wet again. Oh, I'm not really one for formalities, but…" Kyo placed his hand over his heart and bowed. Unlike Donavi, he did so at the waist, used to that method from his father's people. "That's for fixing up my face and head."

Smiling, Marsh repeated the gesture. "And that is for your assistance. Twice you have supported me when I lacked the confidence to do what I must."

Kyo's stomach fluttered. People tended to yell at him far more than thank him for anything. He found it embarrassing but something he could get used to. "Don't worry about it. Sometimes a person just needs a swift kick in the ass. Speaking of which, time for this storm to kick ours again."

They emerged from under the bonnet together, using their hoods in a feeble attempt to keep their heads dry. While he couldn't call this a happy ending for Donavi, at least he still lived. Kyo would make sure no one in Calmarock got hurt.

He glanced back at the wagon. The fact that it and Donavi were left out in the open concerned him. In Mistwell, Sybilla and Blanq were more discreet. But maybe this would be a good thing. Their actions were certain to piss off plenty of people. And when they found themselves overwhelmed, he'd be at the front of the mob.

Chapter 7

A weight lifted from Kyo when he saw a wooden archway with 'Calmarock' engraved in it. Unfortunately, that weight didn't include his soaked clothes. The storm had ceased an hour ago but left him and Marsh no less drenched.

They'd only walked one block into town when Kyo slowed his pace. Calmarock was a mining town, primarily iron. He wouldn't have been surprised if his swords had been forged here. A mine cart track ran through the middle of an intersection up ahead. He figured a place like this would be bustling with people working, yet he could neither hear nor see anyone.

"Where is everyone?" he asked.

"Perhaps they elected to remain indoors even as the storm passed. We are sure to find someone if we keep looking." Marsh took the lead down the main thoroughfare.

The structures here had a similar aesthetic to back home, but an older style. Wooden beams supported the roofs, the front doors rounding at the top instead of a rectangular shape and wooden planks in a crisscross pattern across the bottoms of each story. Kyo examined each building they passed, more than once swearing he saw someone through curtains. How were they supposed to find Sybilla and Blanq if no one was around to ask? If they set up shop in a random building like in Mistwell, it could take hours or days to find them.

Marsh paused in the middle of an intersection. "Something terrible happened here."

The building on the left corner had a massive hole in the wall next to the front door. Another across the street had claw marks in the wooden exterior and shattered windows. Several dark crimson stains were spattered along the road and sides of buildings, sending a shiver up Kyo's spine.

They turned their heads at the sound of a shop bell. Two women carrying bags of food stepped onto the road.

"Let's find out what," Kyo said.

Hustling in their direction, he waved to get their attention. As he got closer, he realized one appeared around his age.

"Oh, hello. I'm surprised to see two young men like you out and about," the older woman said with a wide smile and friendly tone to her voice. She wore a starry-sky-patterned dress and her brown hair short, barely reaching her shoulders. "Not many people are willing to come outside at the moment. What makes you two so brave?"

In contrast to her kind demeanor, the fair-skinned girl about his age appeared as though she were attempting to stab them with her glare, a hand on her hip and foot tapping impatiently.

"Yeah, about that. What exactly happened here?" Kyo asked.

The woman tilted her head. "You don't know? It was dreadful. Very frightening. It's why everyone is staying inside. But you two should be careful. I think we're okay for now, but it could happen again."

Kyo and Marsh exchanged confused looks.

"We only just arrived in town, from Aquarin. Would you care to tell us what this horrible thing was?" Marsh asked.

"Layla, can we go already?" the younger girl asked, each turn of her head whipping the emerald-green ponytail that reached to the back of her knees. "We don't need to give a lesson to these two. And I'm getting hungry."

"That's enough, Krysta. There's no harm in being polite. Besides, look at them." Layla motioned to them with her hand. "They clearly came all the way here in the middle of that dreadful storm."

"I can tell—they look like a couple of drowned saber pups. Do you not take any pride in your appearance?" Krysta sighed and rolled her eyes. Kyo motioned to the storm clouds in the distance, but she continued before he could get a word out. "The short version is someone became corrupted. Do you know what that means?"

Kyo and Marsh nodded.

"Well, he turned completely," Krysta continued. "It took a lot of people to bring him down, and not everyone made it out alive. That was two days ago." She turned to Layla. "Can we go now?"

This girl needed a good slap upside her head. And with each passing second, Kyo became more tempted to give it. But he had to stay out of trouble, for Alden and Ruby's sakes. "Before you do, can you tell us where we can find the chancellor? We have something important to tell them."

"Of course." Layla pointed further into town. "If you go two—no, three—blocks that way then take a right, you should find his office on the left."

"Thank you." Marsh bowed his head. "We appreciate it."

They took two steps before Krysta interjected. "Not that it'll do you any good. Chancellor Barion left

Calmarock. I think he went to Mistwell for something. Can't say when he'll be back."

To Mistwell? Maybe Chancellor Demaskus wanted to tell him about Sybilla and Blanq himself. Talk about terrible timing. Warning him was the best way to spread the word to the rest of town.

"Really? He's gone?" Layla asked.

"You need to pay more attention to your surroundings. I keep telling you that." Krysta stared at Layla with a smile. "Please try to keep your head out of the clouds a bit. Now give me one of those bags. I can carry another one."

Layla shook her head. "I have another idea. Give me the bag you have, and I'd like you to take these two boys to the public showers to get cleaned up then bring them back home for a warm meal."

"What?" Krysta asked with wide, sad eyes. "Why do we need to bring them home?"

"Because they'll get sick if they don't get clean and dry soon. And if I had to guess, they have nowhere to go now that they're here, isn't that right, boys?" Layla asked, turning to look at them.

Marsh cupped his chin. "Well, it is true we have nowhere to stay. But we have something important we must do. There are a pair we are looking for, and it is imperative we find them as soon as possible. They would have come into town earlier today."

"And you mean to greet them like that? Absolutely not. Krysta…" Layla grabbed the paper bag from the girl. "Please get them cleaned up."

"But…"

Layla leaned close so her face nearly touched Krysta's. "You say my head is in the clouds, but I say yours is trapped in a box, trying to ignore anyone's needs but your own. You of all people should know better." She placed a soft kiss on Krysta's forehead. "Now go on. I'll see you soon."

Krysta pouted as Layla walked away. Then she turned and glared at Kyo, but her gaze softened when looking at Marsh. "Fine. Come on and keep up."

She marched down the street, not checking to make sure they followed.

"Well, isn't she a bright ray of sunshine," Kyo muttered.

"Did you say something?" Krysta called back.

"I said your clothes don't fit." At least the top didn't seem to, the long-sleeved, striped shirt exposing her right shoulder.

"I like it this way," she said. "Now shut your mouth and hurry up."

Marsh nudged Kyo. "Let us go along with her and avoid confrontation, please. Perhaps we can eat something at Miss Layla's home beyond the bread you packed. Bread and nothing else."

"Don't talk bad about bread." Kyo could have counted the people they passed on one hand, none more than a few steps away from their homes. Claw marks were etched into front doors, and cracked indents pockmarked the road. It must have been one intense battle against the shade.

Up ahead, a statue caught Kyo's attention. He paused to examine it. Molded from iron, if he had to guess, but he saw no plaque explaining its purpose nor a stand for it to be placed on. Nothing more than a vague human shape hunched forward with clenched fingers, as if in agony. The metal drooped in places, as if the man were melting.

"This is a cheery statue," Kyo said. "Why is it in the middle of the road?"

Krysta approached, running her fingers over its arm. "It's not a statue. It was the person who became a shade."

Marsh gasped, eyes fixated on the iron man. "Does that mean there is a person underneath the metal?"

"What's left of him, yes. Not many people use magic in Calmarock, and the few that do usually practice it for the sake of the town's mining economy. Spells that would make it easier to mine ore or craft weapons, things like that. With the exception of basic medical needs, that is. So, when the poor man turned into a shade and weapons were useless, they had to come up with an alternate method of dealing with it." She shook her head. "A few people were killed before they realized conventional weapons couldn't hurt it. Even my own spells were brushed off."

"So, they covered it with liquid metal? I guess that would do it, huh?" Kyo asked. Taking out a monster that resisted weapons and magic like this — Donavi was right about the people in this town.

"Not that he was the only corrupted person in town." Krysta clenched her fists and slammed one against the metal. "But forget it. Come on. Hurry up so we can get to the showers. I want to get home and eat."

Kyo followed alongside Marsh, taking one last look at the 'statue.' Images of Ruby and Alden transforming filled his head, those dark energies striking down any who came near them. What drastic measures might others, or he, have to take part in to put an end to them if they fully turned? His heart thudded, and he was unable to focus on anything else.

"Do you know how long he was corrupted before he turned?" Kyo asked.

"No," Krysta stated harshly.

Rolling his eyes, Kyo tightened his lips to keep from saying anything that might make them miss out on the food Layla promised.

They walked the rest of the way in silence as they turned down this road and that. Krysta stopped and pointed to a nondescript, one story structure with two separate entrances. The sound of running water reached the streets.

"Here are the showers," she said. "Don't take too long."

Rushing inside to get away from little miss cheerful, Kyo and Marsh entered the male side of the showers. Once out of view, Kyo stripped down, placed his clothes into a metallic box, and pressed the button, activating the heating spell contained within. He turned the shower on and released a long sigh as the hot water hit him, steam filling the area around him.

"How do you think we should go about finding Sybilla and Blanq?" Marsh asked from the next stall.

"I don't know. We can't just go door to door. But if people aren't willing to come out, maybe those two will have a hard time finding victims. And if the chancellor comes back soon, I'm sure he knows a way to get the word out to everyone." Kyo pulled his ponytail from its tie and lathered his hair. "Finally, I don't feel like crap."

"We cannot count on the chancellor. If he returns soon, then all the better. But there is no telling how long he will remain in Mistwell, so whatever plans we make should not include him for the time being. And something else concerns me."

Kyo stood under the flowing water, staring at the wall separating Marsh and him as he listened.

"If people are so unwilling to leave their homes," Marsh said, "it will become impossible to identify any who are corrupted. This could lead to a repeat of what happened here several days ago, perhaps on a heightened scale."

He had a point. The last thing these people needed were multiple shades running rampant across town. Preventing that wasn't their responsibility, but Kyo knew his parents would have found a way to keep it from happening. To think Calmarock didn't have a team of enforcers. He couldn't understand why so few here used magic. Every person had the ability with a little practice. Maybe after the shade attack, the citizens would rethink their opinion on the matter.

"One thing at a time," Kyo said. "Let's deal with Sybilla and Blanq first. So far, they're the only ones who can cure the corruption, so if we want to prevent a repeat, it'd require their cooperation. Probably forced on them, but that's fine."

Once he finished cleaning himself, Kyo dried off with a towel, wrapped it around his waist, and stepped out. Nothing left to do but wait for his clothes to dry.

Marsh joined him a minute later. He peeked into the clothes dryer, frowning. "I know finding them is of the utmost importance, but I suggest we take advantage of Layla and Krysta's hospitality."

"I think we can cut Krysta from that statement." Kyo didn't look forward to meeting her perpetual glare when he stepped outside again. "She's as hospitable as a zu protecting its eggs."

Marsh shrugged. "Regardless, it could be beneficial to have a place where we can rest when needed, as well as prepare proper meals for ourselves. Though I would not feel right making use of their hard-earned food, as I have not brought any cryst with me."

"I brought some from home, though it's not a lot. But I guess we could do a little shopping if we really have too later." Kyo opened the dryer and pulled his clothes out. "Good, finished. I bet the longer we take, the louder Krysta will yell at us." Moving back into the shower stall, he shed the towel and got dressed. He couldn't help but smile from the warm comfort of his own clothes, opting to wear his hoodie instead of wrapping it around his waist.

"Please tell her I will be a bit longer," Marsh said. "Robes take longer to dry."

"Sure." Kyo left the showers, finding Krysta leaning against the wall next to the door. "And here I thought you would have ditched us."

She scoffed. "Layla said to bring you back, so I will. Where's the cleric?"

"His robe is still drying."

"I suppose so." There wasn't much malice behind those words. Even someone like Krysta gave a bit of respect to clerics, it seemed.

"Is Layla your mom?" Kyo asked.

"What business is it of yours?" She glared.

He shrugged. "I'm just curious. But if you won't tell me, I'm sure Layla will anyway."

Krysta opened her mouth and promptly closed it, her lips forming a straight line. "Of course she will," she muttered. "No, she's not, but she may as well be. She was my teacher and caretaker up until a few years ago. I have no idea why she decided to live here of all places, about as far away from home as you could get."

"You're not from Calmarock, then. Just visiting her?"

She nodded. They stood in silence until Marsh emerged.

"Good, let's get going." She motioned for them to follow.

Kyo didn't intend to spend much time at Layla's home. While Marsh had a point of needing a place to rest, Kyo wanted to begin his search as soon as possible. A quick stop to the house, devour some food, then off he'd go. Besides, there was no telling when Cleric Micha's spell would wear off. Sleeping for hours would waste far too much time. He had to find and subdue Sybilla and Blanq before then. Ruby and Alden were counting on it.

Chapter 8

The three mages approached a simple two-story home with a chestnut-brown exterior like all the others. Krysta burst through the front door.

"I'm back, Layla!" She ran straight into the kitchen, leaving Kyo and Marsh behind.

A part of Kyo wanted to turn and leave, explore the town, search high and low for Sybilla and Blanq. What kept him there was the rumbling in his stomach. The food he'd packed helped but couldn't replace a full meal, and doubling over from hunger while confronting those two wouldn't end well.

He stepped inside. A soft maroon couch sat against a wall, with an armchair in the opposite corner. The walls were lined with lifelike pictures, painted and hand drawn, of various individuals he assumed were her family. A rather average-looking living room, with the exception of the wide bookshelf of black wood that held not books but various ceramic figurines too far from the door to see in detail.

As he neared the kitchen, the aroma of various herbs and spices filled Kyo's nostrils. He heard the sizzling before peeking into the kitchen to see thinly sliced potatoes cooking in oil on a frying pan. One of several dishes being prepared, or had been, before Krysta had wrapped her arms tightly around Layla.

"If you don't let go, I might burn dinner," Layla said with a chuckle, even though she had her own arm wrapped around Krysta.

"It smells delicious, Layla," Marsh said. "I apologize for intruding."

Layla waved her hand dismissively. "Nonsense, I'm the one who invited you boys. It shouldn't be much longer now."

Krysta pointed to a cabinet hanging from the wall above the counter. "Make yourselves useful then and set the table."

Marsh opened it, revealing shelves of plates and drinking glasses. He gathered four plates and handed them to Kyo, then took the drinking glasses to place on the table. "We should offer to clean up after dinner too. It is only polite."

Kyo groaned but nodded. More time being wasted. Maybe he should let Marsh take care of that while he got a head start searching the town. It might be rude, but lives were on the line.

"Utensils are in the drawer under the cabinet you opened," Krysta said without looking, her eyes fixed on the food Layla prepared.

Minutes after the table was set, the food was distributed. The potatoes were appetizing enough, but servings of dullfish and—most importantly to Kyo— buttery, flaky rolls had his mouth watering. In his mind, no food could beat bread of nearly any kind.

"We truly appreciate the hospitality," Marsh said, eyes glued to his plate as he shifted impatiently in his seat.

"Yeah, thanks. This looks and smells amazing." Kyo didn't wait, stabbing a potato slice with his fork and taking the first bite, then chasing it down with a sip of bullafruit juice.

"This is a bit much. Layla, don't tell me you went out of your way for these two." Krysta took a roll from the basket and bit into it.

Layla swallowed her food before responding. "Really, you of all people should understand the concept of hospitality and treating everyone with respect. If you were home, I have no doubt you'd do the same."

"Where is that?" Kyo asked.

Layla opened her mouth, but Krysta spoke first. "What's it to you? You sure do like prying into people's business, huh? Really, try to have some class. I guess we have five dullfish at the table instead of four."

Kyo bit down hard on his bread. He aimed his finger toward her plate of food, fully intending to blow it in her face.

But Marsh grabbed his wrist, staring intently at him.

With a grunt, Kyo pulled his hand back and continued eating, noting Krysta's satisfied smirk.

"And here I thought I taught you better than that. People must think you were raised by a good-for-nothing who treats people terribly." Layla frowned.

"I—" Krysta turned to her with wide, sad eyes. "No, Layla, of course not." Sighing, she mumbled a barely audible apology.

A tense silence overtook the kitchen, save the sound of utensils scraping against plates. This girl was a good reason to leave once dinner was finished. The sooner Kyo could leave her behind, the better.

Marsh cleared his throat and waited until all eyes were on him. "Kyo, I believe it would be best to tell them the full story of why we are here. For their own safety above all else."

"Can we tell Layla and not Krysta?" Marsh narrowed his eyes and Kyo shrugged. "It was just a suggestion."

Kyo started from the beginning, though he excluded a few details about the corruption as they were already familiar with it. He told them about Alden, Ruby, Blanq, and Sybilla, as well as their victims and what became of them.

"So, we're here to force them to cure Alden and Ruby and keep them from hurting anyone else," he finished.

Krysta stared at her plate. "That's actually serious. I'd swear you two are lying through your teeth. But the timing of the chancellor's trip to Mistwell does match up. I wonder if Chancellor Demaskus called him there about this issue."

"We wished to warn the chancellor when we came to Calmarock, but his being away means it will be much more difficult to warn the people," Marsh said.

Layla stood and rounded the table. "You three, stay here and finish your meals. Krysta, be a dear and make sure the kitchen gets clean, please."

Shooting from her chair, Krysta grabbed Layla's wrist. "Where are you going?"

"I'm just going over to Mr. Fallus's. If I tell him what these boys just said, the chancellor will find out as soon as he returns. He works closely with the chancellor." Layla embraced Krysta and placed a kiss atop her head. "Now stay here until I come back, okay? I won't be long." She had to force herself from Krysta's arms to leave the house.

"She'd better hurry back," Krysta muttered before continuing to eat.

"Marsh, when did you become a cleric?" Kyo asked through a mouth full of potatoes.

Krysta cringed. "Gross."

Swallowing what food remained in his mouth, Marsh's face fell. "It would have been close to two years ago. I am a cleric at the Oasis chapel, not Aquarin.

However, I was asked to come here to meet other clerics and expand my knowledge."

"Oasis, huh? I went there once as a kid. What kind of magic did you practice before becoming a cleric?" Kyo asked.

"I—" Marsh stared at his plate, poking the fish. "I was…am an orphan. Since I was young. I lived on the streets of Riftdale and had to rely on theft to survive." The fork in his hand shook, and his breathing became heavier. "You may think poorly of me after you hear this, but I ran after doing something terrible." His words came quickly, as if they'd been held at bay for a long time. "I stole something valuable from a family, to sell so I could buy food. But it did not belong to them. It belonged to someone dangerous. The family was killed because of my actions. I had no way of knowing it would happen. I…" Tears streaked down his cheeks.

"Whoa, whoa. Easy there. I guess you've been holding onto that for a while, huh?" Kyo rested his hand on the cleric's back. "I don't think badly about you. You were in a rough place. You had to survive, right? And you didn't know what would happen. Sounds to me like they shouldn't have been involved with dangerous people to begin with. Don't blame yourself."

"I mean, on a technical level it *is* because of your actions." Krysta cleared her throat when Kyo bit his lip in anger at her. "But the dolt is right. I'm sorry you had to go through such a hard time in your life. The events are unfortunate, but you shouldn't put the blame on yourself."

Marsh took in a few sharp, shaky breaths. "Thank you. I will never let myself forget what happened, but I wish to help as many as I can. This is why, when I found myself in Oasis, I went to the temple and asked them to teach me." After a few seconds, a smile crossed his lips. "I appreciate the support from you both." He inhaled deeply and sat back in his chair. "I am all right."

Kyo pat his back. "Good. Just keep doing what you're doing."

The remainder of their meal passed in silence. At least the food was delicious. Kyo finished his third roll, grateful Krysta was too distracted to shoot him any more angry looks merely for existing. Minutes dragged on, enough for Kyo to finish his first helping and get seconds.

When all plates were empty, Marsh stood and collected everyone's dishes and utensils.

"How far is the Fallus residence?" he asked, walking toward the sink.

"One block east and one block north. She shouldn't be long. I suppose it makes sense she's going there. He works in the chancellor's office, so he could get word to him quickly. Maybe use the com-orb in his office to contact Chancellor Demaskus through his own," Krysta said. "Since you got to partake in that delicious meal, you two can handle the cleanup, right?" She strolled into the living room and dropped onto the couch without waiting for a response.

Kyo sighed and collected the drinking glasses, setting them on the counter. "Since you're already washing, I guess I'll dry."

He grabbed a towel off the counter and took whatever Marsh handed to him and dried it, piling the plates on top of one another then setting the utensils down in a disorganized pile. About halfway through, Marsh's actions became noticeably slower, keeping his eyes downcast.

"Hey, you awake?" Kyo asked, gently nudging him.

Marsh blinked and handed him a knife. "Apologies. I can finish this myself. You want to head outside and begin your search, correct?"

Kyo smiled and turned to leave.

"But where will you begin?" Marsh asked. "I know you are in a rush, but it could save a lot of time if we have a plan in place before we start."

Sitting around and making plans had never been Kyo's style. But as much as he wanted to dash out the door and start his search, Marsh had a point. He had no idea where to begin, and for all he knew, Sybilla and Blanq could sit idle for days before making a move. Ruby and Alden didn't have that kind of time.

"Well, what do you suggest?" Kyo asked.

"Despite what we were told, I find it hard to imagine every single resident has remained indoors since the shade attack. After all, we found Layla and Krysta, correct? And we passed several people outside their homes on the way to the showers. I suggest we return to that area and ask anyone we find if they have seen those two come through town. From what you told me, their appearances are rather distinctive, so they are likely to stick out." Marsh cupped his chin, tapping his foot. "Beyond that, you said in Mistwell, they—"

"By the will of the Altruists, shut up!" Krysta shouted from the living room.

Kyo startled then glared at the wall separating the kitchen and living room. "Geez, what is her problem?"

Marsh cleared his throat. "As I was saying," he continued in a lower voice. "You said they used an empty home for their operations. We could also ask if there is any place like that and search it ourselves."

"Not a bad idea. I'm glad you're around. You're more than just a pocket healer." Kyo wrapped an arm around him, squeezing tight. "Well then, if you're going to be the brains of this operation, let's get this cleaned up quickly so we can both go."

Krysta's heavy footsteps echoed as she entered the kitchen. "Do you two hear that?"

"The voices in your head? Sorry, those are only for you," Kyo said.

"No, you dolt! Come here." She waited for them to follow before marching to the front door. She opened it and motioned outside.

A voice came from far off but seemed to resonate across the entire town. "Do not let this horror happen again. We can help you. No more do you have to fear the corruption nor the corrupted."

Kyo recognized that voice. A chill ran down his spine. "It's Sybilla. What does she think she's doing?"

Across and down the road, people poked their heads out of windows and doors.

"I guess we were right about them not being discreet anymore," Kyo said.

Without a word, Krysta dashed down the street.

"And where is she going?" Kyo took off after her with Marsh behind him.

"It is for the best if she leads us to them. But I fear for what they may attempt, should a crowd gather. Especially knowing Sybilla has an affinity for poison spells," Marsh said. They followed as Krysta rounded a corner. "I am prepared to help any way I can."

"Hopefully it won't be necessary," Kyo said. "If we're lucky, the people here can do to them what they did to that shade. After they cure Ruby and Alden, of course."

Some people remained in their homes with open doors and windows, while others took to the streets to follow the voice. The trail of people led away from their homes and toward a hillside with numerous mine cart tracks, discarded tools, and the entrance to a mine. Around an elevated wooden platform, a small crowd gathered.

Above everyone stood Sybilla and Blanq.

Blue and purple energy flowed from an elderly man toward Sybilla's hand then redirected to the pouch at her side. The corruption that had overtaken half his body vanished, and he slumped against her. Blanq moved to set him down gently into a sitting position. Beside him sat several others, one with a starry dress that stood out.

Marsh cupped his chin, completely focused on the spectacle before them. "Fascinating. She truly can drain the magic of others."

"Layla," Krysta gasped, her hands over her mouth. "She's okay, right?"

"As you've just witnessed, the corruption that so worried this man's family and friends, that threatened to turn him into a raging monster, is gone. There is no need to fear a repeat of what happened days ago, that took loved ones from you all," Sybilla shouted, hands in the air as she addressed the growing crowd. "But do not think you have to already be corrupted to seek our help. The corruption takes time to manifest into the visible way we see it. Some of you may already be afflicted and might not know it yet."

Murmurs rose from the crowd, some touching various parts of their bodies as if to feel for the corruption they couldn't see.

"Why are the people up there with you just sitting there? Are they okay? What did you do to them?" Krysta shouted.

Sybilla turned to her, a smirk on her face. "An expected concern. New people are joining the presentation every minute. Pulling magic from another is a tiring experience for them, and they need ample rest to recover from the ordeal. It takes close to a week for their magic to fully recover, corruption-free."

Having had enough of her voice, Kyo ran around the crowd to the platform and climbed it. "You mean if you decide to let them live."

Sybilla looked his way, narrowing her eyes.

He turned to address the crowd. "Don't believe her! They did the same thing in Mistwell. The people they claimed were resting were dead. These two are nothing more than killers."

More mumblings echoed among the crowd.

"But we saw her do it. That man was corrupted before, and now it's gone," a woman shouted, others verbally agreeing.

"I'm not denying they can actually cure it, but they're after something else in doing so. They took in my godfather, and now he's missing." Kyo faced Sybilla. "So, where is he? Where's Alden?"

Blanq ignored him, crouched with their head down.

Sybilla tilted her head. "Have we met?"

Gritting his teeth, Kyo built air around his fist and thrust it forward. He hurled the concentrated wind, hitting her in the gut like a long-distance punch. She hunched over with a grunt, holding her stomach, but stood upright again a moment later.

Many among the crowd gasped, but he ignored them. His strike should have hurt more than that.

"Don't give me that," Kyo said. "My godfather's life is on the line, and I will do anything I have to if it means getting him back." While his magic hadn't fully returned, he hoped to have enough to put up a good fight if necessary.

His attention shifted to Layla, heart rate increasing. The sun sat above the horizon. With so much light, it might be difficult to spot what he hoped wouldn't be there. Taking deep breaths, he crouched beside her and forced her eyelid open with one hand, using the other to cup around it and block the sunlight.

Her eyes had a blue glow.

A chill ran down his spine. He was close by, in the same town as her knowing something might happen, and yet she'd still lost her life. He gritted his teeth and thought of that boy in Oasis. Someone who should have been protected. Not enough vigilance, not quick enough. And like with Alden, this happened because Kyo had sat idle. Again! Krysta needed to know, to see for herself, but how could he bring himself to tell her?

Sybilla's foot met his chest, pushing him onto his back. "I'll have to ask you to leave them alone and let them rest. Such a disrespectful brat."

As Kyo righted himself, Krysta rushed past him, cupping Layla's face.

"Layla. Hey, come on, we should go." Her voice wavered, and she gently slapped Layla's face, shook her by the shoulders, but got no response. "Come on. I don't like these people."

Kyo glared daggers at Sybilla, who kept that cocky smirk on her lips.

"Check her pulse," he muttered.

Krysta rested her fingers against Layla's neck. They held still then shifted, desperate to feel what Kyo knew wasn't there.

"No. No. Why did you come here?" she asked, holding Layla's head against her chest, sobbing. Her body trembled as she rocked.

"What's going on?" a woman cried from the crowd.

"Is she okay?" someone else called. "What did you do?"

Shouts and demands erupted from the group of citizens which continued to grow. Yet Sybilla showed no signs of concern. Keeping her eyes on Kyo, she extended her arm to the side, fingers outstretched toward the crowd.

"Well, I was going to wait until the crowd grew larger, but I suppose it doesn't really matter in the end." Her eyes widened, the smirk growing as puffs of green gas leaked from her fingertips.

"Back away, quickly!" Marsh cried as he moved between the mass of people and the platform, but his voice was drowned out.

Kyo summoned a sword in his right hand and dashed toward Sybilla, slashing down at her wrist. She pulled away in time to avoid being cut and took a step away from the people.

"We saw what you did to those traders on the way here," he said. "We won't let you do it again."

Pointing his sword at her, he glanced between her and Blanq, who continued to remain silent. Not only an alteration mage but a poison spell too. Was Sybilla also well versed in affliction spells, or was it a one-off? This was exactly why even a town like this should have a team of enforcers.

"And you think you can stop us? You're welcome to try, little boy. I was growing tired of the facade anyway. Weren't you, Blanq?" Sybilla asked. Blanq turned their head to look at her but said nothing. "At least you're getting new playthings."

Krysta rose, her arms engulfed in flame. "How dare you."

Tears streamed down her cheeks from her red, puffy eyes. If she clenched her teeth any further, she might shatter them.

"How dare you take her away from me," she screamed, thrusting her hands out and blasting a torrent of flame at Sybilla and Blanq.

Kyo stepped back, shielding his face from the intense heat. Screams erupted from the crowd. Marsh erected a thin, transparent barrier of magic energy, spreading it to cover most of the people behind him. While Kyo would've loved to see Sybilla and Blanq reduced to ash, it'd mean Alden and Ruby were doomed.

"Don't kill them! They still need to cure my godfather," Kyo shouted.

Krysta ignored him, releasing a long, guttural scream as the flames blasted well beyond the platform toward the mine's entrance.

She released a heavy breath, arms falling to her sides. Panting and trembling, her eyes held such intense rage, Kyo might believe if someone told him the fire started from sheer force of will.

Were they dead, or did they somehow survive the onslaught of flame?

Kyo hated that he had to hope for their survival, but he wouldn't have minded if they held on by a thread.

Then, like a child's nightmare, Sybilla and Blanq stepped through what remained of the inferno, the platform under their feet still burning. Kyo's heart nearly stopped. Other than singes and holes in various parts of their clothes, they didn't have any noticeable injuries.

"You're going to have to put a little more power behind your spells than that if you want to hurt us. But don't worry, you might get another chance before you wind up like that husk next to you." Sybilla released a laugh laced with insanity, her eyes wide and wild. Stone encased her hand, ending in sharp points along her fingers. "Let's play."

Chapter 9

Kyo's heart pounded in his ears. Sybilla crouched like a coeurl ready to pounce upon its prey. He summoned his second sword, eyeing her for any sign of movement. His eyes flicked to Blanq, mindful of any assistance they might give their partner.

This was it. Unlike last time, he wouldn't underestimate her. He'd win this fight and force her to tell him where Alden was.

"Everyone, please get back! Return to your homes." Marsh lowered his barrier, motioning for the townspeople behind him to leave.

Some turned and fled, while others backed up more slowly, keeping their eyes on the platform.

A brave, foolish few attempted to approach Sybilla, flexing their burly arms and tightening their fists in a show of physical strength. But a blast of her toxic gas sent them scurrying, covering their faces with Marsh hurrying after them.

Kyo couldn't spare them more than a glance, not wanting to be taken by surprise.

He should strike first, but where? Her ability to turn skin to stone was a bad match for both his weapons and wind spells. Perhaps if he struck quick enough or in a spot without her realizing, she wouldn't be able to defend against it.

Blanq outstretched their arm in front of Sybilla to keep her in place, and a blue glow emitted from their eyes under the hood. Layla and the other victims of their magic rose to their feet, shambling.

"Yes, I know. You don't want me to damage your new toys. Fine, hurry up then." Sybilla's hand returned to flesh, and she crossed her arms over her chest.

"Layla?" Krysta approached her, cupping her cheeks.

Layla's lifeless eyes stared back for a moment then gazed around like a curious child. Sobs escaped Krysta's already red, puffy eyes as she buried her face in her old teacher's neck.

Blanq raised their hand, and the walking corpses turned to approach them.

When Layla attempted to do the same, Krysta held her back.

"No! I don't know what you want with them, but you're not taking her." Krysta wrapped her arms around Layla's waist and hopped off the platform, stumbling when she landed.

Blanq made no move to go after them. Extending both hands to their sides, a white light rose and enveloped them.

"What's going on now?" Kyo asked, squinting.

"They're leaving. Say bye bye." Sybilla smiled and waved to Blanq.

Leaving? What would the spell do; launch them into the air, travel underground? Spells were not cast for transportation purposes. But if Blanq left…

Ruby popped into Kyo's mind, sitting alone and scared in the jail cell. He realized now that there was no way Sybilla would help her willingly. From what he'd seen, she delighted in making people suffer. But Blanq—

the chances were slim at best, but he had no other option.

"Blanq!" Kyo called.

They turned to look his way.

"In Aquarin Port, at the enforcer station, there's a girl named Ruby. She's corrupted, and I don't know how much time she has left. Please, if you can cure her and *not* harm her, I'll owe you one."

Barely a second passed after he spoke before they vanished and the light dissipated. Kyo scanned the crowd, between the buildings, the entrance to the mine, but they were gone without a trace. "How?" he whispered to himself. Teleportation wasn't real, yet he could think of no other way to describe it.

"Well then, where were we?" Sybilla asked.

Kyo glanced over to find even the closest townspeople had moved a considerable distance away. At least he wouldn't have to worry about going out of his way to protect them.

Marsh climbed atop the platform.

"I cannot say for certain if I will be of any use, but I-I will do my best to help you," he said in a shaky voice.

Kyo smiled and tilted his head, cracking his neck. "Glad to hear it. Try to keep your distance. Though that might not matter if they can actually teleport."

"That is something I will have to process later," Marsh said.

"Before we begin, I do have a question. Out of curiosity, would any of you three happen to be summoners?" Sybilla asked. She pointed at Kyo. "Well, I know you're not, but the other two, I suppose. I don't see the markings on the back of your hands, but it doesn't hurt to ask."

"What does that matter?" Krysta asked, ascending the few stairs onto the platform. "The only thing important here is making sure you die here and now." The fury in her eyes matched when she'd attempted to incinerate them. "I'll never forgive you for what you've done."

Kyo took a few steps forward. "I don't care if she dies. But before she does, you need to give me the chance to force answers from her. But I'll give her one more chance." He glared at Sybilla, the amused smile on her lips only fueling his anger. "Where. Is. Alden?"

Sybilla rolled her eyes. "You're like a mimic bird, I swear. You want to know? Well, I'm not telling." She bared her teeth. "The three of you, joining together to protect the townspeople…it brings back horrendous memories. Thankfully I now know better than to go out of my way like that again. All of you monsters deserve to suffer, and turning into shades is the most poetic way for it to happen. Let the outside represent the inside." She gazed toward the people still within view, her voice dropping several octaves. "Every single one of you." She brought the backs of both hands to her lips, kissing a gold ring on her left then the one on her right, muttering. "We will not fall without putting up the fight of our lives. No surrender. Do what it takes to survive."

"Your mantra isn't going to help you." Krysta opened her right hand, a fiery orb appearing before she hurled it at Sybilla's feet. Sybilla jumped to her left but couldn't completely escape the explosion once the firebomb detonated.

Kyo shielded his face with his arms. When he lowered them, he found that, like before, the spell had little effect on Sybilla, her dress more a victim than herself. "She sure is resilient. How much magic does she have?"

Patting the embers off her dress, Sybilla grumbled. "Well, this dress is beyond saving at this point." Several holes and tears large and small had been burned through the dress. "You kids think too highly of yourselves. You won't be the ones to finally kill me."

She hopped off the platform, motioning for them to do the same with her finger.

Krysta jumped off and waved her hands. Long shards of ice appeared in the air and hurled forward.

Sybilla dashed toward them, raising her arm, which not only took on the stone texture again but grew in thickness, using it to bat away the icicles. As soon as the threat was gone, her arm fell to her side and returned to normal.

Kyo ran forward to meet Sybilla and swung one of his swords toward her neck, but she nimbly flipped over the blade. He followed through by spinning around, keeping his momentum, and tried to catch her as she landed, but she did so in a crouch to once again avoid being cut. When he looked down, her stiffened, glowing fingers jabbed into his side.

Pain shot through every nerve in his body. His mouth opened, but no sound came.

The swords fell from his hands, and his body could do nothing but tremble, the pain shooting through every nerve like electricity. For a few seconds, he couldn't move at all, could barely think or breathe.

Sybilla stood and reared her hand back, readying another strike, but a transparent golden barrier appeared between the two. Marsh stood on Kyo's left, hand outstretched to keep the spell going. Grinning, Sybilla thrust her hand forward and shattered the barrier like flimsy glass, gripping Marsh's face. Blue and violet energies streamed from Marsh's body up her arm, diverging at the elbow and into the pouch and without question into her stone.

A glowing red circle appeared under Sybilla's feet, forcing her to release Marsh and avoid the upward explosion. The pillar of fire that followed singed Kyo's sleeve as he and Marsh fell to the side. Though the shock allowed Kyo to move again, he gripped his arm.

"Dammit, watch what you're doing","" Kyo cried out.

"Then get out of the way," Krysta shouted back. Turning her eyes to Sybilla, she gritted her teeth. "If I can't burn you, then I'll just freeze you to death."

A torrent of icy air burst from her hands and enveloped Sybilla, stretching beyond her. It reached as far as the townspeople who backed away, more than one rubbing their bare arms for warmth.

Yet Sybilla closed her eyes and smiled. "I do appreciate the refreshing breeze."

Krysta grunted, the icy air growing more intense, focusing and swirling around Sybilla. The only indication it had some effect was the visible breath escaping her lips, and her arms shielding her face from tiny shards of ice.

Kyo rose on wobbly legs, attempting to still the trembling coursing through him. To be so resistant to their spells, her magic pool had to be well beyond that of an average enforcer. He dismissed his sword, rotating air around his open palm. He may have failed the last time he'd attempted this spell on her, but it was worth a try. Sybilla's overconfidence gave him the time needed to build the spell. The wind spun faster, condensed further, blowing his hair and Marsh's robes about. The air kicked up enough dirt and dust to be seen with the naked eye, first forming an orb in his palm then extending and narrowing into a drill. He ran forward while Sybilla was distracted, braving the icy air.

Lowering her arm, she stared right at him the second before he thrust his spell into her stomach. Once it made contact, it dissipated, leaving his palm resting harmlessly against her.

Dammit, again? His wide eyes met hers.

"You're really bad at this, aren't you?" she asked with an amused chuckle then backhanded him across the face and kicked him in the chest, sending him tumbling back.

Krysta charged at her with another firebomb in her hand. Sybilla crouched, ready to pounce on her, but Marsh put up a barrier between the two. Krysta ran face first into the barrier, dropping the firebomb and barely dove out of the way before it exploded.

She sat on the ground, her right leg reddened from the blast. "You idiot! What are you doing?"

"I-I'm sorry," Marsh stammered. "I thought she'd—"

A shrill laugh cut him off. "Are you kidding me? Honestly, you three are just embarrassing all of us. Look!" Sybilla pointed to the townspeople. "Look at their faces. Even they're embarrassed for you."

Sure enough, some of them had their heads turned, unable to watch. Some that did were cringing or shaking their heads. Kyo didn't doubt they hoped for their victory, but saying things weren't going well was an understatement.

"Like I care!" Kyo rose to his feet, legs shaking from the aftershocks of her previous spell. "We're not putting on a show here."

"I knew you couldn't give me what I wanted, but this has been sad." Sybilla reached into her pouch and took out the orb, gripping it tight. The same energies she absorbed from Marsh, and Kyo back in Mistwell trailed up her arm and into her body. "Oh well, I can still revel in breaking your spirits."

"You failed to mention she could actually use the magic she stole from people," Krysta said, rising to her feet and shifting toward Kyo and Marsh.

"I would have liked to know that too," Kyo said.

As she absorbed more magic from the stone, the green gas returned, circling her feet and growing in density.

"It's amazing how much of a boost the magic of a few random people can give you." Sybilla held her arm out to her side, palm facing the townspeople. As the gas snaked up her body and gathered around her arm, her grin grew more sadistic.

"Marsh, barrier!" Kyo shouted, positioning himself in front of Krysta and the cleric and gathering as much power from within himself as he could.

"Run!" Krysta shouted to the onlookers.

Too late.

The gas erupted from Sybilla's hand, overtaking the people and several blocks of the town within seconds. The excess would have done the same to Kyo and his partners if he wasn't using all his power to keep a circle of air around them and the gas at bay. He groaned and clenched his teeth, bending his knees to brace himself. So much magic flowed within her spell, he wasn't sure he could hold it back. Marsh's grunts were low and deep, attempting to keep a barrier up where Kyo's spell let some of the toxic miasma through.

A thick, green cloud blocked Kyo's vision. He couldn't see the townspeople, the nearest building, or Sybilla. How many people had her spell overtaken? How far into town had it reached?

"This isn't fair," Krysta said with a hitch in her voice. "We can't let her do this."

Kyo breathed easier as the force behind the gas eased. Not allowing his own spell to do the same, he spread the air outward to clear the area.

No sign of Sybilla.

Krysta fell limp at his side, Marsh following a second later.

Kyo turned to have his throat grasped by Sybilla, his eyes staring into those of madness. Her fingers jabbed into his gut, and like before, his body shook and tensed from pain. Another jab then another, and he nearly blacked out, his head swimming.

Fight Sybilla? Defeat her, force her to tell him where Alden was? What a joke.

A slap across the face kept him from losing consciousness, and the grip on his throat eased enough to let him breathe, if he tried hard enough.

"Don't worry. I'm not going to kill you today. It'll be far more delicious to let you watch these people suffer." She adjusted her grip so he could see the gas clearing, people on the ground, coughing, struggling to breathe, some not moving at all. "I used to be like you. Naïve, thinking people were good and worth protecting." Tightening her grip, she spoke through clenched teeth. "But they only care about themselves in the end."

Sybilla tossed him to the ground.

He lay, unable to move, next to Marsh and Krysta. Their eyes were open, wide and moving, but their bodies didn't budge. With each passing second, there were fewer coughs, less moaning in the air, until all went silent.

All the while, Sybilla sat upon an overturned cart near the entrance to the mine, toying with the stone in her hand.

"This should be good enough. About half." Sybilla extended her hand, closing her eyes and inhaling deeply.

Nothing happened at first.

But she remained still, waiting. Then, strands of blue and violet energy raced toward her from all over town and into the stone, so much Kyo had to squint to block out some of the glow.

After what must have been a full minute, Sybilla dropped her arm.

"There we are." She stood and approached, crouching in front of them, glancing from one to the other. "It's much easier if at least some of them are dead." Leaning forward, she brought her face within a breath of Kyo's. "The only reason I'm keeping you alive is so the next time I see you, I can see the look of true fear in your eyes. Don't disappoint me."

Kyo could do nothing but bear the pain stabbing at him, like a thousand needles piercing his skin and nerves as she stood and skipped down the road along the outside of town, hands behind her back and humming to herself. His mind ran wild with images of what he'd see when he regained movement in his neck. The hatred he felt for her would have reached a boiling point but instead did battle with the growing terror that filled him when he pictured her grinning face.

Chapter 10

Complete and utter failure. No four words
described Kyo better as he lay on the hard
ground, body rippling with agony that brought
soundless gasps to his lips. Be like his parents? Even
with two other mages at his side, he could barely touch
Sybilla. And he still didn't know where Alden could be.

To top things off, he managed to turn his head to
see the townspeople who'd been watching the fight, now
lying quiet and unmoving within a dissipating green
cloud. How far had it spread? He managed to push
himself to a sitting position, eyes clenched from pain as
he sucked in air between his teeth. Nobody can save
everyone. But he…he couldn't save a single person.

Sybilla's spell weakened, but not enough to try
standing yet.

"Are you two still with me?" Kyo asked.

"Yes, though unable to move," Marsh responded
without budging a muscle, lying face down against the
dirt.

Heat radiated off Krysta as fire enveloped her
without doing any harm. "She'll wish she had finished
us off. I will hunt her down to the ends of Feracael if I
must." Her voice hitched, followed by a sniffle. "I'll
make her pay."

Kyo carefully moved his right arm forward and back, gauging the pain to get a better feel for when he could move comfortably. His gaze wandered over the nearby homes — the gas had likely seeped into them as well. How many people had died in the past few minutes? Bracing himself, he managed to stand with small ripples of pain around his side where Sybilla's fingers had prodded.

Krysta and Marsh shifted around the same time, regaining movement in their bodies. Marsh wasted no time in attempting to stand, stumbling toward the nearest body, while Krysta's flame had gone out, replaced with tears streaming down her cheeks. On wobbly legs, she made her way to Layla, who gazed around with lifeless eyes. Wrapping her arms around her deceased teacher, she dropped to the ground, sobbing into Layla's chest.

Kyo should have been able to stop this. How could he dare compare himself to his parents? The scene playing out before him could easily include himself and Alden or Ruby and Ren in the near future.

Clenching his fists, he pushed aside the self-hatred and approached the two. Layla gave no indication she noticed Krysta or her touch. Obviously Blanq didn't need to be around after the initial raising.

"I'm sorry. She was…really nice," Kyo said. A moment of silence passed before he spoke again. "What do we do about this?"

Krysta raised her head and placed a soft kiss on Layla's cheek. "I'm not stupid. She's gone, even if she's moving." She sucked in a shaky breath. "I've read stories involving necromancy before. Some fiction, some from real accounts. They called the victims undead and pierced their skulls and brain to put an end to them, to release the magic that raised them. I don't know if her soul is still in there, but if so, I want to set it free."

Fire wouldn't be suitable for a clean end. Ice could do the trick, but instead, Kyo held out his right hand and summoned his sword.

"You can use this if you want." He fought to keep his jaw from trembling too much. Stories were one thing, but he'd never seen a situation like this with his own eyes. It had to be infinitely harder for Krysta. His heart broke for her.

Without looking, she grabbed the hilt of the sword with a shaking hand. "Go away. Please."

Kyo wished he could do more but only nodded and left her behind, wiping a tear from his eye. Layla didn't deserve this. None of Sybilla's victims did. How could she call them all monsters? She didn't even know them.

He crouched next to Marsh, who had his purple glowing hands on a woman's chest, and asked, "Can you help any of them?"

Marsh looked up from the young woman lying at his feet. "I do not know. Even should we find more survivors, it is the same process as how I removed the poison from Donavi, and you saw how I struggled with that. I may be able to save a few, but I only have so much magic to spend. I wish Cleric Micha were here, but even then, I do not doubt many have already passed."

Standing, Kyo stared at the front door of the nearest home, not wanting to look at the bodies strewn about the road. Perhaps there were survivors inside. He opened the door and covered his face with his sleeve as residual gas escaped, blasting it away with a burst of wind. A sweep of the home revealed no one inside. They may have been among those on the road or, with any luck, safe elsewhere in town.

When he emerged, the woman Marsh had been working on sat up, dazed but alive. Thank goodness *someone* made it. She took a quick look around, startled, and released a gasp before she broke down crying.

As Marsh attempted to console her, Krysta returned, dragging Kyo's blade along the ground with fresh blood around the tip. He couldn't find it in himself to say anything about it, so he just called it back, the sword vanishing from her hand.

"I'll go back for her when I figure out what to do," she said barely above a whisper.

Kyo put his arm around her, and she leaned into it.

"With so many gone, I imagine several funeral pyres will be used. You can follow us for now, if you do not know where to go," Marsh said. She simply nodded. "Kyo, you can clear any gas we come across, correct?"

"Yeah, no problem." As they progressed down the block, Kyo checked more homes while Krysta and Marsh looked for signs of life in the bodies they passed, finding about one survivor for every fifty or more bodies staring lifelessly at the sky or attempting to shield one another. A mixture of rage and sadness swirled inside Kyo. He did his best to keep his emotions in check. "All these people. Parents, siblings, neighbors…"

Even when he took a moment to close his eyes, he still saw the bodies. Among the sorrow, his mind filled with images of doing the most horrible, painful things to Sybilla.

"No," Marsh said, checking for a pulse on a woman, shaking his head, and then moving on. "Do not try to piece together who they were, who they are leaving behind. Do not write their eulogy."

"You mean don't treat them like people now that they're dead? Should I forget Layla too?" Krysta asked angrily.

Marsh didn't look at her and kept his tone steady. "Do you think clerics could maintain their sanity if they did? With all the death and sorrow they see during their lives?"

Krysta didn't answer, shifting her eyes to the ground.

"It is one of the first things we are taught," Marsh said. "Mental separation."

They reached the first major intersection of town, remnants of the gas in all three directions as far as they could see. Kyo cleared what he could before they moved on. Beyond the initial group close to the mine, they didn't see many bodies outside, more having died in their homes the farther into town they went.

Another hour or two passed, the sun below horizon on the other side of the trees. Block after block was thoroughly checked, Kyo reaching the limit of his magic due to how much gas he had to blow away. At least what few survivors they found were willing to help in the search for others. Upon reaching a main thoroughfare, they saw a large crowd gathered, paused at the limit of where Sybilla's spell reached. Once Kyo cleared the way between himself and the crowd, they cautiously moved forward, multiple voices asking what had happened.

Marsh explained the situation. Probably for the best. Kyo doubted he'd keep their attention as much as anyone wearing cleric robes. In turn, Marsh asked what had happened on their end.

"Not much, yah," a man told him. "We heard the commotion all the way across town. Explosions and such. When we finally decided to check it out, this wall of gas came right for us. It stopped before it could reach us though, yah."

"Strange too. It stopped right at the road that splits the town in half." A woman pointed down the road leading back toward the entrance Kyo and Marsh had walked through upon their arrival. "A clean cut halfway through town."

Sybilla must have figured she could get what she wanted, while also causing plenty of emotional trauma in survivors by leaving half the town alive. At least that was Kyo's theory, based on how much she enjoyed his own emotional suffering related to Alden.

"Few we passed along the way survived," Marsh said, unable to meet the gazes of the townspeople. They had found no more than ten survivors. "But there are many roads and homes we were not able to check. Are there any clerics among you?"

A young woman in a white robe weaved her way through the crowd. "There're a few of us from the clinic."

Krysta's lips parted then closed again. The fist at her side trembled like her breathing.

So Kyo spoke instead. "Not all the streets are fully clear of the gas, but if you can help in any way, please help us find any survivors."

"You got it," the cleric said, turning to the crowd. She motioned for the other clerics to join her. "Form a line in front of each of us. C'mon, hurry it up now. Each group will take a different street. Don't go wanderin' far from yer cleric, in case ya need their assistance."

Kyo turned to stare down the street, trying to get an idea of how many he'd have to clear. It took so little magic, but after the fight, he wouldn't be able to keep at it much longer.

"We may as well get started." He took a few steps. Then the whole world spun.

Before he registered what happened, he found himself face first on the road. All of the energy in his body left him at once. If he'd been left alone for even a few seconds, he would have passed out right there.

"Kyo," Marsh cried, kneeling at his side.

"I can't...keep my eyes open. Can barely move," Kyo mumbled.

"Krysta, help me get him up." Marsh draped one arm around his shoulders, and Krysta did the same. "Remember what Cleric Micha said. He gave you extra stamina, but once it wore off, you had to get proper rest. No excuses."

Breathing deeply and clenching his eyes, Kyo struggled to stay awake. "But…the people…and Sybilla."

"Can he rest back at your home?" Marsh asked.

Krysta huffed. "Yes, yes. Come on, you dolt."

Whether seconds or minutes passed after Krysta's insult, Kyo couldn't tell. All he knew was he passed out before reaching the house.

* * *

When Kyo woke, the sun shone brightly through the window. He rested his arm over his eyes to block it out and get a few extra minutes of sleep before the events that had transpired registered in his mind. The bed was larger than his own at home, with decorative pillows against the headboard. On the opposite wall, a vanity mirror sat atop a small, white desk with a similarly colored stool. The room didn't have a closet, but a wardrobe cupboard stood against the left wall. A room like this had to be decorated by someone much older than himself or Krysta. Could this be Layla's room? It felt odd using it after what had happened, so he wasted no time in leaving and heading downstairs.

"It's about time you got up," Krysta said, seated on the couch.

Marsh, who sat next to her, smiled. "Did you sleep well? How do you feel?"

"Sluggish." It took more effort than it should have to move, like Kyo had weights strapped to his body. Rotating his shoulder, he paced about the living room to loosen up. "How long was I out?"

"It's early afternoon. You passed out yesterday." Krysta sat in an oddly regal position, legs crossed at the ankles and hands folded on her lap. If she was trying to pass herself off as a proper lady, it wouldn't fool Kyo.

"Geez. What about the town, the search? Did anything else happen?" Kyo's pacing quickened.

Marsh shook his head. "Only a handful of survivors were found in the east side of town. About as many as one could count on two hands. Those we helped were lucky we found them so soon." He sighed, resting his hand on a closed tome at his side. "A tragedy like this will certainly be recorded in history for a long time to come."

No question remained in Kyo's mind that Sybilla was the most dangerous of the duo. They were all terribly lacking in skill compared to her. She'd beaten them into the ground without even trying. She could cause so much damage, but the most burning question remained: why?

He turned to Krysta. "I'm sorry about Layla. She was a sweet woman. Great cook too."

"Layla used to look after me when I was young. She lived with my family and helped raise me. A few years ago, she retired and settled here. I missed her, so I came to visit." A sad smile crossed Krysta's lips. "It was like old times again. Like she never left. All I could do was bring her to the others who didn't make it, to be burned and buried with them."

A tome lay open at Krysta's side as well. Reaching into his enchanted pouch, he felt around until his fingers grazed the leather cover of his own spell tome. While he might not have a fondness for studying history, literature, or many other subjects, he'd gladly take the initiative in studying spells. He had to force his hand off the tome to keep himself from opening it mid-conversation.

"So, what do we do?" he asked instead.

"I will never forgive them. Either of them." Krysta's teeth clenched. If looks could kill, the wooden floor would have rotted away in that moment. "I refuse to just sit here and do nothing. They're going to pay for what they did to her and the rest of Calmarock."

"That didn't exactly work out well before. Or did you forget they basically walked out of your fire like it was a refreshing sauna?" Kyo submitted to his desire and pulled the tome from his pouch, flipping through the pages. "Even without using that stone, they're way out of our league."

"So, what?" Krysta stood and stomped her foot. "You want to just do nothing? Because I don't need you two, you know."

"No, just making sure you both know what we're in for. I'd prefer not to try fighting them again, leave that to the enforcers. But if we do, we're likely to get our asses kicked." Kyo turned to Marsh. "You know you don't have to come. I'm going for Alden, her for Layla. But if you'd rather head back to your chapel, it's okay."

Marsh placed his tome on his lap, flipping the pages until he came to a section about poison and venom. "The wise thing would be to find a more skilled cleric to join the two of you. But perhaps your recklessness is rubbing off on me because I do not want to leave. I know if I did, I would simply spend my time worrying about your fates. So, I suppose my only option is to become a better cleric for you. Though it would be smart to warn anyone we can about Sybilla and Blanq. If they plan to leave Kattelink Island and head north to Terrorigo, we had best head back to Aquarin."

"If we leave now, we'll make it before nightfall. I'll pack some food for us." Krysta headed for the kitchen, and the sounds of cabinets and the refrigerator opening and closing reached the living room. "Even if they head to the mainland, we can still be of some use. We should talk to Aquarin's chancellor. She can spread the word to other towns and cities to keep an eye out for them."

Marsh stood, holding his closed tome at his side, a finger saving the page. "It would be best to leave out no details about the events that transpired and the pair themselves."

Krysta spoke from the kitchen. "Necromancy was banished hundreds of years ago. I can't imagine how Blanq even learned it. But we'd best make sure everyone knows Sybilla is the most dangerous." A few minutes later, she appeared from the kitchen and patted her pouch. "Okay, let's get going."

"I don't know when they'll set up the funeral pyre, but are you sure you don't want to be here for that?" Kyo asked.

She shook her head. "For all I know, it could be days before that happens. Even if it's tonight, that's hours of delay we can't afford." She gripped her pouch tightly. "She's already gone, her soul on its way to the Flow. I'm sure I'll see her again someday, but she'd understand if I don't stay."

Together, they left the house and traveled through town to the dirt path connecting to Aquarin. With any luck, they could avoid fighting Sybilla again, though the idea of thrusting his fist firmly in her face was tempting to Kyo. The weight on his shoulders related to Ruby and Alden hadn't lessened one bit. He'd asked Blanq to help Ruby, and he'd check on her when they returned to Aquarin, but the chances of anything coming of it were slim at best. But he'd done all he could for her. And he clearly couldn't force answers about Alden from the pair. If the enforcers hadn't made any progress in finding him, then his already paper-thin hope would rip to shreds.

Chapter 11

irds chirping, footsteps along the dirt trail, and the rustling of leaves were all Kyo heard for most of the return trip to Aquarin Port, something he found surprising since they had a new—and often loud—travel companion. Krysta insulted him maybe twice during the trek through the forest, far less than he expected. More important things took precedence. Each had a tome open as they walked, resulting in more than one of them tripping over elevated ground or walking face first into an outstretched branch.

Krysta elected to keep her practice to ice spells, not taking the risk of lighting the forest on fire. Marsh had no actual victims to heal, so he went back and forth between creating barriers and visualizing removing poison from an imaginary person's lungs. The spell Kyo had attempted and failed to cast twice against Sybilla became the focus of his training, though when the others complained about the excess wind disturbing them, he remained about twenty paces behind.

Glancing at the darkening sky through the canopy above, Kyo wished he could enjoy the serenity of the forest. He'd taken lengthy breaks between attempted spellcasting so as not to drain his magic in case something unexpected happened. Having little magic to rely on remained fresh in his mind, but it didn't require Sybilla for such fatigue to overtake him. He could do it to himself if he wasn't careful.

But one more attempt wouldn't hurt.

Keeping his palm up, air rotated above it, condensing then forming the shape of a drill. The hard part was keeping it together while pressing it against something else. He thrust his palm against the next tree within reach, and though he felt some resistance, the spell only lasted a second before dispersing.

"Dammit."

The bark of the slim tree cracked and splintered, but not enough for him to feel proud. The tree shook then rose into the air.

He took several hasty steps back, watching as several trees around the one he'd damaged followed suit. "Whoa, did I piss you off or something?"

Kyo stared down at the shell of another massive tortoise, like the one on the way to Calmarock. Or maybe the same one, he wasn't sure. Stepping forward, he reached out to touch it, rough against his skin and partially coated in moss. Marsh and Krysta joined him, a slight smile on each of their lips.

"I don't remember seeing one of these on my way down here," Krysta said.

"They don't move much. Sometimes they can go months without budging." Kyo ran his fingers over its leathery skin. "Or so I heard."

Marsh grinned. "So, you do study."

The tortoise released a low groan, taking several steps left then right, rotating its body before slumping back onto the ground with a thud.

Kyo patted its shell. "Not a care in the world, huh? Want to switch places?"

"Come on. We should be almost there," Krysta said, waving her hand for them to follow.

Sure enough, the outskirts of Aquarin came into view no more than fifteen minutes later, where the dirt path turned into a cobblestone road. And at the start of that road stood two enforcers Kyo didn't recognize.

"Stop there," one ordered. He approached and circled them. "They appear to be fine. No outward symptoms."

"Are you searching for people afflicted with the corruption?" Marsh asked.

"That's right," the other enforcer said, brushing some of her lengthy blue hair behind her ear. "We have orders from the chancellor to take any corrupted citizens we find and bring them to the enforcer station. For safety reasons, of course."

"Okay, you three are free to go." The first enforcer motioned for them to move along. "But be careful. It may be best to stay inside until we figure out how to handle this situation."

"Has word gotten to you about what happened in Calmarock yesterday?" Marsh asked.

The blue-haired enforcer nodded. "I'm afraid so. We sent a few enforcers and clerics to help early this morning. I've heard Mistwell has sent their own as well. Good to see the three of you made it out okay. Now go on."

Krysta glanced over her shoulder at the enforcers as they walked past them. "I'm willing to bet they couldn't afford to send too much help in case something similar happened here. We should head straight to the chancellor's office before it gets too late."

"Not that I don't want to go with you to do that, but I want to see Ruby first," Kyo said. Not knowing if Blanq went out of their way to help her ate at his mind. He had to know one way or another.

"Well, I suppose the enforcer station is on the way. Just don't take too long." Krysta took the lead, walking down the main thoroughfare of the town that led all the way to the port.

"How do you know the layout of Aquarin so well?" Kyo asked.

Krysta glanced behind her with a smirk. "This isn't my first time here, you know. I'm quite well traveled. Not something a homebody islander would understand."

Kyo grumbled under his breath but said nothing. He preferred seeing that attitude over her being emotionally distraught.

The enforcer station sat ahead on the right, but not far beyond stood a small group, including two enforcers Kyo *did* recognize. More importantly, there were several among the group with a shadowy aura over half their bodies. As they drew closer, they heard the angry cries and sorrowful wails of those clinging to the corrupted people. Among the small group, five were half cloaked in shadow, while another eight had no visible signs of affliction.

"I'm sorry, but it's for the safety of everyone. We have strict orders," Karu said, binding a corrupted man's wrists behind his back with the same cuffs they'd put on Kyo.

"We're here to get help," a woman protested. "How can we do that if you take us all into custody? You're just guaranteeing they'll turn into shades at this rate."

Milo cuffed the woman, drawing angry shouts from the others, corrupted and uncorrupted alike. "You've all been in close contact for days on your way here. We can't take any risks." He ignored the outcry and grabbed a young girl's wrist, attempting to pull her along.

"Let go," she cried, yanking her hand from Milo's grasp.

A man in a russet trench coat with deep bronze skin moved to push Milo away.

But Milo's hand extended, glowing and ready to cast a spell. "This is a precaution for everyone's safety. I'm not trying to take her from you. But if you all won't come willingly, we will have to use force."

A golden rope wrapped around Milo's arms, binding them to his sides and pulling him back until he fell.

At the other end of the magic rope, Marsh stared with wide, angry eyes, his jaw clenched. "Do not dare separate a child from her parent." His hands trembled as they gripped the rope. "I and the Altruist, Tutelvus, will not forgive such an act."

Kyo preferred not to start a fight with the enforcers, but Marsh making the first move filled him with more confidence that stopping this was right. So what if the order came from a chancellor? As Karu closed in on Marsh, Kyo summoned one of his swords and pointed the tip at him.

Karu met Kyo's eyes, but neither budged. "Don't do this, kid. Or you'll be in the station for much longer than a few hours."

"What you're doing is wrong." Krysta stood between the enforcers and the citizens. "And you call yourselves protectors of the people?"

"We are no Aurora." Milo positioned his palm to face Marsh and knocked him back with a torrent of water.

The rope vanished, and Milo stood, marching toward him, but stopped when Kyo's second blade neared his throat.

"Our duty is to protect this town," Milo said. "Even from its own reckless people."

"You're not using your head. Taking those who are corrupted, I get it. But you have no reason to take those that aren't, like that kid." Kyo's gaze darted between the two enforcers. "If you could catch the corruption from close contact, what about me? I brought Ruby here, remember? Wouldn't I have been corrupted by now too?"

Karu's face softened, his eyes shifting back and forth as if processing Kyo's words.

"Our orders are to—" Milo started.

"Your orders come from a lack of information and an excess of fear," Krysta said, flames engulfing her hands. "If you lock them up with the corrupted who become shades, the others will have no way to protect themselves. It's important for those in your position to be able to think for themselves and determine what's right."

Marsh joined Kyo at his side, hands extended toward both enforcers in a calming gesture. Karu glanced between Krysta and Marsh then lowered his hands. Slowly, the other three followed suit.

"Five corrupted," Marsh said. "Were they all afflicted at the same time?"

Kyo kept his eyes on both enforcers in case they tried anything. Though he wondered if the situation would turn out the same if Marsh and his cleric robes weren't present.

"We don't know." Karu glanced back at the people who remained both angry and scared, keeping loved ones close while glaring intensely. "They all came on a boat from Oasis. So long as they're corrupted, they pose a threat, whether they intend to or not."

A young man stepped forward, one hand gripped by an elderly man supported by a cane. "Word has been spreading of a pair that can cure the corruption. They've been traveling all over the island. We came hoping they could help us. But we didn't get far before they tried arresting us." He pointed angrily at the enforcers. "Just for the crime of being here."

Milo groaned. "Do you have any idea how dangerous a shade can be?"

"Extremely," Karu added. "As far as that duo you're referring to, we've heard unsavory tales about them. Isn't that right?" He turned to Kyo, and a moment later, all eyes focused on him.

Kyo sighed and groaned. He didn't feel like telling the whole story again, so he kept his explanation brief. "They're dangerous. Those two are the reason my godfather is missing, and they've killed people. In fact, we just came from Calmarock." He gulped. Images of the bodies flashed in his mind, and a shiver ran through his body. He tried to imagine a beautiful star-filled sky in hopes of beating back those memories. "Because of them, about half the town is dead."

Gasps rang out, fear in people's eyes.

"That must be an exaggeration, yah. No way that could be true," a woman said.

"We've heard of the attack on Calmarock. But half…" Karu cupped his chin, his breathing heavy. "I didn't realize it was that bad."

"We were on our way to the chancellor's office to give her more specific details. But that's an accurate estimation." Krysta's voice trailed off.

"It can't be. Half the town?" Milo said.

Marsh nodded. "I'm afraid it is true. Clerics certainly among the dead. I would be willing to say whatever aid Aquarin and Mistwell have sent will be insufficient. In fact, I plan to return to the chapel and see if Cleric Micha, or whoever may be there currently, can also lend assistance. Even if only to properly handle the bodies."

Karu's eyes were wide, glancing between Marsh and the corrupted, as if trying to determine which was more important to deal with. "Now, I *do* wonder if more should be sent. But if something happens here…"

A loud groan tore everyone's attention toward the elderly man, one hand on his cane, the other holding his head. His chest heaved, and he hunched forward more than before.

"Grandpa!" the younger man cried. "Are you okay? What's wrong?"

The old man panted, each time his voice growing more high pitched. An explosion of shadowy energy erupted from his body, coupled with a piercing screech that left everyone covering their ears.

Kyo's jaw clenched as tightly as his eyes, trying to drown out the sound as best he could. His palms pressed firmly against his ears, but his head throbbed. The screech ceased, and he slowly lowered his hands.

"That sound. I've heard it before, in Calmarock," Krysta said. She grabbed the little girl's yellow sundress, pulling her away from the group. "Right before the attack."

The shadowy pulses faded, and among the crowd who sought help and compassion stood a monster. Kyo never would have guessed seconds ago it had been an old man who could barely stand.

Before them was a deep void in humanoid shape, except for a pair of bright golden eyes. Shadow seeped off its body and vanished like smoke from a flame. If he stared closely enough, he could see glimpses of the old man's vest or gray hair as the void that coated its body shifted continuously. Without any of the limitations the once weak old man had, it turned its head, taking in those around it, then grabbed its grandson by the throat.

Chapter 12

Kyo stared in horrified awe at the shadowy creature who had been an elderly man a moment before. No longer weak and struggling to stand, it had the strength to lift the young man off the ground with one arm, his feet dangling in the air.

So this was a shade, the creature anyone afflicted with the corruption turned into.

Piercing yellow eyes glared as its grip tightened. Everyone else remained frozen in place, mouths agape.

Kyo summoned a sword in his right hand, launched himself with wind from his feet, and slashed at the shade's arm. The shadowy energy caught his blade before it could do any damage to the flesh underneath. He raised his sword and tried again to the same effect.

The grandson's struggling weakened, arms falling to his sides as his face turned blue.

"Dammit! Let go," Kyo shouted, thrusting his blade at the shade's face, again causing no harm.

"Grab him," Milo shouted.

Kyo obeyed, dismissing his sword and wrapping his arms around the man from behind as a jet of water blasted the shade. It knocked the monster back and loosened its grip enough to free the man, who inhaled deeply and lay coughing on the ground.

Marsh rushed to kneel at the man's side, placing his fingers to his throat. "He should be okay. Although I cannot say the same for everyone if that creature cannot be dealt with."

"What are you all doing?" Krysta shouted. "Get away. Run!" Looking down at the young girl whose gloved hand she still held, she pointed to the man in the trench coat. "Is that your dad?" The girl nodded. "You two need to leave. Find somewhere safe."

"Krysta, move!" Kyo shouted.

Krysta turned to see the shade nearly upon her. Fire engulfed her left hand while her right swung the young girl behind her. Before she could launch an attack, the man in the trench coat jumped between them, slashing a long polearm at the shade in a wide horizontal arc. Though it didn't seem to do any damage, it momentarily stopped the shade's advance.

"You're going out of your way to protect Rosette, so I've got your back, kid." His free hand slicked the front of his chestnut hair so it spiked up, and he placed his left foot forward, reaffirming his grip on the shaft of his polearm. The weapon's spear tip jutted out from what looked like an axe blade, making it useful for more than stabbing forward.

While the shade's attention remained focused on the man, those who had been questioned by the enforcers took the chance to run.

"Milo, help them! I'm going to make sure the corrupted don't get far." Karu ran off, attempting to herd everyone in the same direction.

"My grandfather." Still releasing the occasional cough, the shade's grandson managed to stand on shaky legs. He stared at Marsh, tears welling in his eyes. "Can anything be done for him?"

Marsh didn't answer his question. "You need to run. It is too dangerous here. We will do what we can."

The man obliged but didn't go far, retreating to an alley between two buildings and peeking out from behind the wall.

Marsh and Kyo joined Krysta at her side.

"Roland, be careful," Rosette shouted as he dodged the shade's slashes and parried them with the metal shaft of his weapon.

Kyo ran around Roland and extended his hands, took a deep breath then blasted air at the shade's feet, taking out its legs from under it. Roland took the chance to stab down into the creature, but it had no more effect than before. Purple bolts of pure magical energy shot from Milo's fingers, exploding upon contact with the shade.

Yet seconds later, it returned to its feet as if nothing had happened.

"How durable is this thing? It's like fighting Sybilla all over again," Kyo said. Strategies swam through his head on how to defeat it using the spells they had at their disposal. Fire, ice, wind—they could all do immense damage, but if they didn't have enough magic to put behind the spells, it wouldn't matter.

The shade focused on Milo and ran at him, releasing a high-pitched screech. Marsh hurled his golden rope at the shade, wrapping it around its waist, but it tore through it like paper. Milo fired more magic bolts, but he may as well have not done anything. It wrapped its long, pointed fingers around his head, slamming him into the ground hard enough to crack the cobblestone, then chucked him through the nearest building.

Kyo hoped Milo had enough magic to keep the attack from killing him. "Geez! Let's try to make sure that doesn't happen to us."

The shade turned its head to stare at the remaining five, releasing a guttural growl.

"Hey, kid with the green hair, I don't have much to my name, but I'll owe you big if you can keep Rosette safe, got it?" Roland tightened his grip, the spear tip glowing midnight blue.

Rosette stomped her foot. "Let me help. I'm not defenseless."

"Don't argue," Roland said. "Keep your distance from that thing, kiddo. We're not dealing with some pissed off cockatrice here."

The shade took off in a sprint toward them. Krysta extended her hand, icicles jutting from the ground, sharp points that threatened to skewer the monster, but all they did was shatter as it ran through them with minimal effort. Marsh attempted to slow it with a barrier placed in its path, but the shade tore through it as easily as his rope.

While everyone else leaped from its path, Roland slashing at its side while doing so, Kyo used wind to jump high over the shade and land behind it. His sword appeared again, and he attempted to stab it in the back while running behind it. But the shadowy aura kept the blade at bay. Grunting, he used all his physical strength to push the sword forward before the shade backhanded him across the face, sending him tumbling across the road. His vision flashed, pain stabbing at his neck. It took a few seconds to stop seeing double.

Marsh knelt beside him. "Are you well?"

"Fantastic, thanks. How are you?" Kyo groaned and rubbed his fingers into his aching neck muscles. Blood trickled down the side of his face.

Krysta attempted to keep the shade back with a jet of flame, which did nothing to deter the creature. Roland stole its attention by slashing its arm. So far, being struck by the glowing blade upset it more than any other attack.

The shade reared its claws back, ready to strike Roland, then paused.

Turning its head, it stared into the distance then released another terrible screech. Everyone covered their ears, groaning.

"This again? Maybe if I stab it in the mouth, it'll shut up!" Kyo shouted.

The screech ceased, but another, identical screech echoed in response. A crash, then an enforcer was flung from the station into an adjacent building and remained slumped against the wall. A second shade emerged from the station, heading their way. The shades examined each other like curious saber pups. Then together, they turned and approached the young mages.

As they drew closer, Kyo's body tensed. Beneath the shifting void of the second shade, he could make out hints of enforcers' robes from Mistwell.

Blanq hadn't helped Ruby. Kyo had failed her.

"I'm so sorry," he muttered, tensing his jaw and trying not to let tears flow — trying and failing — at the thought of her alone, scared, and waiting for him to help her, then realizing that help wouldn't come. "I tried my best. I really did."

"I would suggest a retreat, but if we leave…" Marsh didn't need to finish his statement.

They were all that kept the shades from going on a rampage throughout the town. They couldn't put so much as a scratch on the creatures.

"Kyo, I am sorry, truly. But you must save the mourning for later." Marsh pulled him along to rejoin the others.

Roland grabbed Rosette's wrist and stepped back. "Kiddo, you keep your distance, but it looks like we could use some help after all."

The girl stared up at him for a moment then glanced around with worried eyes. "Are you sure I should help *that* way? I can punch them or something."

"I don't think that's going to help with these things," Roland said. "In a case like this, I don't think most people will mind."

Nodding, Rosette interlaced her fingers and held her hands to her chest.

"Altruist Guardian, I seek thine aid." Each word she spoke echoed in the air. A faint blue glow emitted from beneath her black gloves. "In these darkest of times, when all hope fades."

Another blue light glowed from her forehead in the shape of a double helix with all but one strand connecting, a filled dot between two parts of the disconnected strands.

"To protect the life which thine hath laid." Raw magical energy seeped from her body, surrounding her small frame and rotating like a slow-motion twister. "In this time of need, I call you by name. Ignivus!"

Her magical energy shot into the sky then vanished. A flame erupted in front of her, easily reaching taller than any building in town. When it faded, not a lick of ember remained.

In its place stood a creature with red-and-black patterned skin and slicked-back hair composed of fire. Its upper half appeared similar in shape to a human, with claws instead of fingers, but it had thick, digitigrade legs. The creature stood a head taller than Roland.

Kyo couldn't believe it, and the wide eyes of Krysta and Marsh showed their shock as well. Rosette was a summoner, calling upon the avatars of the pantheon themselves. Everyone knew of summoners, but they were so rare he'd never met one before, and he'd certainly never witnessed a summoning.

But now the avatar of a deity stood before him. It was all he could do to keep from reaching out and touching it out of sheer curiosity.

The aggressive screech of a shade shook Kyo from his awed trance. "Well…okay then. If we lose with what's basically a deity fighting with us, I'm calling bullshit."

Kyo could process this and ask questions later. For now, they had shades to take out. This thought brought a pang to his chest. The shades had until recently been ill, frightened people. But what choice did he have? Even Sybilla and Blanq could do nothing once the transformation had taken place, or so they said. Their fate was sealed.

Don't write their eulogy. Kyo repeated Marsh's words in his mind, though it did nothing to calm his pounding heart. He'd at least wait until they were out of danger.

Ignivus jumped at one of the shades, knocking it back across the road with its fist and bellowing fire from its mouth in a follow-up attack. Roland dashed at the other, white energy surrounding his blade before he slashed down. It left a gash in the road without the blade touching it, yet the damage to the shade remained minimal, a faint line through the shadowy aura.

Kyo built air around his palm, determined to try the spell again that had failed against Sybilla. The shade knocked Roland back, a barrier appearing a second too late. It not only failed to protect Roland but defended the shade from Krysta's unannounced flame.

"Marsh! Pay attention to what others are doing," Krysta shouted.

Marsh cursed himself. "I apologize!"

"Then how about this? No one get in my way." Kyo launched himself at the shade, thrusting the wind drill at its chest.

The shade moved its hand in the way at the last second, catching the spell. While the wind couldn't push past the shadowy aura, its secondary effect had begun. The wind drill compressed, but before anything more could happen, the shade screeched in Kyo's face, startling him, and grabbed his fist, spell and all.

The creature that was once Ruby slammed him against the ground, knocking the air from his lungs, then flung him into Roland.

A few seconds later, Ignivus landed beside them, skidding across the road. Standing side by side, the shades growled and stared down their prey. Another blast of flame from Ignivus had them shielding themselves with their arms. Krysta joined the Altruist, adding her own flame to the mix. Both shades took a step back.

"Krysta, stand next to Ignivus," Kyo said. He rushed to stand between them, hands outstretched, each expelling torrents of air.

The flames roared with increased intensity.

The shades screeched but not the same ear-piercing one from earlier, not as loud or aggressive. It sounded as though they were in pain. Their arms flailed through the fire.

At last, something they did had an effect.

"Keep going, Ignivus!" Rosette shouted.

Kyo grunted, feeding as much magic as he could into his support of the other two, and ducked his head to ward off the intense heat that might cook him if he wasn't careful. But if he drained himself completely, he'd be defenseless. One strike like before from the shades would be enough to kill him.

Magic bolts flew from the opposite direction, joining in the assault. Milo stood with his hand outstretched, trickles of blood running down his face.

Krysta's flame died off, and Ignivus's shortly after. Kyo cut his spell, panting, and keeping his eyes on the inferno that engulfed the shades in the middle of the road.

Silence filled the air as everyone stared, waiting for any sign their efforts weren't in vain.

"Do you think we got them?" Kyo asked.

"If nothing else, we should have injured them, I hope." Krysta tucked strands of hair behind her ear.

The shades burst from the flames, claws bared.

They charged forward, arms reared and ready to strike. Their eyes flashed as they chose their targets, one heading for Ignivus, while the one who had been Ruby aimed for Kyo.

A line of barriers appeared, separating the shades from their potential victims.

"Get back," a feminine voice called.

Unlike Marsh's barriers, the shades slashed at them but couldn't break through. Both shades working together caused small cracks to form in the first barrier, with three more untouched.

Kyo and Krysta backed away as the air above the barriers crackled with electricity. Bolt after bolt struck the shades. They screeched and writhed, but the bolts kept coming, a thunderous boom after each.

Once the cries ceased, so too did the lightning.

Kyo dared open his eyes as the barriers vanished. The shades lay in a heap, unmoving.

A young woman with braided brunette hair draped over one shoulder and an older man with a light caramel complexion, wrinkled skin, and wild, white hair approached the bodies.

The man lifted one of the shade's arms and then let it drop. "Seems like that did the trick, yah. A couple of tough customers, these two."

"This is getting bad. What would happen if there were ten or twenty of these things loose in a city?" the woman asked, her voice soft and breathy. Her eyes rose and locked onto Ignivus. She offered a faint smile and turned her attention back to the shades. "That enforcer was with several other corrupted. They could turn in a matter of hours or minutes."

"Excuse me," Marsh said, approaching the pair. "Thank you for your assistance. I do not believe we would have survived without it. But may I ask who you are?"

The man grinned and placed a hand on Marsh's head, ruffling his hair. "Don't you worry, little cleric. We're just a curious party who like to help where we can."

Kyo's heart skipped a beat. He'd heard those words before—or rather, that excuse. Eyeing the pair, he had a strong suspicion of who they were. Not by name but there could be no other explanation as to how they were able to take out the shades so easily. The amount of power required to do so with such ease couldn't be conjured by an average mage. That power, their excuse, and their pale green robes—no insignia, nothing special about them. As plain as could be so as not to stand out.

Milo approached, and the woman stopped him to work on healing his injuries. The old man's grandson rushed from his hiding place, kneeling by what used to be his grandfather, sobbing.

The shadowy aura did not completely fade but dissipated enough to reveal Ruby's face.

Kyo's fists clenched. Such a cruel fate. Even if they weren't friends, he wouldn't have ever wished something like this on her. How would Ren react when he found out? Kyo crouched beside her, resting a hand atop her head.

"I'm sorry. I tried my best." Kyo inhaled deeply and swallowed hard to compose himself. "I hope you find some peace when you return to the Flow."

It had become normal to mimic those words, having been repeated by so many after his parents died. He hoped it was true, the energy composing the human soul returning to the flow of natural magic within the world. And he hoped peace could be found there.

Chapter 13

Kyo couldn't tear his eyes from Ruby as the last rays of sunshine bathed her body. He held her hand, unwilling to let go. After all she'd been through over the past couple days, her face finally showed some semblance of peace.

His body and breath shook. He truly was helpless. When it came to Sybilla and Blanq, at least he could take action and fight, even if the chances of success were slim. But the corruption… He couldn't do anything to help the afflicted. All he could do was watch until they inevitably turned into vicious monsters. As much as he wanted to find Alden, he hoped he wouldn't have to witness his turn. Although it took victims varying lengths of time to turn, he couldn't imagine Alden had much longer.

Marsh placed a hand on Kyo's shoulder. "I am sorry. But do not blame yourself. You did all you could."

Kyo nodded, ignoring the tears running down his cheeks. Through his blurred vision, he looked up in time to see Ignivus fade away into a mass of sparkling red lights, like gem shards floating into the air and vanishing.

"Ruby?" a voice called.

Kyo turned to see Ren, eyes wide, panting and sweating as he dashed toward them and pushed Kyo aside.

"Ruby…" Ren's voice was barely above a whisper. His arms trembled as he pulled his sister into his arms. "What happened to her?"

Taking a deep breath, Kyo opened his mouth to respond, but the threat of sobbing made him close it again. Recounting the whole story would undoubtedly make him break down. Ren's sobs and the hurt on his face already brought Kyo to the edge. Ruby deserved to go home and return to her life. The inability to point his finger at someone and say, 'They did this' had sadness and anger fighting for dominance.

"They fell victim to the corruption that's been spreading," Krysta said, crouching next to him and the man mourning his grandfather. "There was nothing anyone could do. But Kyo tried his best to help her." She brushed a bit of hair from Ruby's face. "I'm sorry. I lost a woman who was like a mother to me yesterday." Her fist clenched against her lap. "You're not alone."

Ren buried his face in Ruby's neck, bawling and holding her against him. "My sister. She's…my best friend."

"We'll bring you home and celebrate your life," the young man said, gripping his grandfather's hand.

Kyo gripped his hair, looking anywhere but ahead of him. Marsh and Krysta's cheeks weren't dry either. So much death. Did his parents deal with things like this, only to come back home with big smiles on their faces? How many of those smiles were faked for him?

Milo placed his fist over his chest and nodded and then broke away from the woman healing him. He stood behind Ren. "Come on. Why don't we make arrangements to return them home?"

Nodding, Ren stabilized himself enough to pick up his sister while the other man carried his grandfather.

"Milo, has there been any progress on finding Alden?" Kyo asked.

"No, sorry," Milo said then turned his eyes to Rosette, squinting. "Make sure you restrain that little monster too," he said before heading down the street with the two mourning men shuffling behind him.

Roland marched in Milo's direction, fists clenched at his side. "Why that ungrateful little—"

Rosette grabbed his hand, and he paused.

"It's okay. Don't start another fight," she said, her voice meek.

Roland trembled and inhaled deeply then crouched to embrace her.

"What a jerk," Kyo said, glaring at Milo's back.

"This damn corruption. What is going on?" Krysta asked, grunting in frustration.

A valid question, and Kyo suspected they could get answers from their mysterious saviors. He wouldn't let them leave without confirming his suspicions about them. With Ruby being taken away, he calmed his breathing and managed to stop the tears from flowing.

"Speaking of…" the young woman said. "It was extremely reckless of the five of you to engage a shade, let alone two. Especially for a little girl." She gestured at Rosette then glared at Krysta. "And especially for you, Your Highness."

Kyo wiped the tears from his cheeks with the back of his sleeve. "Please, she already acts like a damn princess. Don't encourage her."

"Well, there's a good reason for that, yah." The older man stared Krysta in the eyes. "You're a long way from Alderdeem. His majesty has been worried sick about you. You've done a good job avoiding the royal guard he sent to look for you, yah."

His majesty? Kyo groaned, hoping it wasn't true. He'd never seen a princess wear cut-off denim shorts, but it would explain her *'I'm so much better than you'* attitude. She didn't need more of a reason to justify it. But was he really to believe she was royalty? Then again, he'd never met a princess before. Alderdeem was the last remaining region to have a monarchy.

All eyes were on Krysta, who glared daggers at both of her accusers. "I am my own person, and I will do as I please. If that means leaving the palace, then so be it."

"Are you really a princess?" Rosette asked, eyes wide with a cheek-squishing smile.

Krysta's scowl faded into a soft smile. "Yes, I really am."

Rosette squealed and covered her mouth to hide her obvious glee.

"And do you think it wise, such an important person wandering alone, unguarded?" the young woman asked. "What if someone recognized you? Decided to kidnap you for ransom — or worse?"

Krysta placed a hand on her hip. "Funny because until a second ago, Estella, no one here had any idea I was a princess. Until you and Garret opened your big mouths."

Estella's lips parted then closed.

Garret chuckled. "She got us there, yah. I suppose that's on us. Still, Your Highness, won't you please return home?"

"First, stop calling me that," Krysta said. "Second, no. I will return home when I am ready. And certainly not before I avenge Layla."

Roland cleared his throat. "I don't know what's really going on here, but we'll leave you all to it. We're just going to…"

He took Rosette's hand and made it a single step before Rosette yanked his arm, her creased eyebrows and clenched lips showing she had no intention of leaving. He sighed and remained still, letting his eyes wander.

"Engaging in battle with a shade is beyond reckless, yah. Though I guess the concept is a new one so you may not have known." Garret's gaze shifted from one mage to another. "What exactly is going on here?"

Kyo rolled his eyes so far up he thought he'd see his brain. "Fine. I don't even feel like arguing right now."

They explained the situation yet again, Marsh jumping in when he came into the story and Krysta doing the same.

"So, Sybilla and Blanq are the pair we've heard rumors about. This is a dangerous development," Estella said, more to herself than anyone else. "Pretending to cure the corruption to collect magic…and bodies."

"The idea of a necromancer isn't very comforting, nah," Garret said.

"They're not pretending though. They really can cure it. Figures the only ones who can have no intention of helping people," Kyo said. "But it seems you two know more about what's going on than we do. Care to share?"

Estella shook her head. "Such information is reserved for chancellors and His Majesty. The princess is not in a role of authority to receive that information."

Krysta narrowed her eyes. "I'll find out either way. If me returning home and standing in the room as you give a report to my uncle or calling for a meeting of all chancellors is what it takes, I *will* learn what you know."

Covering her mouth with her hand, Estella exhaled from her nose. "We might really get it from Cedric later, but she has a point."

"Who's Cedric?" Kyo asked.

Everyone gathered close to listen. Rosette pulled Roland and used her other hand to grip the bottom of Krysta's shirt, which brought a smile to the princess's face.

"A colleague of ours, helping in the investigation. As far as the corruption is concerned, we don't know what the source is or if there even is one. It's possible it could be like any other illness in the way it forms and spreads, yah." Garret's eyes met Rosette's. He stuck his tongue out and crossed his eyes, making the girl giggle. Estella nudged his side hard. "Just having fun, yah. Anyway, we're still looking into possibilities and theories about how it started, though not much progress has been made."

"It doesn't seem like it can transfer from one person to another. But from what our information shows, those who have become corrupted so far did so within a full day of each other or less. Thankfully, there haven't been those who have become corrupted in every town and city. A few here and there, but the majority are here on Kattelink Island." Estella paced as she spoke. "One theory is that each of them became afflicted with the corruption around the same time, but certain factors such as age and overall health determined how quickly they turned into shades." She focused her eyes on Kyo. "How did Blanq and Sybilla cure them?"

"She drained them of their magic. Every bit, I guess. It left them exhausted, but the corruption faded away after that. She said their magic would return in time, like normal. Oh yeah, she also said it didn't affect the body but the magic itself." Kyo shrugged. "It'd be nice if more people could learn to do that."

Garret cupped his chin. "I know forcibly draining the magic of someone else seems like just another spell, but it shouldn't be possible, nah. It isn't like spells that affect another's body. Over the centuries, there have been mages who have theorized and tried to perform a spell that directly affects another's magic. And all have resulted in failure. It simply doesn't work, nah. I can't imagine how she could have figured it out."

"And to think we came here trying to stay away from the corruption. We can't catch a break," Roland said with a deep sigh.

"At least the lady said we can't catch it from someone else." Rosette stared up at him with a hopeful smile.

Roland smirked and ruffled her hair. "True, that's one thing going for us, kiddo. We just need to find a safe place to settle down for a while."

Marsh hesitantly raised his hand. "You really will not tell us who you are? Knowing Krysta is in fact a princess, as well as investigating the corruption and having the power to easily defeat two shades. Though I suppose Krysta could tell us herself."

"As we said," Estella began, "We're just a curious party."

"Liar." Kyo focused his attention on the two of them. "I know that line." His lips formed the faintest hint of a smile. "You're members of the Aurora."

It was a bold statement. Many believed them to be nothing more than a story about a group who worked behind the scenes to ensure a better tomorrow for Feracael. Something to make them feel someone out there was looking out for them. But they were far more than a story and dealt with great dangers most people never learned about.

"And what makes you say that?" Garret asked, stroking his chin.

Kyo met Krysta's gaze. Her wide eyes either suggested she thought he was an idiot for suggesting it or impressed he knew the truth.

"Because that's what you always tell people who ask," he said. "My parents were members too."

Garret's eyes narrowed, leaning closer so their faces almost touched. "No, it couldn't be, nah." Righting himself, he looked Kyo up and down. "What's your name?"

"Kyo Sonata."

Garret's smile almost reached his ears. "I don't believe it! Little Kyo Sonata. Well, not so little anymore, nah." He placed both hands on Kyo's shoulders and shook him. "Look at you, so big now. Not that I ever actually met you in person."

"He's telling the truth?" Estella asked.

Garret didn't look away from Kyo. "It was before you joined. Iris was his mother, and Kei was his father. They were members all right and certainly liked to get into mischief. I see that's a trait you inherited, yah." He pulled away and cleared his throat. "My condolences. Your parents were amazing people. Wouldn't ever shut up about you."

Kyo offered a weak grin. "Thanks. Yeah, they were great. Maybe you can tell me about them sometime."

"I'd be happy to, maybe when all of this corruption nonsense calms down, ya."

"Royalty and Aurora." Marsh pinched the bridge of his nose. "I will have to speak with Cleric Micha about what he has gotten me into."

"I never would have thought such a dolt would have parents who were Aurora," Krysta said with a smirk. "I can't put faces to them, but the names ring a bell. I'm sure they came to the palace when I was younger. If you plan on living up to such amazing people, you'd better work much harder."

Kyo glared at her then turned to Marsh. "Don't think so hard about it. Her being a princess just means she's a spoiled brat, which we already knew anyway by her attitude. So, nothing has really changed, right?"

Garret stared intently at Kyo. "I'm sure Kyo here would be far more skilled if his parents were still around to teach him, yah. I remember Kei saying you liked wind spells like him. Is that still the case?"

Turning his palm up, Kyo pulled some magic, and air circulated above his hand. "Yeah, it is."

"You know, Kei had an interesting spell that almost made him untouchable. It was really something, yah. Something about stretching his magic out of him like strands to feel the air around him. Then he could feel anything moving and act accordingly." Grinning, Garret raised a finger, and electricity sparked from the tip. "Made it a fun game to see if I could get close enough to give him a little shock."

Kyo chuckled. His dad playing such a game sounded like him. No doubt his mother participated in her own way. Knowing her, probably trying to travel through shadows to get at his dad. He felt a sudden pang of guilt for the happy thoughts after what had happened to Ruby only minutes before.

"We still need to speak to the chancellor," Krysta said with a sigh.

"We can take care of that." Estella grabbed Garret's arm, pulling him away. "But it was nice to meet you. And Your Highness, we will be obligated to inform your uncle of your whereabouts."

Krysta waved her hand dismissively.

"You kids be careful. Stay away from Sybilla and Blanq and any shades, understood? You can leave this to us, yah," Garret said, giving a friendly wave as he walked backward.

Leave it to them. Kyo would love nothing more, and for the most part, he fully intended to take them up on that offer. But he couldn't let the weight drop from his shoulders until he knew Alden was safe. At least regarding Sybilla and Blanq, they could take comfort in knowing the Aurora were on the case, and with any luck, he shouldn't have to see their faces again.

That left him with the question of where to go from here. As much as they craved it, getting revenge with their own hands wasn't an option. It'd result in a repeat of Calmarock. Or worse. He needed time to sit down and think about how to move forward while not further risking his life. With any luck, he could find Alden and bring him home without having to encounter Sybilla again. While he felt confident the Aurora could handle the cold-blooded killers, Sybilla's spoken desire to see him and his friends again made him nauseous with nerves.

Chapter 14

As the sun dipped below the horizon and the first stars were glimmering in the night sky, Kyo and his friends stood alone in the middle of the street. He doubted anyone nearby would come outside again for a while. At least no innocents were killed, a better situation than in Calmarock when they'd dealt with their shade.

"We should find a place to sleep," Kyo said.

"I can direct us to an inn." Marsh took the lead down the road.

Rosette tugged on Roland's hand. "We need to sleep somewhere too, right?"

Roland nodded and followed.

Turning to Krysta, Kyo forced a smirk. "A princess. That's perfect."

"What's so perfect about it?" she asked.

"It means I get to legitimately call you a royal pain in the ass."

Krysta's lips parted to say something, but after Rosette giggled, she sighed and let it drop. "Well, it's not as important as Rosette here. A summoner. That's really something."

Rosette glanced down. "Is that okay?"

"Of course. You really helped us out back there. Thanks a lot." Kyo had no idea if the Altruist would have allowed them to win without Garret and Estella's interference, but it did hold its own against a shade, at least for a short duration. "Pretty cool, huh, Marsh?"

"I suppose so," Marsh said hesitantly. When he looked back at Rosette and the frown on her face, he did the same. "Do not worry. I have no problems with you, Rosette. And I thank you for your assistance. You too…Roland, was it?"

Roland nodded.

A smile returned to Rosette's face. "You don't like the idea of summoning, do you? I'm not the Altruist's master. They gave us the power to summon them because they wanted to help us. And I always thank them when they do."

"It is an uncomfortable thought. But I have never heard the reasoning from a summoner's own lips before. I promise to consider it," Marsh said before covering a yawn.

"You're a good girl." Roland pulled Rosette close to his side and rubbed her back. "And I appreciate the rest of you helping to keep her safe. I owe you big time."

They turned a corner, still not a soul in sight. Kyo bet the shade's screeching kept people inside more than the sounds of combat. No doubt he'd be hearing it echo in his mind when he tried to sleep. But he wouldn't let them scare him into inaction. After another loss, he mentally berated himself and his casual approach to training his magic and became more determined to do something about it. The wind drill spell he'd been working on would annoy the others, so instead he decided to consider how he might approach the spell Garret had spoken of.

Exhaling slowly, he released the tension from his body. Used to expelling magic from his hands and feet, his muscles tightened as he tried to let it seep from everywhere. Thin strands of magical energy leaked from him, not dense enough to see, but he could feel them like an extension of his body. They stretched like tendrils and expanded their influence into the air. The amount needed wasn't as much as his wind drill at first, but it was a spell designed to be maintained for a longer time and required much more focus, so best if he didn't try for too long. Once he paid more attention to his surroundings, he registered Krysta introducing them to Roland and Rosette.

"Were you two not with someone who was corrupted?" Marsh asked.

"No, it's just the two of us." Roland turned to stare south toward the ocean. Reaching into his trench coat, he pulled out a flask, popped the top, and took a swig. "Guess you can call us stowaways."

"Why stow away on a—" Kyo stumbled as he nearly tripped over something. He turned his head to see Marsh motionless on the ground.

Something caused the air his magical energy manipulated to tremble. Like an instinctual warning, he jumped to the side and spun around but saw nothing.

"Is Marsh okay?" Krysta asked. Before she could take a step, she too fell forward, her body unmoving, save her eyes staring wide at Kyo.

Roland fell next, and Rosette froze, her breath hitching in her throat.

"Well, well," a familiar voice said. "Looks like you've become a bit nimbler."

Kyo shuddered, his spell fading.

Behind Rosette, Sybilla's form appeared, like someone wiping the dirt from a window to reveal her. He clicked his tongue. Camouflage must have been another way she used her alteration magic. Kyo turned to Marsh, whose eyes also darted around in a panic. Paralyzed like in Calmarock.

"What is it this time?" Kyo asked, the slight waver in his voice betraying the false confidence he hoped to show. Unfortunately, he had less control over his shaking legs. It took a second to register that Sybilla's hands were wrapped loosely around Rosette's throat, fingernails slightly digging into her skin.

"Don't be that way. I thought I told you to show me fear next time I saw you. Do you really want to disappoint me?" Sybilla crouched behind Rosette and tightened her grip, the young girl squealing through clenched teeth, hands tight at her sides.

Kyo's heart thumped so hard he thought it'd be visible through his shirt. Where were the Aurora? If it came to a fight, he and Rosette couldn't take her alone. "You still didn't answer me. What do you want?"

"While watching your little skirmish with the shades, I noticed something that piqued my interest, that's all." Sybilla brushed her nose against Rosette's shoulder-length blond hair. "To think I'd find something as rare as a summoner so easily."

Kyo recalled her asking if they were summoners back in Calmarock. This couldn't be good for the kid. "She's just a kid. Leave her alone."

His fists clenched as he resisted the urge to summon his swords or conjure a spell. One false move and Rosette was done for. Once again, he found himself responsible for protecting someone. He'd failed in Calmarock. He'd failed Ruby. If he had to watch a little girl die due to his own weakness, he wouldn't be able to live with himself.

Not again.

Sybilla's nails dragged up and down over Rosette's neck. "People usually tend to fall into two categories: those who like summoners and see them as special and those who dislike them and think they shouldn't have deities at their beck and call. I don't care either way, although they can be rather dangerous if left unchecked."

Kyo met Rosette's eyes. Frightened, yes, but there was more. She glanced down then over her shoulder as best she could. What was she trying to get across to him?

"If you hurt her, I'll make sure you regret being born," Roland managed to say through a jaw that barely budged.

"You are a bold one, aren't you? Let's put that to the test." The glow from Sybilla's index and middle fingers radiated in the darkness, but the streetlamps lit the area enough to show two droplets of green liquid leaving those fingers and sliding down Rosette's neck.

Rosette's eyes clenched, and her body trembled as she sucked air in through her teeth. Kyo swore he could hear a slight sizzle. Sybilla really was an unstable sociopath.

He ground his teeth together, wanting to blast her through every building in town. "You're such a coward, hiding behind a kid."

"Get off me," Rosette said through gritted teeth. Her small fists trembled at her sides.

Around the corner behind Kyo, a pair of voices grew louder. Someone was coming, and if they got caught up in this, he bet Sybilla could easily kill them without compromising her advantage with Rosette. She'd killed more than enough people already. Their footsteps reached his ears. He didn't want to see any more innocent people die, but what could he do?

The streetlamps dimmed.

No, everything did, as if a blanket of darkness fell over them. He couldn't see his hand in front of his face, let alone anyone else. Would Sybilla try to take advantage of the sudden darkness in some way? If so, he had no means of stopping her.

The voices—a man and woman—passed him as if not noticing anything unusual, casually chatting about the food they'd just eaten. Kyo strained his ears to get a grasp of what went on around him, yet he made out nothing but the footsteps and voices as they faded away. When silence fell upon them, the darkness faded. No one had moved, not even Sybilla, who remained crouched behind Rosette.

"Seems like one of you knows quite the handy trick. I'd say that was a good decision. If they'd noticed what I was doing…" Sybilla giggled. "I would have had to silence them. Now then, where was I? Hmm, oh, I believe I was deciding whether the world would be better off with one less summoner. What do you think?" She leaned forward to look at Rosette's face. "Well, not you. No one cares what you think."

That unexpected darkness could have been Kyo's chance to do something, but even after it passed, he couldn't think of how to properly take advantage of it. Once more, his eyes met Rosette's, which were performing the same motions: down, behind. Sybilla sat behind her, so that was obvious. Below were Sybilla's hands wrapped around Rosette's throat, but how could he get her to loosen her grip? If Rosette had an idea, he hoped she could pull it off with a distraction.

Air circulated around Kyo's fist, strong enough to be of some use but not so much it'd disturb anything nearby. He didn't often cast spells to be controlled from a distance, but prayed he could do so without arousing suspicion. Eyeing a trash bin near a shop entrance behind Sybilla, he focused on the air around his fist, letting it fall to the ground and glide across the road.

"Let go of her, and I might not roast you alive," Krysta said.

"Yes, because you did such an amazing job at that before, didn't you? I might ask you to try again, just because the nights can be a bit chilly near the water," Sybilla said with a smirk.

Kyo couldn't see his spell, but he could feel it. He stared at Krysta until their eyes met and motioned to Sybilla with his head and mouthed for her to keep talking.

"Well, maybe you'd prefer to be frozen then." Krysta spoke with more ease, though so far showed no other sign of being able to move her body. "I'll freeze your hair and snap it off until you're bald."

Sybilla gasped. "How dare you. Threatening to mar beauty like mine. Clearly you have no taste."

Almost there. The further the spell went, the less he could control it, but he managed until it reached the trash can. The air burst upward, toppling the trash can with as much subtlety as a rock through a window.

"Garret! Estella!" he said, trying to sound relieved.

Sybilla turned to look behind her. Rosette took the chance to kick backward. What Kyo expected was for her to have the wind knocked out of her, or maybe she'd use the force of the kick to push herself forward and away from her captor. Instead, the kick sent Sybilla flying with a shriek then tumbling backward until she came to a stop with her dress-covered ass in the air.

"Whoa!" Kyo's eyes widened, and his slacked jaw shifted to a smile as Rosette ran to him. "Damn, kid, that was awesome."

As impressive as the display was, he got equal pleasure out of seeing Sybilla on the receiving end of an attack like that. Rosette clung to his side, and he placed a hand on her back, the other summoning a sword.

Sybilla rolled forward and hopped to her feet, stumbling and rubbing her stomach. "Seems there's more to you than just a summoner, huh? Little brat."

Kyo moved Rosette so he stood in front of her. If he had to fight, he couldn't do it with her clinging to him. Not that he had any hope of winning, but imagining his parents in his place, he'd never forgive himself if he didn't try.

Sybilla's grunts became chuckles, and then she howled with laughter. "This sure has gotten interesting." Clapping once, a sweet smile graced her lips that would have fooled anyone who hadn't met her before. "Congratulations, you all won't be dying…tonight."

"Wait, what? Why?" Kyo stiffened and clicked his tongue once the words left his lips.

"If you're so against living to see the sun rise, I can always change my mind. But I thought of something even more fun." Strolling toward Roland, Sybilla stepped on his back and dug the heel of her shoe into him. Even she had to know that wouldn't cause him much pain so long as he had enough magic in him. "Like I told you before, you all remind me of someone—well, a group of someone's who were just as caring, just as naïve. Wanting to help where they could, to validate themselves. I'm going to let you live so I can show you the hard way what a mistake that is. Just how I learned. Besides, I don't intend to make it easy for those Aurora to find me."

"You think we're just going to let you toy with us?" Kyo asked.

Sybilla strolled to Marsh and crouched, lightly prodding his cheek with her finger like a curious child.

"To be honest, your compliance isn't a factor." Standing again, she brushed her hands over her dress to straighten it. "I want you to see what's to come. To see what I'm working toward. Then you'll understand how weak and helpless you are." Her hand absently grazed over the pouch hanging from her side. Shifting her eyes to Rosette, Sybilla licked her lips. "No matter how things progress, I'll be sure to see *you* again, little summoner."

Sybilla turned her back to them and skipped down the road, grabbing a lamp post and twirling around it.

"And be sure not to ruin my fun. If you ever want to see your uncorrupted Alden again, you'll stick around," she said in a singsong voice, leaving them behind without looking back.

Chapter 15

Kyo remained as still as his friends on the ground. Sybilla's last words… Could he trust them? It didn't seem like something she said to get a rise out of him. She hadn't even looked at him when she'd said it. Gripping his hair, he took a deep breath as he fought between relief and skepticism.

"Roland, can you move?" Rosette crouched beside him, shaking him.

"Not too much yet," Roland said. "But it'll be okay, kiddo. Don't worry."

Kyo could consider what Sybilla meant later. He walked toward Roland and Rosette, purposely stepping on Krysta's back on his way to them.

"Hey!" Krysta cried out.

"Sorry, didn't see you." Standing beside Rosette, Kyo patted her head. "You've both been victims of Sybilla. Welcome to the club. Don't worry. The paralysis will wear off soon." He grabbed Roland's arms and struggled to pull him off the road and lean him against the closest shop in a seated position. After doing the same with Krysta and Marsh, he sat next to them, waiting for them to regain movement.

No one spoke while they waited. Kyo rested his forehead against his propped knee, wanting to forget their latest encounter with that insane woman. Twice they should have been killed, and twice they were spared because she thought it'd be fun. How long until their luck ran out? He glanced at Rosette, curled up against Roland's side. There was no way he could leave her and Roland when Sybilla had taken a special interest in the kid. Then there was Alden. Could he really be okay? And if so, why did they want to keep him?

When the others regained movement in their bodies, Marsh led them down the street on wobbly legs to an inn two blocks away, where they pulled together their cryst—mostly low-value red and white coins—and rented a single room. As the last one to enter, Kyo closed the door behind him, ensuring no one unseen could sneak in. The room had two beds and a chair in the corner, so no one should have to sleep on the floor. So far it seemed a waste packing his sleeping bag. A desk sat against the opposite wall from the beds and a wardrobe closet near the door. Not a lot of extras, but so long as they had some place soft and warm to sleep, Kyo didn't care.

"I apologize for the two of you getting mixed up in this," Marsh said, taking a seat in the corner chair. "Sybilla should not have become your problem."

Roland sat on the edge of a bed, pulling Rosette into his lap and examining the burn marks on her neck as she clung to him. "It's not your fault. Rosette being a summoner attracts attention, both good and bad. Though I have to admit, this is one of the more extreme situations. But there's no way I'm going to let her touch Rosette again."

Marsh rose from the chair and placed his hands gently over Rosette's neck, casting a healing spell. Though when he pulled back, the marks remained as noticeable as ever. "The pain should be about gone, but I can't seem to heal the marks left behind."

"It's okay. It feels better. Thanks." Rosette forced a smile at Marsh who took his seat again.

"I really don't like that she can be invisible, watching from any corner." Krysta took a seat on the same bed as Roland and grabbed a pillow to hug against her chest. "We don't need that paranoia on top of everything else."

As if in response, Marsh closed the curtains.

"My question is, why did it suddenly get so dark when those two people walked by us?" Kyo asked.

Roland pointed to Marsh with his thumb. "You have the cleric to thank for that. Unusual spell for someone like him but probably for the best in that situation."

"I may have only become a cleric recently, but that does not mean I did not practice magic before then." Marsh frowned, glancing to the side.

"I take it that's a spell you made use of when living on the street?" Krysta asked.

Marsh nodded. "One of several, yes. Again, as a means of surviving."

"It's terrible you had to live like that. I wouldn't wish that on anybody in Alderdeem or elsewhere. But you being here now shows you were, and are, strong," Krysta said with a smile.

Roland turned his eyes to Marsh. "I don't know the full story, but if you spent time living on the street and you're now a cleric, that shows a lot about you. Strength, resolve, and I can't imagine a cleric with bad moral character. So, keep your eyes up, not on the ground, kid."

Marsh's smile widened, and he fell limp on the couch. "Thank you. That is very kind."

"So, what about you, *Your Highness*? Why leave your luxurious palace and life of wealth and whatever else you have?" Kyo asked.

"Are we all taking turns telling our life stories now?" Krysta asked, crossing her arms over her chest.

Kyo shrugged. "May as well. We're all stuck together until Sybilla is dealt with. The way I see it, she has an interest in us. If we go our separate ways, she'll probably hunt us down one by one just for the fun of it. So, why not get to know each other better?"

"Easy for you to say. Everyone here has already heard your story several times." Krysta waved her hand dismissively. "It's getting exhausting, honestly."

"Rosette, do you remember the only place left that has a king?" Roland asked.

The young girl's lips tightened. "Um...Alderdeem, right?"

"That's right." Roland then looked at Krysta. "Need to keep up her education somehow, since we don't stay in one place for long. So, random trivia seems to do the trick."

"Is that really the best way to educate her?" Kyo asked.

"It's fine. We both like the nomad lifestyle we've got, right?" Roland ruffled Rosette's hair. "We get to see all sorts of places."

"It'd be nice to have an actual home though," Rosette said with a frown.

"We've tried, remember? Some people just don't like summoners around. Traveling around like we do is oddly the safest way to raise you." Roland kissed Rosette's head, but it did nothing to brighten her mood.

The life of a summoner must have been hard. Kyo knew not everyone liked them, but he never expected people would go so far as to chase them from their homes, especially a kid. But he bet it wasn't easy for Roland either.

A loud bang came from the hallway, causing everyone to jump or tense up. Several loud footsteps drew closer and closer before a door opened and closed again.

"Geez." Kyo sighed, his heart pounding. That woman had really gotten into his head. He needed a distraction from his paranoia.

When Kyo poked Krysta with his foot, she slapped it away.

"I left home, okay?" she said. "You think being a princess is wonderful? Always being told how to talk, how to walk, eat, dress, people trying to control every aspect of your life. I couldn't take it anymore and wanted some freedom. To make my own choices, to not know what would happen tomorrow." Upon seeing Rosette's deepening frown, she reached out and held her hand. "It has been three months, so I do miss my family. I guess I'll go back home after all of this is over. But if they try going overboard again, I'm right back out the door. I never asked to be heir to the throne, and I don't want it."

"The grass is always greener on the other side, as they say," Roland said.

"And it was Layla that brought you to Calmarock?" Marsh asked.

Krysta hugged the pillow tighter. "For years she helped raise me and teach me at the palace. Then a few years ago, she decided to live a quieter life on this darn island. I wanted to see her again, so I came to visit. Then the shade and Sybilla and Blanq…"

She shook her head and fell silent. Rosette patted the back of Krysta's hand.

"I'm sorry for your loss. It seems things have become intense on this island. We never would have come if we knew." Roland stripped himself of his trench coat, letting it drop to the floor. "When it comes to Rosette and me, there isn't much to tell. I'm sure you know feelings on summoners are split. We can never spend too much time in one place because, while we come across plenty who are friendly to us, even think Rosette is amazing, which she is…" Rosette smiled at him, and he smiled back. "The few whose hatred manifests into violence ensure we're constantly moving around. Can't risk anything happening to her, you know?"

"But we can try to stay. I'm not little anymore." Rosette thrust her fist into her palm. "I'm ten. We can make them leave us alone."

"It's too risky, kiddo. I won't let anything happen to you." Roland's gaze rose. "They don't usually mind her summoning an Altruist, but the fact she's even capable of summoning a Relinquished frightens them."

The summoning of a Relinquished occurred so infrequently, Kyo hadn't considered the possibility. He'd learned they always left death and devastation in their wake, on par with what Sybilla had done to Calmarock at minimum. "You don't think she can take care of herself? It sure looked like she could, the way she kicked Sybilla across the road. That memory will bring a smile to my face for a long time."

Rosette flexed her arm. "I started learning to be a brawler a while ago so I could protect myself if Roland wasn't around. That lady is scary…but I also want to punch her really hard."

Of all of them, Rosette appeared to be the least affected by the thought of Sybilla, despite what had happened. What must she have gone through in her life to take this so lightly?

"Adding to that, it doesn't hurt that summoners naturally have a larger magic pool than most people, making her a little powerhouse, which in turn reflects on the avatars she summons," Roland said.

Kyo raised a brow. "What do you mean?"

"Golden rule of summoning, kid. The power of a pantheon's avatar is equivalent to the power that summoned it. In most cases, it means the avatar is as strong as the summoner. But it only takes one careless moment for something to happen you can't take back. So, we try to avoid situations like that." Roland motioned for Rosette to join him. She crawled into his lap and wrapped her arms around him.

"So, that's why you were stowaways. It sounds like such a harsh way to live. Has it always been this way?" Krysta asked.

A sigh escaped Roland's lips. "Yep. Ever since I found her as a baby. I do the best I can though."

"Oh, so you are not her biological father, then. I would not have guessed." Marsh sat slouched in the chair, eyes half open.

"When my mom and dad saw I was a summoner, Roland said they tried to drown me in a river." Rosette's words were so casual and spoken with a straight face. She removed her gloves, holding her hands up and showing off the double helix with the dot in the middle engraved in the back of her hands. "See? We're born with the pantheon symbol like this, so people can tell right when we're born. But Roland said I was a few months old when it happened, so I guess they tried for a while."

Krysta frowned, grabbing Rosette and holding her against her chest. "I'm so sorry. You poor girl, having to live a life like that, with parents so terrible."

"It's okay." Rosette's words were muffled against Krysta's shirt. She pulled away, inhaling deeply. "I have Roland, and he's great. And one day, we'll find somewhere we can live where no one will chase us away. I know it."

Her words deepened Krysta's frown, and she held the young girl tighter.

"As luck would have it, I happened by at the right time to stop them. So, they shoved her into my arms and ran off. And the rest is history." Roland pulled the flask from his coat and took a swig. "It sure was rough at first, being so unexpected. But it was well worth it."

Marsh covered his mouth as he yawned. "You sound like a wonderful father."

"Thanks for not minding me being a summoner," Rosette said with wide, adorable eyes.

Roland chuckled. "Rational people won't think you'll summon a Relinquished. Even if she summoned one for some reason, it wouldn't be like those worst-case scenarios you read about in history books. Take the summoning of Saecluvus in Goruza about a hundred years or so ago. A group angry about increased taxes on the poor sought to get revenge."

Kyo groaned. "What, a history lesson?"

Roland pointed at him. "You kids are here, which means you're not home studying. So don't complain. Anyway, most of the bigger historical events involving Relinquished are due to a situation where a group of people give their magic to a summoner, who used it all during the summoning. Remember the golden rule I just mentioned? The Relinquished went on a rampage, and the entire town was utterly erased from existence. Well, dissolved, I think is the appropriate term." He sighed and poked Rosette's forehead. "But most people don't think of the context. They just go by base information and let their fear fill in the rest."

"But I won't summon a Relinquished, promise!" Rosette held her hand up as a sign of her word.

"Hey, I believe you. Don't need to convince me," Kyo said. "On the topic of places to live, you could try Mistwell on the other side of the island. It's a pretty nice place, real homey."

Kyo shifted to lay on his back. With any luck, he and Alden would return there together. He used to think their life was boring, uneventful, but now he'd take it any day over dealing with insane mages and shades. At least until he became an Aurora. When Alden came home, Kyo would never take him for granted again. For a few seconds, he closed his eyes and imagined them eating dinner and laughing while poking fun at each other. It would happen again. It had to.

"Traveling across the island doesn't sound like a good idea for now, with its shade problem. Though as long as Sybilla has a specific interest in Rosette, I guess she and I don't have a choice but to stick close to wherever the Aurora are." Roland stretched his arms above his head and groaned. "You kids are all right. Glad it's you we ran into. It isn't too late, but after what happened earlier, you should all get plenty of sleep. We can talk about what we're going to do tomorrow." Roland stood, facing Marsh. "You take the bed with Kyo. I can use the chair—I've slept in far more uncomfortable places than that."

Marsh shook his head. "You may have the bed. Besides, I am too tired to move now. While living on the streets for years, I have learned to sleep anywhere."

Roland shrugged and laid down next to Kyo.

Kyo sat on the edge of the bed. "I think I'll stay up for a bit, keep watch."

Since he'd woken up so late earlier that day, staying up to keep watch for a while made sense. He doubted he'd be able to fall asleep easily anyway.

Reaching into his pouch, Kyo pulled out a small, round container with a clear gel inside. He scooped some with his finger and rubbed it against his teeth to clean them, the others doing the same. Krysta and Rosette got comfortable under the blanket, and Marsh hadn't even closed his container before passing out.

Kyo turned the light off then stared at the ceiling. All of his worries kept his mind occupied. He couldn't calm his heart, nor stop his leg from shaking. While she couldn't possibly be in the room with them, that didn't stop his imagination from running wild. Knowing Sybilla could be anywhere, he trembled at the thought of facing her yet again. At least if she came after them overnight, she couldn't get in without them hearing a window or door break down.

Then there was Alden and whether Kyo should trust the indication that his godfather might be cured. After failing to help Ruby, Kyo wanted to believe he could still save Alden. But why would they be so interested in keeping Alden in the first place? They used him to get the stone hidden in Mistwell, so why hold on to him? And where could he be? With their ability to teleport, he could be anywhere. He stretched his arms above his head in a fruitless effort to calm his body. Even if he wanted to, there would be no point in searching for Alden without more information. Sybilla certainly wouldn't reveal anything if directly asked. And so far, Blanq hadn't uttered a single word. He grimaced as it felt like a pit opened in his stomach, admitting to himself he could do nothing but leave it to the enforcers and the Aurora, if Sybilla didn't ambush them again.

He turned his head, taking a moment to watch as the others lay comfortably in bed with their eyes closed. It had only been one day since he met Marsh and Krysta, and a couple hours for the other two. Yet it felt like they all belonged together. There was something to be said about the bonds that could form as comrades in arms, fighting for their lives. He'd do anything to avoid fighting Sybilla again. With each passing hour the desire to ensure their safety became more of a priority.

Chapter 16

If Kyo kept his eyes closed, maybe he could convince his body it hadn't woken up in the middle of the night. He didn't know how many hours he stared at the ceiling or poked a dark corner of the room with his sword to ensure Sybilla hadn't slipped in before sleep finally took him. A slow shuffling across the room didn't help. When he peeked with one eye, the moonlight revealed a long ponytail leaving the room.

What was Krysta doing up so late? Well, if she decided to stay up all night, then that was her business. Kyo turned onto his side, tightening the comforter around him. Exhaling, he let his head sink into the soft pillow, but seconds later, his eyes opened as scenes of Krysta sobbing over Layla's body played in his mind.

He rose and swung his legs over the side of the bed. "Dammit."

Alone time with Krysta wasn't exactly on his list of things to look forward to, but he knew the guilt he'd feel if he didn't check and make sure she was all right. After rubbing his eyes for a few seconds too long, he stood and staggered through the door and into the upstairs hallway. He'd check up on her, then go back to bed. Quick and easy.

The bottom floor of the inn had tables and chairs set up like a small tavern, all of which were cloaked in darkness, save for one table in the far corner. Krysta sat in a chair with her face buried in her hands, illuminated by a lit candle on the table. Her sobs and shaky breaths carried throughout the room.

Inhaling sharply, Kyo forced himself to cross the room. As soon as his hand gripped the back of a chair, Krysta fell silent. He sat and propped his head up with his hand, elbow on the table. "Want to talk?"

Narrow, bloodshot eyes glared at him from between parted fingers. "No."

"Give it a try. If you keep it all in, it'll break your soul."

"Where did you hear something like that?"

Kyo smiled weakly. "Alden said that to me after my parents died. I tried to keep to myself, stayed in my room, wouldn't talk to anyone. Heh, my pillow got wet from crying after a while." He flicked his finger, weak bursts of air making the candle flame dance. "Alden wanted to give me space, but eventually he forced me out. Looking back, it was probably for the best. I would have kept myself in a cycle of sadness if he hadn't."

After a moment's hesitation, Krysta wiped the tears from her face and looked at him with puffy eyes. "I suppose that makes sense. It's just… Layla was… It's like losing my mother." She clenched her fingers into a fist, and the candle flame stretched to match the height of the candlestick. "And I cannot rest until *they* suffer for what they've done. And not just to Layla but all of Calmarock."

He grunted in agreement. Even if he didn't have the connection to Calmarock that Krysta had, he wanted Sybilla and Blanq to pay for their actions too. But while he had come to accept the reality of the situation, it didn't seem like she had. "You're right. Those two need to get the swift ass-kicking that's coming to them. But not from us."

"So, you're just going to give up?" She stood and slammed her fists on the table. "After what they've done?"

Kyo remained silent for several seconds, listening for opening doors or footsteps in case her outburst had disturbed any of the inn's patrons. He didn't need someone marching down the stairs to yell at them for disturbing their sleep. When no one came, he sighed and focused on Krysta. "Of course not. If nothing else, I'm not going home until I find Alden, wherever they put him. But when it comes to fighting them… Well, you remember what happened the other day. We could hardly put a scratch on Sybilla. And what if Blanq joined the fight?" His body tensed from the frustration of what he had to admit. "We're nowhere near strong enough to take them on. As much as I would love to bring them down with my own two hands, we have to leave it to the Aurora. Now that they're involved, we should be able to rest easy knowing this will be dealt with."

Krysta sat, almost growling through clenched teeth. "If I come across them again, I won't run away."

He sighed, unable to agree with that sentiment, though he kept his lips tight so as not to argue. Her desire was natural, though ruled by her emotions from recent events. Days ago, he thought the same but came to his senses after two firm beat downs. If they did encounter those two again, he may have to force Krysta away. Better to change the subject.

"So, what was it like with Layla?" he asked. "When she lived with you, I mean."

Hugging herself, Krysta stared into the flame. "She was very kind. And patient. I was a bit restless as a child, which made things more difficult for her. But she never raised her voice. She was both my nanny and my teacher. And sometimes my playmate. Layla always humored me when I wanted to hide from her. A difficult game in a large palace."

"It sounds like she had her work cut out for her."

"Time spent with her was a relief. With her, I felt so free to be myself. With my parents…" She closed her eyes and sighed then stared at the candle. "I know it's not fair to complain about my parents, since yours are, well…"

Kyo waved his hand dismissively. Even if his parents were gone, he still recognized not all parents were great. "Don't worry about it."

"I know they love me. They really do. They're just so frustrating." She placed her finger within the candle flame, her skin not even reddening from the heat. "My uncle is the king, and my parents don't mind. They enjoy the life that comes with being royalty with minimal responsibility. But he has no children of his own, so I'm next in line for the throne. And to my parents, this means I must walk a certain way, talk a certain way, even smile the way a princess would. Around them, I can't be myself." Her eyes met Kyo's. "I don't know why I'm telling *you* this."

He shrugged. "You need to get it out. Trust me, I get it. When my parents were killed, I had Alden to vent to. You need someone like that too."

Krysta raised her finger, the flame duplicated, one in the candle and one on her fingertip. "I miss Layla so much. She had so many years ahead of her." She wiped away a tear with her sleeve. "I do hope she finds peace in the Flow. Maybe I'll see her there when it's my time." She coated her other index finger in ice and held the flame up to it, watching the ice slowly melt. "I wonder what it's like. Is it just our souls floating within a sea of natural magic?"

"Everyone else wonders the same thing. We won't know until we die." Kyo hadn't expected such a deep conversation. At this time, he should be asleep, escaping such worries. But if he were honest with himself, he didn't mind too much. He hadn't spoken to anyone about such things in years. "But let's not rush that. I'm sure Layla and my parents would be pissed if we wound up there so soon after them."

"I know." Krysta grunted and tore her eyes from her fingers to look at him with a raised eyebrow. "You don't have to answer this if you don't want to, but your parents were Aurora, right? But you said they were killed. Who, or what, could have done that to them?"

This question had run through his mind nearly every day for the past six years. They were powerful heroes who, in his mind, could not be beaten.

Except they had been. Taken away from him by a faceless, nameless person.

His jaw clenched, wishing he had a face to go with his burning hatred. He and Alden were given vague information about the event. With the Aurora here in Aquarin, he'd have to make it a point to ask one of them what they knew.

"I wish I knew," he finally said. "Somehow, a single person was able to take them both out. That's all we were told."

"That's not right. If anyone deserves to know what happened, it's you two." Krysta stood, the ice and flame vanishing from her fingers. "This is a lot to take in." Pacing, she wrapped her arms around her stomach. "Mages who are that powerful and are a danger to everyone. I mean, it's not like we didn't know they existed, but it hits much harder when you see it for yourself." She paused and turned her focus on Kyo. "Didn't you say you wanted to be an Aurora? Do you still want that?"

"Absolutely," he said as he stood. He might be uncertain about many things recently, but becoming an Aurora was not one of them. "If anything, this whole situation makes me want to become one even more. I have no delusions about becoming one anytime soon like I did before, but when it happens, I can help prevent situations like in Calmarock. And put a stop to psychopaths like Sybilla and Blanq. But for this situation, we'll have to leave it to Garret and Estella."

"And Cedric, apparently. I've met him a few times in recent years. Honestly, I feel a bit more at ease knowing he's involved." She sat on a nearby table, crossing one leg over another.

Such a heavy discussion had lessened Kyo's fatigue, the weight easing from his eyes. He might not be able to fall asleep again. "What's special about this Cedric guy?"

"Well, I don't know many details about him honestly. But whenever my uncle asked something of him, it got done with little to no issue. He always looked relieved when Cedric took on a request himself." Krysta uncrossed her legs and drummed her fingers on her knees while her feet kicked lightly. "I've listened in on a few of their conversations, even if I wasn't supposed to." A grin spread across her lips. "I assume Garret and Estella will relay what we told them to him."

"I hope they let us know as soon as they make some progress." With a sly smirk, he placed his hand upon his stomach and bowed at the waist. "But with Her Highness in our group, maybe they'll feel obligated to anyway."

Krysta rolled her eyes. "I don't want to hear you call me that again. So long as I am away from Alderdeem, I am Krysta, nothing more."

"You didn't think to change your name after you left home?"

"I did. The only reason you know me as Krysta is because you met me in Calmarock. Everywhere else I'd been, I chose a different name to go by." She silently chuckled. "I tried that in Calmarock too, but Layla let my real name slip so often there was no point in keeping up the charade."

Layla had seemed a bit absent minded, so he could believe that.

Kyo righted himself. "What are you going to do once Sybilla and Blanq are dealt with? Will you go home?"

Sighing deeply, she hunched forward and leaned her arms on her thighs. "Maybe. As frustrating as my parents are, I do miss them. And my uncle. And with the corruption spreading, I want to make sure they're okay."

"Yeah, I'm sure that's best. Good luck getting away again though. They'll keep a close eye on you once you're back. Trust me, I've wandered away more than once, and Alden hardly let me leave the house for a while afterwards." He chuckled. "He got so mad when I'd go to Solitude Pass on my own before I was even a teenager. At the time, I thought he was overreacting, but looking back, I get it."

Krysta pointed at him. "Speaking of which, a thought has been going through my mind. According to your story about what happened in Mistwell, whatever that stone is that Sybilla uses—she got it from there, right?"

"Yeah. Funny enough, I was looking for it that same morning. Though I didn't know what I was actually looking for, I just knew it was something powerful." He shrugged. "Now I'd be happy if I never see the damn thing again."

"Something like that would be under some protection, wouldn't it? Enchantments, for example."

Kyo grumbled. "I know what you're getting at. They might have used Alden to retrieve the stone. It'd make sense if it were Alden's job to hide and enchant it to protect it from...well, people like me I guess."

"Which is why he didn't wind up like the others you found. They needed him." She narrowed her eyes. "So, the question becomes, did he help them willingly?"

"Now hold on." He clenched his jaw. How dare she insinuate such a thing. "If he did help them get it, you can bet it was some sort of blackmail. They'd already met me—maybe they used me as leverage. Or the whole town. Mistwell could have easily seen the same loss of life as Calmarock. For all we know, he saved lives by giving them the stone."

"Saved lives?" Krysta stood and shoved Kyo. She kept her voice low, but there was no mistaking the deep tone and fury behind her words. "Layla is dead! Half of Calmarock is gone. And Sybilla used that damn stone to do it. Watch what you say, you idiot."

"You don't know the details of what happened. If Alden refused, they could have found another way to get it and leveled Mistwell in the process. There are too many unknowns to make an assumption like that." Kyo returned Krysta's aggravation, shoving her shoulder. "So, *you* should be the one to watch it."

"Maybe you're right, and maybe I am. But I'll definitely be keeping it in mind for the time being. If he's even partially to blame for what happened, then he deserves whatever punishment would be coming to him." She marched toward the stairs then paused and turned to him. "I'll be sure to get whatever information the Aurora learn from their investigation."

In her anger, she stomped up the stairs with clear disregard for anyone who may be sleeping.

Kyo wanted to scream, but he tightened his jaw and released a long, low groan instead, his whole body shaking. As if Alden would ever willingly help them if he had a choice. Knowing sleep would be impossible, he left the inn, the cool, salty air making him regret leaving his hoodie in the room. But he wouldn't be going back in there anytime soon. He didn't want to look at Krysta.

Rubbing his arms for warmth, he sauntered down the road. Krysta's assumption wouldn't leave his mind. Alden would never do such a thing, certainly not without them holding something over him. Krysta made it sound like he was in league with them from the beginning. Kyo bet they were keeping Alden somewhere so he wouldn't be able to go to the enforcers. But for how long? And why not kill him to keep him quiet? Assuming they hadn't, he didn't want to think about what they could have in mind for him in the future if he still lived.

Chapter 17

In the dead of night, with the moon the primary light source aside from spread-out streetlamps, Sybilla could appear around any corner, emerge from any shadow. At least the moon was nearly full, chasing away some of the darkness. Though given her tendency to play with her victims—not to mention her desire for them to see what she had planned—Kyo hoped he wouldn't have to worry about that as he traversed the streets of Aquarin. Not entirely confident, his steps hastened when in the dark and slowed under the light of the occasional streetlamp powered by magic-tech, giving off a dark blue hue instead of the more common red flame like back home.

With no destination in mind, he absently wandered wherever his legs took him. Given the hour and the earlier shade attack, Aquarin was like a ghost town. Not a soul in sight and no sound aside from the faint echo of his footsteps. The port sat too far down the hill for him to hear any splash the sea might make against the pier or docked ships. If not for the fear of Sybilla, he would consider it peaceful.

His gaze darted around when he came upon the damaged buildings and road, remnants of their battle a few hours before. Did the dent and cracks he stepped on come from when the shade slammed Milo's head into the ground or from someone's spell? At this point, the whole fight came as little more than a blur to his mind. In the heat of the moment, he was more than willing to face off against the shades, but in retrospect, he wished never to come across one again. They were strong and durable. The memories of their screeches made him shudder, and if he'd faced one alone, his life would've ended in minutes. Unfortunately, no one knew how long the corruption would last or how far it would spread. All he could do was hope the Aurora could find its source — assuming one existed — and put an end to it.

He made his way further up the hill and paused, spotting rubble on the road. The enforcer's station would need to be repaired after Ruby had destroyed much of the front exterior and who knew how much of the interior.

Don't write their eulogy.

Marsh had a valid point, but how could he not when he personally knew the victim? Ruby's trembling voice and Ren's sobs flashed in his mind. He took a long, deep breath to steady his emotions and tried to push away the thoughts.

Kyo approached the building next door, disconnected from the enforcer's station, and jumped onto the roof. He dropped into the adjacent road then leaped atop the building across the street. Stars littered the night sky, as if someone had sprinkled glitter across it. Out at sea, he bet the view was even more impressive. Keeping his eyes glued to the starry sky, he filled his thoughts with images of stargazing with his parents. It always helped to calm him. Already his body loosened, arms dangling at his sides as he let his mind wander, drawing imaginary lines between each sparkling dot to make a new shape.

Minutes passed like mere seconds. By the time he could focus his thoughts again, the moon had shifted from where he'd last seen it. He couldn't go the entire night without trying to sleep again. At least by this point, Krysta was either asleep or wouldn't acknowledge his presence if he returned to the room and slipped back into bed. And as unlikely as it was that Sybilla would find him tonight, he didn't want to take that chance any longer.

Something shifted in the corner of his eye. Kyo turned his attention to the chancellor's office, similar in design to the one in Mistwell, including its three-story structure. But it had its own town symbol on the highest floor's exterior, a painted carving of a ship atop a wave. The entire building shifted, as if he'd stared into a puddle and a ripple distorted the previously perfect reflection.

"What the… Maybe I'm more tired than I thought." Kyo rubbed his eyes, and when he looked again, the rippling continued for another second before ceasing. "That's not normal."

Instead of searching for the correct roads to get to his destination, he made his way in a straight line to the office by jumping onto rooftops block after block and descending onto the road.

From the closest roof, he saw two enforcers standing guard outside the door. But why would they be here this time of night? Every window from his view remained dark. Perhaps the chancellor stayed late doing some last-minute work, probably related to the shade attack earlier. He didn't envy her job. Even though the theory made sense, it didn't account for the odd distortion he saw. An idea struck him like a rock to the head. Back home, it became second nature to avoid enforcers at night, since they often didn't approve of whatever he might be doing so late. Tonight, he had nothing to worry about by approaching them, admittedly a new feeling but one that allowed him to breathe easier.

Kyo hopped down from the roof. As he drew closer, the air rippled around him again. The two guards that stood at either side of the door were slumped against the wall.

He froze, staring at them for a moment, then frantically looked to his sides and behind him. Taking a large step back, the air rippled again, the two guards once more standing with eyes open. Could this be some sort of illusion spell?

Kyo stepped with haste toward one of the guards, once again slumped over after the first step. He reached out, pressing his fingers to her neck. The enforcer had a pulse. A second later, she inhaled deeply then released it with a slight snore.

"Sleeping on the job, huh?" Kyo sighed, relieved he hadn't found a corpse. Calmarock had shown him enough of those.

Kyo checked the other enforcer and confirmed he too was fast asleep.

"Come on, wake up. Something weird is going on." He gently shook the enforcer by the shoulders but got no response. "Don't hate me for this." Reeling his hand back, he gave the man a firm slap across the face. The crack of his hand against the enforcer's cheek made Kyo cringe, and yet the man still didn't stir.

Turning to the front door, Kyo narrowed his eyes. Putting the guards to sleep, an illusion over the building—someone inside didn't want to be disturbed. His heart pounded as he pushed a hand against the door, finding it unlocked.

Please don't be Sybilla. Repeating this in his mind, he opened the door and stepped inside. Sprawled out on the floor were two more enforcers, one of them Karu. After confirming their chests rose and fell, Kyo looked around but saw no sign of anyone else, which sent a chill down his spine. Karu had been with the corrupted people from the ship Roland and Rosette had come here on. So where were they?

Kyo jumped as a thud sounded from the second floor. Taking a moment to breathe deep and calm his heart, he made for the half-spiral stairs then traversed the hallway as silently as possible. He stopped in front of a large pair of thick wooden doors and heard the occasional footstep on the other side.

Please not Sybilla.

But he had to know what was happening. If the corrupted people were loose, Aquarin was in for a rude awakening. Gulping hard, he rested a trembling hand against the door and pushed it open.

The walls to the left and right were lined with bookshelves without enough space to add one more tome. Of similar design, the desk was crafted of deep black wood. To its right, a man stared at him, hunched over, arms dangling in front of him, and his eyes glowing blue. Behind the desk sat Blanq, paused with a mug in their hands, and against their lips.

At least Kyo saw no sign of Sybilla, but that didn't mean his heart didn't threaten to leap out of his chest. He may have preferred taking on Sybilla again over being turned into some mindless undead. A simple death had to be a better fate. His fists clenched at his side as that fear shifted to anger. Turning people into walking corpses, taking Alden from him, and Layla's final fate.

A sword materialized in his hand, and he pointed it at Blanq. "Where is Alden?"

Blanq sipped their beverage then lowered the mug, saying nothing. The faint scent of chocolate wafted across Kyo's nose. Sitting alone in the chancellor's office drinking heated chocolate? Relaxation time was over.

Kyo stomped to the desk, keeping an eye on the undead but leaving most of his focus for Blanq. "One last time. Where is he? I'm tired of asking, and I *will* get my answers tonight."

The tip of his sword pressed against Blanq's robe at their throat. If they made any move, Kyo would strike first.

"Not here," Blanq said in a high, meek voice. "But he is unharmed."

Kyo hadn't expected that. Narrowing his eyes, he raised the tip of his sword to catch Blanq's hood. As he raised it, the shadow covering Blanq's face also receded. It must have been an enchantment on the robe or the hood itself. Kyo flipped the hood back, revealing a girl who couldn't have been any older than him. Striking blue eyes stared back at him behind a curtain of unkempt dirty-blond hair. Between her pale skin, button nose, and a small dimple on each cheek, he couldn't find any word to describe her other than…cute.

Blanq's overall appearance and apparent age left him with more questions but none as important as those he'd had before tonight.

He blinked hard, refocusing his mind and positioning the tip of his sword back to her throat. "How am I supposed to trust you when you say that?"

Showing no concern over the sword, she brought her mug around it to take another sip. "If you've already decided not to trust my answer, then why are you asking the question? There is no logical sense in that approach."

Kyo's lips tightened. Why did he get the feeling that was a roundabout way of calling him stupid? "Then let's try another approach. What exactly do you mean by 'he is unharmed'?"

Blanq lightly ran her finger over the edge of the blade then took a few seconds to examine the unbroken skin. "To elaborate, we have done what you've asked of us and removed the corruption from him the night you left him with us. Since then, we have done no harm to him, physically or mentally."

Free of the corruption? And Alden hadn't been turned into one of those undead? Kyo wanted to believe her, to let hope and relief wash over him. But Sybilla was the type to enjoy toying with her enemies. It was reasonable to assume Blanq could be the same way. Even if she'd given no indication of having the same mentality, the fact she worked with Sybilla said a lot.

He realized his breathing had grown heavy and tried to calm himself, fighting the shivers running through his body. "Then what have you done with him? Why can't you let him return home?"

Blanq raised the mug to her lips, taking another sip and said nothing. Yet she kept her eyes on Kyo's the whole time. If she intended to test his patience, then Kyo would make sure it'd come back to bite her.

"If you're not going to tell me by choice, I have no problem making you talk." Kyo narrowed his eyes and tightened his grip around the hilt of his sword.

He knew his words sounded like someone desperate who might surrender their morals to get what he wanted, but he didn't care. Finding Alden and bringing him home mattered far too much for him to worry about that. Shifting his blade, he thrust forward at her shoulder. His jaw clenched as he stared where the blade tore through the robe and stabbed at her flesh. Yet the skin didn't break. He grunted, putting more strength behind the push, yet it was like trying to stab the shade all over again.

"You underestimate Sybilla and me. I theorize that you believe you had a difficult time with her due to her use of the accrue stone and her defensive spells. Yet even without those, your chances of defeating her in battle alone would amount to less than half a percent. Against me, I would place your chances just short of two percent." Blanq glanced at her shoulder. "Even so, your efforts are leaving an unpleasant sensation."

Kyo attempted one last thrust, flexing the muscles in his arm and releasing a low grunt. Yet he still couldn't break the skin enough to release even a trickle of blood.

He pulled back, dismissed the sword, and gulped hard. How much magic did that small body of hers store to be able to withstand a sharp blade like that? If he'd tried the same against an enforcer, certainly he would have left some wound. The idea sent shivers throughout his entire body, but he had to at least entertain the idea that Sybilla and Blanq could be on the same level as an Aurora.

Cupping her chin, Blanq tilted her head. "Although you do not fight alone, so that must be taken into account. As I understand it, you now have a summoner and a lancer among your party. That makes it five. Given the groups array of spells and skills and taking into account their lack of experience working together, when put against Sybilla…"

Blanq's eyes darted back and forth as she mumbled to herself.

"I don't care about your damn calculations." Kyo kicked the front of the desk, a loud thud echoing within the room that made Blanq's eyes widen and even got the attention of the undead man who stared at him while holding a pen in his hand. Kyo didn't need to stand there and listen to her prove mathematically how much weaker he and the others were compared to the two of them.

Whether through words or force, he couldn't get the information he wanted from her. Something she said did catch his attention though. Any information he could get from her could be useful, so if she was willing to answer, he may as well ask.

"So, it's called an accrue stone? That thing you took from Mistwell?" Maybe the Aurora had heard of it.

Blanq nodded and raised the mug, finishing the heated chocolate.

"It was probably protected by enchantments among other things, right? You used Alden to get to it."

Again, Blanq nodded.

Krysta's accusation echoed in his mind. He could put the idea to rest with one question. "Did he help you willingly?"

Blanq stared at him for a moment then turned her attention to the undead man who held the pen in front of his face as if it were a magic-tech marvel. She slid a sheet of paper across the desk in front of him. The man's head tilted down, and he stared for a long moment before placing the pen to paper. His body swayed back and forth as he slowly scribbled on the page.

"Progress is coming quickly now," Blanq whispered.

Kyo didn't know what to think. Wasn't she simply controlling him to make him scribble? He dismissed the thought with a scoff. "Was this guy was one of the corrupted people who were gathered earlier today? Where are the rest of them?"

"Gone," Blanq said without moving her attention from the undead man.

"Gone, she says," Kyo mumbled under his breath. "I'm so sick of this. The corruption, Alden is missing, Sybilla is killing people, you're turning them into walking corpses, and I want it to stop!" A sword materialized in his hand.

But when he remembered the previous attempts to do her harm, it vanished, and he released a frustrated shout. There had to be more he could do, but try as he might, no ideas came to him. If he went to get the others, nothing could stop her from leaving in the meantime. In fact, he doubted he could stop her from leaving at all. Which made him wonder why she stuck around.

"Are they safe?" She'd revealed Alden's status to him, so it couldn't hurt to ask.

Nodding, Blanq reached a hand to the undead man's cheek and caressed it. "This one was mid-transformation. He is more useful this way."

"And I'm guessing you won't tell me what you do with them, will you?" Kyo asked.

She gave no response.

"Of course not. I bet you didn't even check Ruby. Though given you work with someone like Sybilla, you're no less a monster than she is. I bet you love all of this."

With a gentle touch, Blanq took the pen from the man's hand and cupped his chin, turning his head slightly as if examining his face. "She had already been turned. Nothing can be done for such a person."

"So, you did check?" But why would she in the first place? Probably to see if Ruby could be turned into one of her undead puppets. Since that didn't happen, maybe she couldn't raise people after they turned into shades.

"You have strong empathy for others. It's admirable. Is it a result of losing your parents when you were young?" Blanq asked. Her words sounded like the type of teasing he'd heard from Sybilla, and few things angered him like when that woman spoke.

"So, what if it is?" Kyo shouted, the heat in his face growing. He snatched her mug and threw it against the wall. "You think I'll let you get away with mocking me about it? And what would you know about empathy anyway?"

Blanq shook her head. "It was not mockery. I ask because I understand. My parents were murdered before my eyes when I was young. Every emotion you felt in relation to your parent's death, I have also experienced." She kept her gaze to the undead man, who idly running his finger over what remained of the beverage on the wall. "You are lucky to have Alden."

Kyo didn't need her to tell him that. Even when he'd acted like a brat in retrospect, he had always been glad to have Alden to go home to. He didn't need to be as analytical as Marsh to put the pieces together. Nothing about her past excused her current actions, of course. But he couldn't deny the pang of sympathy for her, his angry scowl softening, though his eyes remained narrowed.

"And your answer to that loss was necromancy?" he asked.

She lowered her head, took the undead man's hand in hers, and made for the door. "Yes."

Kyo dashed in front of them, hand out and palm facing them, air ready to blast at them. "You think I'm going to let you leave?"

Blanq tilted her head. "Do you think you can stop me?" She pulled the hood over her head, shadow once again covering her face. Then she raised her hand in the air. "You must start thinking beyond the capacity of a dullfish."

On either side of her as well as behind, people appeared one after another, transparent and sickly green. What looked like flesh hung loose from their faces and exposed bodies. Their eyes were sunken deep pits that looked to consume him. His body quaked as much as his breath as he took a step back. If she could raise dead bodies, maybe summoning spirits really was possible. No wonder such magic had been banned.

Then they were upon him, flying through the air, through him, around him. With shouts reaching a higher pitch than he knew his voice could make, he blasted air in random direction with one hand and swung a summoned sword with the other. Books flew off shelves, papers scattered across the floor, but he didn't care so long as he could be rid of these spirits. Panting, slashing, blasting, all the while his ears assailed by their high-pitched wails.

Then as quickly as they appeared, they vanished.

Kyo took several deep, shaky breaths and focused on the floor, trying to calm his pounding heart. "What the…"

When he looked around the room, Blanq was gone, as was her undead minion. He dashed to the door and looked over the balcony to the first floor but only saw Karu and the other enforcer sound asleep.

With his heart still pounding, he braced himself on the railing and stumbled down the hall and the stairs. Kyo checked to be sure no further harm had come to the enforcers before wandering away from the chancellor's office. He looked back, and the two enforcers outside the door were still slumped against the ground.

Blanq's illusion must have lifted. Could those spirits have been mere illusions too? Given the nature of her magic, he couldn't say for sure. He could speculate on that later. At the moment, what mattered was finding an enforcer, an Aurora, someone to tell about Blanq and the missing corrupted, before they have more shades to deal with. So much for sleeping tonight.

Chapter 18

Kyo's body still shuddered from the frightening spirits Blanq had conjured as he ventured through Aquarin in the dead of night. In addition, realizing he couldn't break through her natural magic defenses chilled him to the core, with no reason to doubt it'd be the same with Sybilla. He was tempted to find someone to put him under a sleep spell with instructions not to wake him until this whole situation blew over and let everyone else deal with this crap. Her statement about Alden was the only reason he didn't give it serious consideration. Those last words to him were the same as those Alden would often say to him. It couldn't have been a coincidence.

At least the enforcers were asleep and, as far as he saw, unharmed. But with the enforcer's station in its current state and not having seen anyone while passing it, finding someone to help would be difficult.

Or maybe not.

Someone stuck in a sleep spell might fall under the jurisdiction of a cleric. He could get Karu and the other enforcers' help if he figured out where their chapel was.

A familiar sight up ahead helped push such thoughts away for the moment—burn marks on the road from Krysta and Ignivus.

"Okay, so I'm back here," Kyo whispered to himself, turning at an intersection he'd nearly passed.

A familiar, high-pitched screech filled the air. He froze, his heart almost leaping from his chest. Trying to control his panic, he spun around but found no sign of a shade nearby.

Another screech then another.

Could it be the corrupted people who should have been at the chancellor's office?

Every instinct told him to run in the opposite direction. Even with a team of five, they couldn't take out two shades. What could he hope to do alone? Best case scenario, he could help people get away safely. That was what his parents would've done and without the hesitation that kept him firmly rooted to the spot. Kyo swore trying to be like his parents would send him to an early grave, but the regret of doing nothing would eat him alive.

He fought his tremors and slapped himself in the face a few times. "Get it together. You can do this."

Kyo took a deep, shaky breath and, with wobbly legs, leaped onto the roof of the nearest house. He immediately saw where to go by the illumination of every light turned on in a whole block. Screams of terror accompanied the screeches of the shades, and silhouettes rushed by the windows of lit second-story rooms. Traveling from rooftop to rooftop brought him one street away from the affected area in under a minute. More lights turned on in neighboring homes and those behind them. The screams were bound to wake up the entire town at this rate but hopefully get Garret and Estella's attention in the process.

A woman crashed through a second-story window and fell hard onto the road. Kyo shuddered at the moment of impact, jaw tightening as he swore he heard a crack. Exhaling hard, he forced himself to move, jumped to the ground, and crouched at her side. Her body trembled, and her breathing came out in labored gasps. Deep claw marks tore through her top and into her chest. At least she'd survived, but for how much longer, he couldn't say.

"Come on, stay with me," he said. "I'll bring you to the chapel...somehow."

The crash of house siding hitting the ground made him startle and brought his attention to the window she'd fallen from in time to see a shade leap for them both. Kyo shot his hands up and blasted the shade with a focused torrent of wind, enough to send it tumbling to the ground not far from them.

As the creature rose to its feet, people barreled out of their homes, running down the street, some turning on their heels when they saw the shade. More shades crashed through the walls and windows of homes, totaling four. Most people fled without looking back. Others attempted to keep them at bay with spells. Purple ropes sprayed from a woman's fingertips, wrapping around a shade, who tore through it like paper.

The one targeting Kyo charged him and the injured woman.

Kyo summoned a blade in his hand but didn't know what to do with it. Their fight earlier in the evening flashed in his mind. They couldn't harm the shades. He couldn't harm Blanq. Why was he so pathetically weak? How could he protect this woman, let alone the others now pouring into the streets to escape the shades that appeared out of nowhere? If he tried moving her, he risked making her situation worse.

Sweat coated his brow, and his grip tightened around the hilt.

He rose and stepped away from the woman but didn't want to be too far in case another got her in its sights. Distracting this one would take everything he had. Kyo didn't have time to turn his attention away from the single shade to count how many there were, but he guessed close to a dozen. How many more were still inside the homes where their former loved ones couldn't make it outside?

Kyo swung his arm out and hurled a burst of wind at the shade's feet. It tripped and fell on its face. The shade rose to a crouch and jumped for him, slashing with its claws. He leaped back but not fast enough, cringing as it tore through his shirt and flesh with sharp, fiery pain. It tried again, but he jumped to the roof behind him, taking a deep breath and running his fingers over the wound.

They came away bloody. The gashes were deep, dripping blood down his stomach. Though frightening and stinging like a dozen wasps, he had to ignore them as best he could and focus on surviving. If he could move, he could fight. Healing would have to come later.

The shade dug its claws into the exterior of the house, climbing after him.

"You stupid piece of crap. Let's see how you like it." Kyo jumped, summoning his second blade and thrust both at its head.

They hit their mark, and he used them to drag the creature back to the ground. The muscles in his arms and shoulders flexed as he tried digging the tips into the shade. But again, his strength couldn't get past the shadowy aura. As it rose, he pulled his swords back. He formed a cross with his swords in time to protect himself from its next slash, the force sending the flat ends of the blades knocking against his face.

Kyo shook his head and found himself between the shade and the woman. Another shade hovered over her, as if to determine if she still breathed. He threw his swords wildly at the shade, one bouncing off its arm, the other striking its head and falling at its feet. Of course, he didn't injure it.

But it turned its head, yellow eyes flashing as it stepped away from the woman.

Both swords vanished and reappeared in his hands. For the time being, the woman remained safe but at the cost of two shades wanting to rip him apart. He couldn't keep dodging forever; they'd catch him eventually. Being killed in battle wasn't appealing, but the idea of being torn apart while still alive left his legs quaking.

Kyo glanced toward where he knew the inn was, debating on running away and looking for help, even if it meant leaving others to die. If he tried, he could probably lose the shades by leaping from rooftops. It would be easy, from a physical perspective. But his mind wouldn't allow it, locking his feet to the ground. Already, he clicked his tongue and mentally berated himself for such cowardly thoughts, but the self-hatred did nothing to quell the fear making his body shake and slowing his movements.

A purple-and-black aura surrounded the shades, raising them into the air.

They frantically looked around, lashing their limbs about helplessly. Beyond them, a similar fate befell other shades as well. More rose into the air every second, some even crashing through roofs to do so.

In total, there had to be close to twenty hovering above the homes in this block of town.

"Estella, hurry!" a voice called. Atop a roof stood a man Kyo didn't know, his arms raised. The light from lanterns and bedrooms revealed a bland green robe similar to Garret and Estella's. Kyo sighed in relief.

From the ground, a flurry of purple arrows composed purely of magical energy pelted a shade. After a few seconds, the volley ceased, and the shade fell to the ground, motionless. Estella held a glowing bow — also made of raw magic, similar in color and make to the arrows — sighted her next target and attacked.

A shade behind Kyo screeched. Even he could tell the difference between the earlier cries and the panic in this one. He turned to see the purple-and-black aura compress around the shade, crushing its body until the screeching stopped. It dropped, its body contorted into an unrecognizable form. Gruesome though the display was, it hinted at the type of spell the man used. Gravity.

One by one, the shades were pierced by arrows, entering their bodies and flying out the other side, and sent falling to the ground until all were motionless. Kyo thought Garret had put on an impressive display earlier, but dispatching so many shades at once? He could hardly imagine that level of power.

For a moment, he forgot where he was. How far did he have to go to match their level? Could it even be done? Compared to these titans of magic, he felt like nothing more than a newborn baby. His hands trembled, though not from disappointment in himself. Such powerful mages would have no problem taking down Sybilla and Blanq. Once he returned home with Alden, he could focus far more on his goal to be like them.

Kyo grunted, his chest burning where the shade had slashed it. If the screams and commotion hadn't already woken everyone, he'd have to stir Marsh from sleep to heal him.

At some point, the gravity man had made his way to the ground and now headed his way.

"Estella, search the block for any who need help," the man said.

"On it." Estella turned her back to them.

"Estella, wait!" Kyo called. "Please, she needs help. Now." He pointed to the woman who still lay untouched, her movements so slight he may have imagined them. Staring hard, he held his breath for a few seconds then released it upon seeing her chest rise and fall.

The man brushed some blond hair from his face, examining Kyo and exposing his unusual eyes in the process. It looked as though he had a target painted on his pupils, the iris at the center and two black circles around it.

"He's injured too. Several gashes on his chest." The man placed two fingers on opposite ends of one of Kyo's wounds and gently spread it, drawing a throaty grunt from him. "Flesh wounds but deep."

Estella knelt and placed one hand on the woman's chest. The other hand almost dismissively threw green sparkling energy at Kyo without looking as the woman's entire body glowed.

He flinched then realized what she threw was a spell. A green aura similar to the woman's surrounded his chest. His skin heated, and the wounds closed and repaired before his eyes, the pain receding until scars were all that remained. He ran his fingers over each and took a deep breath — even puffed out his chest — and felt nothing more than a slight sting.

"I appreciate it." Kyo placed his fist over his chest and bowed at the waist. He couldn't help but notice the way she panted while working. How much magic had she poured into each arrow to pierce and kill a shade?

"I'm not sure whether to call you brave or stupid," the man said, his eyes returning to normal.

"Well, that makes two of us," Kyo mumbled.

Sighing, the man held out his hand. "Cedric Felmont. I'm a member of the Aurora alongside Garret and Estella, who I believe you've already met." Kyo shook his hand. "I've been meaning to do this for six years, so let me do it now. I'm sorry about your parents, truly. But I want you to rest assured the man who killed them was slain soon after. I saw to that myself."

Kyo stared at Cedric, examining his stoic face. This man had avenged his parents? "I…um, thanks. Really. I'd heard the one responsible had been taken care of but didn't know details." His pulse pounded in his ears. He'd never gotten a full story and wouldn't pass down a chance to hear it. "Who was it?"

"He was a fellow member, unfortunately. You deserve to know — his name was Zeshin Valeheart. I never fully learned what he was up to that your parents meant to stop, but the point is moot, I suppose." He turned to watch Estella stand and run off. The woman she'd healed sat up, groaning. "Do try to keep yourself alive though. It would be an insult to their memory if you died so young."

The woman cried, pulling her knees to her chest. Cedric stuffed his hands in the pockets of his dark green robe, which did nothing to hide the tremors running through them.

Kyo mouthed the man's name, committing it to memory. Betrayed by one of their own, someone they trusted. He bared his teeth, a new wave of fury over his parents' death washing over him, the fact Zeshin had died years ago acting as little comfort.

A chorus of sobs and cries from those around him pulled him from his thoughts. He could think about this later, discuss it with Alden.

Releasing a heavy breath helped steady him as he focused on Cedric's shaking arms. "You okay? You seem…shaky."

"Don't worry about it. I'm all right. Having to cast spells like that minutes after rising from sleep can be a bit stressful on the body. Now then, it seems I have some work to do. Did you happen to see anything before this happened?" Cedric narrowed his eyes.

Kyo shook his head. "No, I only came here because I heard the screams. Couldn't really ignore it."

"As I said, brave or stupid. But not unlike your parents."

"There's an issue at the chancellor's office though." Kyo went into detail about his earlier experience.

Cedric glanced behind him at Estella. "If it's a sleep spell, Estella should have enough energy after this to deal with it. About the missing corrupted though, the enforcers will need to investigate and see if any of these shades match those who are missing."

Kyo glanced past Cedric, but as soon as his gaze fell upon the blood and several mangled bodies, he clenched his eyes shut and shuddered. Those poor people. Thank goodness the Aurora arrived before even more perished.

"On the topic of Sybilla or Blanq—" he started.

"We're doing the best we can as far as that goes. We're also keeping informed of any unauthorized sailing of ships or passengers meeting their descriptions. If they leave the island, we'll know." Cedric turned his back and walked in the direction Estella had run. "You should get some rest and keep yourself safe."

They couldn't be watching *too* closely if they'd missed Blanq less than an hour ago. "It might not be that easy. Sybilla is an alteration mage, and I've seen her camouflage herself. And Blanq can use illusions spells."

Cedric paused and looked over his shoulder. "Is that so? Useful information. I appreciate it."

With nothing more to do here and no desire to stick around, Kyo returned to his search for the inn. He couldn't wait to return to bed, surrounded by people he trusted. Their presence would make the horrors he was bound to see when he closed his eyes a bit more bearable. When he arrived at their room, everyone sat or stood wide awake.

Krysta approached him first with loud stomps. "Where on Feracael have you been? We wake up to the sound of more shades and you're still not back in bed. Not like I care too much, but you had Marsh and Rosette beside themselves with worry." She shoved him. "Try to think before you act, will you?"

Kyo pushed past her and went straight for the bed, falling face first. "Sorry, sorry. But the shades have been dealt with, so you don't have to worry about it anymore."

"Did Garret and Estella show up again?" Roland asked.

"Estella and Cedric, actually. I'll tell you about it tomorrow." Kyo rolled onto his back and yawned. The short battle exhausted him, and his conversation with Cedric had brought a sense of calm to his mind. At least enough he thought sleep was possible.

Marsh appeared at his side, placing a hand on his torn shirt. "What happened? You were injured?"

Kyo waved him away. "By a shade. Estella took care of it. She didn't even have to touch me to heal it."

"I'm glad you're okay," Rosette said from the other side of the bed.

Smiling, Kyo reached out his hand, and Rosette took it.

"Thanks. No need to worry anymore, okay?" He turned the light off.

After bits of murmuring amongst each other, everyone returned to their places to get some sleep. By talking to them tomorrow, he hoped to get some answers and make a few connections. Even if at this point his own weakness disgusted him, knowing he'd provided useful information to the Aurora brought a smile to his lips. That may be their best place in this situation, providing information to those who could do the real fighting. Not a bad position to be in.

Nice and safe, he hoped.

Chapter 19

Sitting at a table at the inn's main floor, Kyo's eyes closed as he savored the salty garlic bread in his mouth. Few things could put a smile on his face more than some form of flavored bread. Especially if he got his hands on it fresh from the oven. Combine his favorite food with getting what'd been on his mind off his chest to the others, and he could breathe easier, as if he could stop lugging around a sack of rocks.

"Do you actually believe what Blanq told you?" Marsh asked before taking a bite of his breakfast sausage.

"If this girl is partners with that crazy Sybilla woman, I wouldn't advise trusting what she says." Roland took a sip of coffee from his mug, and Rosette dug into her scrambled eggs.

"I still can't believe you tried to deal with her on your own," Krysta said. "You're going to get yourself killed if you're not smarter about what you do." Unlike Marsh, she carefully used her fork and knife to cut a piece off her sausage before eating it.

"Yeah, yeah. What's done is done, right?" Not wanting to finish his bread too quickly, Kyo set what remained down to work on his own eggs. "And at first, I didn't believe her, but now I think there's reason to."

"Maybe a word stronger than 'dolt' should be considered." Krysta stabbed her sausage, scraping the fork over the plate in the process.

"It was what she said right before she left. 'Consider thinking beyond the capacity of a dullfish.' Alden has said that to me plenty of times growing up when I'd get in trouble, word for word. It can't be a coincidence." Kyo sighed and propped his chin in his hand. "I can only assume they're keeping him so he doesn't go running to the enforcers."

Roland poked Kyo's arm with the end of his fork. "Elbows off the table."

Kyo rolled his eyes but complied.

"If that is indeed the case, then it hints at Alden and Blanq having at least idle conversation during his time with them. Given that, perhaps we should not outright dismiss her claim," Marsh said.

"Um…" Rosette stared down, fiddling with her hands under the table. "Didn't you say something about a stone or something?"

"Blanq called it an accrue stone. It's what they took from Mistwell. I bet the chancellor is freaking out about it, but I wonder about the rest of Mistwell," Kyo said.

Krysta pointed her fork at Kyo. "Hard to say. Something like that shouldn't be common knowledge. But you found out about it, so it wasn't too well-kept a secret. I'll bet Chancellor Demaskus is beside himself though." She tapped the fork against the plate a few times. "And if some sort of fuss was made about it missing, it would have been after you left, so you wouldn't have heard about it."

"But is that the only one? Or are there more of those acute stones?" Rosette asked.

"Accrue," Roland corrected.

"Accrue," she repeated. When Roland nodded, she smiled.

More than one? Kyo knew nothing about the accrue stone from Mistwell, but he had no reason to doubt there could be more. He could feel his face grow pale imagining what Sybilla could achieve with multiple stones. "I do *not* want to imagine that."

"But if they needed Alden to get the one from Mistwell…" Krysta glared at Kyo before continuing. "Then it could better explain why they are holding on to him." She walked to Rosette and wrapped her arms around the young girl. "You just might be a little genius."

Rosette giggled, hugging Krysta's arms.

"Of course she is. I'm her parent and teacher—what did you expect?" Roland said with a smirk. "I told you our nomad lifestyle was good for her. Nothing beats experience from the real world."

"Usually, Alden does small jobs like making someone's weapon be on fire all the time or have some kid's toy be able to fly." Kyo scooped the last of his eggs on his fork. "But enchantments can be a legitimate way to keep people away from something. Like forcing you to turn away from whatever you're trying to get without you even noticing or hiding it in plain sight. I wonder if they already know where the other stones are, assuming there are any."

Krysta returned to her seat to finish her food. "The two of them having more power to draw from is not something we need."

"This situation keeps getting more dangerous." Roland sighed then turned to Rosette. "Finished?" She nodded, and he took her plate, as well as the others, to form one neat pile.

Together, they left the inn and headed west toward the main avenue of town.

"This could be perfect. I don't have any intention of fighting Sybilla again, and I'm sure none of you do either. But we don't have to. All we have to do is find

Alden and rescue him. If they don't have him, they can't get more accrue stones. Then our part is done, and we let the Aurora deal with actually taking them down and putting an end to all of this." Kyo clapped his hands. "And of course, I get my godfather back."

Roland turned his head, brow raised. "If it were that easy, wouldn't you have found him already?"

Kyo held up a finger. "Ah, but this time, we get the Aurora to help. Since it'll hurt Sybilla and Blanq's plans going forward, they're bound to agree."

"I can't believe I'm saying this, but it's not actually a bad idea," Krysta said. "Though it all hinges on Rosette's theory being correct. But that should be easy to confirm."

"How would we do that?" Marsh asked.

Krysta turned her head, flipping her hair and smacking Kyo in the face with her long ponytail. "Simple, we ask Chancellor Demaskus directly. All I have to do is visit Chancellor Ambers here in Aquarin. I'm certain I can convince her to let me use her com-orb to contact him directly."

Rosette tugged on Roland's trench coat. "What's a com-orb?"

"It lets you talk to someone who is far away," he said, "as long as they have one too."

"Whoa. I want to see it!" Rosette exclaimed.

"Come on, I know the way." Krysta led them down one street after another, expertly navigating until they arrived at the three-story building.

Upon entering the office, two enforcers standing by the door kept their eyes on them. None Kyo knew by name though. He hoped those he'd seen last night were okay and resting.

A wide desk sat near the opposite wall. Behind it, a woman glanced up after several seconds. "May I help you?"

"Hello, Tori," Krysta started. "I believe it's been a few years since I've been here. I am Krysta Rose, Princess of Alderdeem, and I'd like to meet with Chancellor Ambers on some sudden but important business."

Tori squinted, looking Krysta up and down, then paused on her face. "Oh my, yes, it is you, isn't it? I hardly recognized you with your attire and colored hair. I'll bring you upstairs right away." She waved for them to follow her up a set of half-circle stairs. "You've sure gotten bigger and prettier since the last time I saw you. How is your family doing?"

"The same as always, really. Which I would say is a good thing." Krysta kept up small talk for the quick trip to the chancellor's office.

Tori knocked on the heavy wooden door then entered. "Chancellor, sorry for the interruption. Her Highness Krysta Rose is here to see you."

"What? Really?" a woman's voice called from inside. "By all means, show her in."

Krysta glanced back at the others. "You all better wait out here. Chancellor Demaskus might not tell us what we want to know if others are listening."

She stepped inside, and Tori took the chance to return downstairs. The door closed behind her but then opened again a crack. Kyo leaned his ear toward the door to listen in, struggling to find a comfortable position while the other three did the same.

"Your highness, it has been far too long. Look how big you've gotten. And your hair, I can't help but wonder if your parents approve, but between you and me, it looks absolutely wonderful," Chancellor Ambers said in a singsong voice.

"Thank you. I'm glad you like it," Krysta said, her voice muffled.

Kyo peeked through the crack. Chancellor Ambers had Krysta's face in her bosom during a tight embrace. When they parted, they moved out of sight.

"Now then, what brings you on this sudden visit?" Several footsteps and a creak suggested Chancellor Ambers returned to her chair behind the desk. "And without your uncle, as well. Have you come into your own, doing diplomatic work without a watchful eye?"

"Well, it's not quite like that. You see, I've been away from home for some time now and have had some awful experiences. I even had to fight off a shade or three." Krysta added a shiver to her voice. "It's been truly frightening. And all thanks to those two. You know the ones. I believe their names were Sybilla and Blanq?"

"Oh no, I had no idea you've had such a time of it. You should have come to see me right away." Chancellor Amber's voice became sullen. "But yes, I'm familiar with the two you're speaking of. After hearing about what happened in Calmarock, I've sent a few clerics and enforcers to help there. Unfortunately, with obvious evidence those two are here, I cannot afford to do more. And after last night's shade attacks, we are all lucky the...er, well..."

"It's all right," Krysta said. "I know of the Aurora. I've met several of them when they came to speak to my uncle over the years."

"I see. Yes, I suppose you would have. But let me guess—after all of this, you wish to return home?"

Krysta paced in front of the desk, hands behind her back. "Well, yes. But not yet. Actually, I came to ask if I could borrow your com-orb to contact Chancellor Demaskus."

"Chancellor Demaskus? Whatever for?"

"There is something I need to confirm with him. This information could be useful to the Aurora in their attempts to put a stop to all of this. Those two haven't reached Alderdeem yet, but as princess, it is my duty to ensure that they do not pose a threat to my people. So, anything I can do to bring a swift end to this situation must be done." Krysta walked toward the left wall and returned with a blue crystal orb in both hands the size of a large melon. "May I use this?"

"I don't see why not. Especially if you think you can help stop those two. I couldn't imagine a repeat of Calmarock here."

For a few seconds, neither spoke. There was a brief flash of light. Kyo couldn't see what they were doing—they'd moved out of view—but a moment later, he heard the familiar voice of an old man.

"Oh-ho, Your Highness. I didn't expect to hear from you." Chancellor Demaskus said, "Though it isn't unwelcome."

"I'm here too." Chancellor Ambers put on a cheery voice. "But her highness insisted on speaking to you while she was here."

Krysta cleared her throat. "First, I'd like to send my condolences for those who were lost due to Sybilla and Blanq's treachery while they were in Mistwell. On top of that, another citizen had gone missing, correct? Alden Somera?"

There was a brief pause before Chancellor Demaskus replied. "You certainly are well informed. I can only imagine how such news reached Alderdeem so quickly. But yes, that is the case. I thank you for your kind words. However, you are slightly mistaken. Two are missing currently: Alden Somera, and his godson, Kyo Sonata."

"Well, allow me to bring your mind a bit of peace," Krysta said. "I know this information because I have been on Kattelink Island for some time now. And in fact, I've had the…pleasure to run into Kyo. He is safe and took it upon himself to chase after Alden."

Chancellor Demaskus's sigh of relief was probably heard downstairs. "That does bring me some peace of mind, yes. It does sound like him. He's rash and a bit temperamental, but he has a good heart."

A smile spread across Kyo's face. He didn't have a particular interest in what the old man thought of him, but the words were still appreciated.

"On to the reason I am contacting you. It is my understanding that Sybilla and Blanq have acquired some sort of...orb, or stone, that they've been using to help them unleash chaos wherever they go. Would you happen to know anything about it?" Krysta kept her voice polite, not a trace of accusation. Even so, silence again lingered in the air. "I have already spoken with the Aurora, and I'm sure this information would be very helpful in their attempts to bring those two to justice. But to put the pieces together, we need confirmation."

The chancellor's sigh filled the room. "I suppose there's no point in trying to keep it a secret from you. Yes, that stone did in fact come from Mistwell. It was kept hidden, protected. I thought it remained well hidden and its existence secret, but I suppose my arrogance made me lazy. After all, Kyo knew of it, though that may be due to his godfather being the one to use enchantments to protect it." Chancellor Demaskus's voice grew firm. "But this information does not leave this discussion, understood? The fewer people know about the accrue stone, the better."

"I wholeheartedly agree. We've already seen what devastation can be caused with it. And this is the only stone of its type that you know of?" Krysta asked.

Chancellor Demaskus cleared his throat. "Unfortunately, no. I am aware that at least one more exists. Though I don't know its location, I do know who does, and precautions are being taken."

Kyo tensed and clicked his tongue. He would have been happier if Rosette's theory had been wrong. But at least this gave rescuing Alden more urgency and a better chance the Aurora would help.

"I see. Then I will relay this information to the Aurora here in Aquarin when I see them next. I appreciate your time, Chancellor." Krysta and Chancellor Ambers said their farewells to Chancellor Demaskus.

Kyo and the others stepped away from the door, having heard all they needed. They were right, and that meant Sybilla couldn't be allowed to get any more accrue stones. If she knew to find one in Mistwell, she likely knew where the other one was as well. And with this knowledge, the probability of Alden no longer being corrupted and alive had shot up considerably. Kyo had to tense his jaw to contain his glee.

The door opened, and Krysta left the room, silently motioning for them to follow her. Once outside, she had a smug grin on her face. "See? I may not like being a princess, but I have to admit it comes with a few perks."

"I would agree. And now we seem to have a more complete picture." Marsh's voice trailed off, his lips tightening before he spoke again. "Unfortunately, it is not a pretty one. Blanq and Sybilla's goals remained a mystery, but I believe last night's events revealed them."

"You mean the shades?" Roland asked.

Marsh nodded. "Kyo mentioned there were around twenty in total. Remember, Estella and Garret told us that even if two people are corrupted at the same time, when they turn seems to vary depending on a number of factors. To have so many turn all at once in such close proximity, I cannot help but suspect Sybilla is somehow responsible."

"But she said she and Blanq had nothing to do with the corruption," Kyo said.

Marsh cupped his chin, staring down as he walked. "They have nothing to do with the creation of the corruption itself. But if they have unique knowledge on how to cure it, they could also have knowledge on how to spread it. This is only a theory, mind you."

Kyo yanked Marsh by the robe in time to prevent him from walking into a lamppost while he remained deep in thought.

"So, what do we do now?" Rosette asked.

"The first thing we do is obvious." Krysta turned to walk backward, facing the others. "We need to find the Aurora again."

Chapter 20

With a plan in mind and renewed hope, Kyo led the way to the port. It might not have been the best plan, and it relied heavily on the Aurora doing their part. But if it worked, he could return home with Alden. It had only been a few days, but it felt like weeks since he'd left Mistwell. And though he might not say it out loud, he would be lost without his new companions. After what they'd been through together, it felt as though he'd known them for a long time.

"So, why are we going down to the port?" Krysta asked.

Kyo struggled not to outpace the others, eager to get their plan underway. "Cedric said they were keeping a close eye on it in case Sybilla and Blanq decided to head north. It's the only lead we have on where to find them."

Families and individuals wandered the port, examining goods at various vendor stalls, waiting to be seated at restaurants, or killing time before their ship began boarding. Even so, wide empty spaces separated them. Kyo bet not many were brave enough to leave their homes yet, or they were people who had arrived in Aquarin that day.

The aroma of various cooked meats and fish dominated the air. It would have made Kyo drool if he hadn't eaten minutes ago. He froze as he caught sight of a food stand selling his undisputed favorite food.

"One second!" He dashed to the stall, waited behind the single person in line, and ordered. A minute later, he returned with a wide smile, holding freshly baked bread of golden brown, stretched long then twisted around itself, glazed in light butter, and rained on with salt. No food reached his heart more than a soft twisty.

"Are you kidding? We just ate. Don't waste your cryst on things you don't need," Roland said, pointing at him.

"I'll always waste my cryst on one of these. It's not like I have enough for it to be useful in another way." Kyo took another bite and walked on with the others in tow.

They headed to the western end of the port and stopped at the last ship in the line, a massive metal structure that would require a large team to operate. The gangplank stretched from dock to deck.

"If they were to steal a ship, I doubt it would be one like this," Marsh said.

Roland looked the ship up and down. "What do you think, kiddo? This would have been a better ship to stow away in than that passenger ship, right?"

Rosette shook her head. "I liked that other ship. It had nice people on it."

"Nice and corrupted," Roland muttered.

"It's not their fault," Rosette said, punching his arm.

Roland rubbed his arm, chuckling. "I know, I know. I'm just glad they didn't turn while we were at sea. So then, where to next?"

"I suggest if the port is the place to be, we simply walk toward the other end and keep our eyes open."

Marsh took the lead, staring out to sea. "It could be a good thing if we find nothing unusual, as it would mean Sybilla and Blanq have not left and neither has Alden. The Aurora would likely give most of their attention to smaller vessels. Aquarin is certainly smaller than Oasis, so that would benefit us."

"Speaking of, if we do head to Terrorigo, do you plan on seeing Cleric Micah first?" Kyo asked.

Marsh smiled. "I do not think that is necessary. If I know him, he insisted on heading to Calmarock to help those in need. I will see him again when all of this is dealt with."

They headed east, keeping their eyes open for the plain green robes the Aurora wore, though the sparkling blue sea, docked ships, and clear sky were more than distracting. Rosette ran to a fountain and scooped up a handful of cryst, which earned her a few disapproving looks from passersby. Marsh attempted to lecture her, but Roland smiled his approval.

Nearly thirty minutes later, Kyo spotted a familiar green robe and head of blond hair. Cedric stood listening to a man shout and point angrily at the sea. Kyo hadn't expected to find one of them so soon. His luck may be turning around.

"Having a fun morning?" Kyo asked.

Cedric turned, shifting his eyes between all five mages. "So, this is the rest of your party Garret mentioned. Sorry, but I'm in the middle of a lead."

"Yeah, buzz off. I've got an emergency on my hands, yah!" The man waved his hand dismissively. "The only reason I'm telling you is because a stolen fishing boat is apparently low on the enforcer's priority list these days."

"I understand," Cedric said with no emotion on his face. "Please calm down. It's something I want to investigate as well."

The man gritted his teeth. "Oh, I'll calm down when I get my boat back. Until then I'll raise such a ruckus the Relinquished will be shaking from their realm."

A high-pitched cackle caught the man's attention, and he glared daggers at an old woman sitting on a crate.

"This has been a delight to witness," she said. "I knew karma would come for you eventually."

"Get out of here, you old hag," the man yelled. "This doesn't concern you, nah."

"Oh, but it does. Because I saw who took your precious boat. I can give a solid description. The question is, should I?" The woman smirked. "Maybe I'll let you writhe in your anxiety for a bit longer."

"If you think I won't—"

Cedric pushed the man in the chest to keep him from advancing on the old woman then approached her himself. "Would you be kind enough to tell me instead? I have a suspicion about who is responsible, but if I'm right, they are dangerous people who need to be dealt with immediately."

The old woman narrowed her eyes, glancing between him and the angry boat owner. "I suppose I could, with the condition you don't tell him. That man has a nasty habit of price gouging for his services and sabotaging his competition. I know for a fact he's done damage to other vessels to keep them from going out to sea, giving him free rein of the fishing area, then charging double what they're worth because he brought back the only catch of the day."

"T-That's not true! You can't prove a thing."

Cedric looked back at the man, his pupils noticeably smaller. After a moment, he turned back to the old woman. "You have a deal."

He leaned in close, and she whispered in his ear. After thanking her, he walked away, ignoring the man shouting for him. Kyo and the others followed, keeping up with his brisk pace.

"So, was it them?" Kyo asked.

"It was. I suppose they thought a small fishing vessel would take longer to be noticed as missing. Though I'd be surprised if they could make the trip on something so small." Cedric kept his eyes on the ships, as if looking for something.

"It's good to know their teleportation spells can't reach across the sea. But they do have a head start on us," Kyo said.

Cedric paused in front of a ship then turned his gaze to Krysta. "Us? You still plan on getting involved with this, Your Highness?"

"Stop calling me that," Krysta said. "And yes, I do. In fact, we had an idea that we wanted to run past you."

The ship Cedric stared at had people boarding, a man at the bottom of the gangplank checking their passes.

"The Swordfish will be departing in one hour for Oasis," he called.

Cedric approached the man, holding up two fingers. After a brief exchange, he handed over some cryst for two tickets.

"I highly advise you to stay here and let us handle this," Cedric said.

"We will not," Krysta said, placing her hands on her hips. "Don't worry. We have no intention of getting in harm's way again, but we can still help in other ways. We need to see this through."

Cedric sighed and pinched the bridge of his nose. "Your uncle would not be pleased. Especially if something happens to you. But I have no actual authority to stop you, Your Highness, so do as you will. If you want to inform me of some plan, however, wait until Garret arrives so you don't have to repeat yourself.

He fell behind, absolutely insisting on browsing a souvenir shop. Not a care in the world, that one."

He tucked the tickets into a pocket on the breast of his robe.

"Where is the woman? Estella, right?" Roland asked.

"She's already taken our airship north," Cedric said. "We sent her ahead to Oasis, just in case. Seems to have been the right call."

Kyo reached into his pouch, feeling around for the coin he had left after partially paying for the inn. "I might have enough. Maybe. How much is a ticket?"

"Four hundred cryst per person," Cedric said.

Sighing, Kyo pulled his hand from his pouch. "Nevermind."

"Apologies, but while I may have enough to pay for myself, I do not have the required cryst with me. I only brought so much with me from Oasis." Marsh's lips tightened. "What do we do?"

After a brief silence, Krysta groaned. "You all owe me big. If we don't put a stop to Sybilla and Blanq in Oasis, I'll put you to work at the palace to pay me back."

Despite the annoyance in her voice, she approached the man at the gangplank and held up five fingers. The exchange was made, and she returned, handing a ticket to each.

"Wow, for how much you don't like being a princess, you sure do use its perks a lot." Kyo took his ticket, grateful one of them had a deep pouch.

"One more word about it, and I'll burn yours," Krysta said, holding up a finger with a small flame flickering on the tip.

Kyo tucked the ticket into his pocket so she couldn't get to it. With their destination set, he searched the port for a green robe and wild, white hair.

About fifteen minutes passed before Garret arrived, and the first thing he did was put his arm around Cedric's shoulders, listening to his update on the situation. "Looks like you were right about the port, yah. Once this is over, I owe you a drink or dessert of your choice."

Cedric's face remained neutral, but he didn't force Garret away either.

"The souvenir shop didn't have anything worth getting, nah," he said with a wide smile. "But what can you do?"

"The princess and her party are joining us, whether we want them to or not, it seems. Since we're all here, we may as well board." Cedric broke from Garret's hold and led the way up the gangplank.

Once on board, they all found themselves a secluded section of railing to lean against. Krysta took the chance to explain their plan, as well as their theories about multiple accrue stones and Alden's purpose to Sybilla and Blanq.

Garret patted Cedric on the back. "Well, it sure doesn't sound like a bad idea, nah. Cedric here would be your best bet in focusing the search on Alden with those perception spells of his. Even so, we'd still advise you all not to get involved directly. You've done more than enough, yah. If you run into them again, you might not survive."

"If we can leave them to you, we'll gladly do it. But I'm not going to sit around when I could be searching for Alden. I doubt they'd leave him behind on Kattelink Island." Kyo stared at the open sea, his stomach doing flips. The last time he'd left the island, he'd been a child. He could only remember flashes of the trip—his parents by his side, warm beaches, and the tragedy that took place. "Besides, you need all the help you can get. Oasis is the only port they could reach in that small boat they took, if even that, and if we miss them there, there's no telling where across the continent they could go. We have to stop them there."

Cedric tapped his fingers on the railing. "I hate to admit you have a point. I'll do what I can with the search. It sounds like Blanq and Alden have frequent communication. Focusing on finding any hints of her illusions will be a good first step. I'll think further on it during the trip. I suggest you all take the chance to rest and prepare. Few strategies survive contact with the enemy."

Cedric pushed from the railing and wandered off.

"He sure is a bundle of joy, huh?" Kyo asked.

Garret laughed. "That's just how he is, yah. Don't take it personally. But he's right. You all should relax on this trip. It'll take a couple days."

"Hey, Garret. Since we have time, I wanted to ask you something." Hesitating, Kyo glanced at the others then pulled Garret away to find a private place for them to talk. He brought him to the bow of the ship, leaning against the railing, staring up at the blue sky. "So, uh, can you tell me about my parents? I mean, it's not like I don't know them. But I figure you could probably tell me things about them I haven't heard."

"It'd be an honor." Garret hopped onto the railing, supporting himself with his hands. "Well, they were great people, of course. Always wanting to help others. And they had a mischievous streak, not afraid to break some rules occasionally. In fact, I think they enjoyed it."

This brought a chuckle from Kyo. At home, they wanted Kyo to follow the rules, be polite, and do things the right way. Those hypocrites. "I'll have to bring that up next time I talk to them."

This earned a side glance from Garret. Speaking to their portraits back home would be the first thing he did when he returned.

"Of course, they never stopped talking about you, nah. You were their pride and joy and their main motivation for doing what they did. They wanted the world to be a better place for you to grow up in. But as loving a pair as they were, they were also fierce in battle." Garret slapped Kyo's arm as if to get his attention, like he didn't already have it. "You should have seen it, yah. There was this situation involving a hydra, vicious creature that would sprout more heads when you took one off. Not quite a Leviathan, but it was big and dangerous all the same. Threatened to take out a whole coastal town far to the west of Terrorigo. While your father focused on defending the town and its people, your mother took on the beast herself. And boy did she. I've never seen such a shower of blood, nah. Using her daggers and hopping through shadows, she not only carved that creature up to save the town but gave them enough meat to feed everyone. So of course, they held a celebration that night, with plenty to go around."

Kyo's eyes were wide, and Garret had his full attention. He'd never heard this story before, and his heart swelled with the new information. Even if he hadn't been there to witness it, he could easily picture it in his head. Especially his mom's viciousness. One of her favorite pastimes involved the Festival of Nightmares each year. She always got a kick out of bursting from the shadows to frighten him and his dad, falling into a fit of giggles afterwards. The memory still made him shiver.

"That's incredible. They told me a few stories, but I guess it wasn't until after seeing you all in action that I started to get a sense of just how powerful they were." Kyo couldn't get rid of the smile on his face.

"Understandable, yah," Garret said. "You were young and inexperienced when you heard those stories after all, so you didn't have anything to compare them to."

Garret told him more stories, and Kyo could picture each one clearly in his head. When the ship's magic-tech engines rumbled, using a combination of water and wind spells, Garret departed as well, leaving Kyo by himself.

Though Kyo wanted to hear more stories, he had work to do. Even if their intention was to not get directly involved with Sybilla and Blanq again, it was like Cedric said—things didn't always go as planned. Much of this trip would have to be spent with his tome open, practicing spells in case the unexpected happened.

Chapter 21

The light bob of the ship combined with the salty sea air and sunny sky made for a welcome respite. Kyo closed his eyes and enjoyed the movement between practicing spells, his mind relatively clear and at more peace than he'd felt in days. So much, in fact, that he fought to keep himself from dozing off as he sat against the companionway. Relaxing between spells was nice, but he had to maintain focus. While not planning to fight against Sybilla again, he didn't want to be caught off guard.

Opening his eyes and exhaling, he stared at the pages of his tome, held open against the breeze by his boot resting on the edge. The pages held diagrams with descriptions on how to channel his magic and the wind it created in order to perform the spell. At this point, he mostly grasped the concept. The problem remained keeping it stable as he pushed it against something or someone. Air was, by its nature, free flowing, requiring focus and power to condense.

But knowing his father could do it drove him on.

Kyo held open his hand, palm up, the air circulating above it. Condensing and rotating rapidly, it took the shape of a drill, not a part he had difficulty with. Unfortunately, he had nothing to press it up against to test if it would maintain its form and pressure. Kyo wasn't out to damage the ship and didn't feel like dealing with the consequences of doing so. So he went with the option that made practicing more difficult and draining.

Air formed above his other hand, and he struggled to create the drill form necessary while maintaining one spell already. Slow, deep breaths left his lips as the air attempted to condense. His brow creased as the spell took form, but the more it did, the less stable the other became. Pausing the second spell, he attempted to reform the first but finally gasped as he lost both.

"Dammit." Kyo leaned his head back and wiped sweat from his forehead. He should have been grateful his progress had advanced since he'd started a couple hours ago, but the desired result still felt so far off.

Paws padded across the deck. Kyo turned his head to stare at a saber large enough for him to ride. It had snow white fur, its canines stretching well beyond its jaw. Before he could react, its rough tongue licked the entire side of his head, leaving his face wet and hair sticking up.

"Oh, come on." He wiped the saliva off with his hoodie, sighed, and reached out to pet its head, its long tail wagging and a purr emitting from its throat. "You're a curious one, huh?"

"I'm so sorry about that!" A man ran over and grabbed the saber by the collar, pulling the creature away. "Come, Raithy. We'll have to put a leash on you after all."

Kyo smiled until he heard boots on his right.

"Working hard, huh kid?" Roland asked, standing next to Kyo, ankles crossed and leaning against the companionway.

Kyo looked up at him, shrugging. "Trying to. Even if we don't face off against Sybilla again, we could run into a shade or two."

The shades made his heart pound each time he thought of them. Yet they didn't send the chill through him like Sybilla did.

"Yeah, the world is becoming a dangerous place. Nothing wrong with being prepared." Roland glanced down at the tome. "Looks like an advanced spell you're working on there. You sure you don't want to try something simpler first?"

Shaking his head, Kyo closed the tome and set it next to him then stretched his legs out. "It's my dad's tome. And this spell was one of his go-to's."

"They were Aurora, right? That sounds tough to live up to. A lot of power to gain and a dangerous road ahead." Roland smirked. "Though, I guess you're getting used to the danger part, huh?"

"Well, not by choice." Kyo tightened his hair tie then brushed the front of his hair with his fingers. When he had time, looking into bobby pins would be a good idea. "But if they could do it, so can I."

"So, you want to be just like them? You sure that's the best thing to do?" Roland asked.

Kyo narrowed his eyes at him. "Of course it is. Why wouldn't it be? They were powerful, helped people in need, they were great parents, and—"

"Whoa, whoa. Easy there." Roland held his hands up defensively. "I wasn't looking to insult them, you know. All I'm saying is, being inspired by them is great and all, but don't try so hard to be like them that you stop being you. Trust me, sometimes your unique decisions can make all the difference." He turned his head, watching Rosette with a smile. She was near the taffrail, her fists up close to her face, throwing punches and the occasional kick at the air. "I didn't have much in the way of role models growing up, to put it lightly. But no one else I know would have taken Rosette in like I did."

There was nothing wrong with wanting to be like his parents. Kyo made his own decisions, which had all led him here. Sure, he may have based those decisions on what they might do, but he didn't see a problem with that. Truthfully, he had no idea what he was doing. So, he needed a guide to help him, that was all.

Kyo watched Rosette practice too. "She's a good kid. You're doing a great job with her."

"Thanks, I appreciate that." Roland ruffled Kyo's hair and lightly pushed his head away. Kyo grumbled, fixing his hair again, and swore he saw a tear fall from Roland's eye. "That Sybilla is going to pay for touching Rosette. For scarring her like that. I'm fine with letting the Aurora deal out punishment, so long as it gets done. I don't like the obligation of going where the Aurora go for the sake of safety. The sooner this is dealt with, the sooner Rosette and I can comfortably travel where we please."

Kyo struggled to stand, and his legs wobbled when he did, a clear sign he needed a longer break from his spellcasting. "It'll happen, you'll see. They deal with crazy stuff like this all the time." Stretching his arms above his head, he released a heavy yawn. "You sure you don't want to find a place for the two of you to settle down?"

"No matter where we go, there will always be people who will dislike her, and a few that will let that dislike go too far. And it only takes one a single moment to take her away from me." Roland's brow creased, and his fists tightened. "Besides, living this way has done wonders for her. She's smart and tough."

"I won't deny that. Even so, she's still a kid missing out on being one." Kyo stood and stretched his arms above his head again then patted Roland's shoulder. Rosette being so cheerful despite her way of life was a miracle. She deserved to settle down somewhere. "Don't let the reason she's not experiencing a real childhood be because you're afraid."

With a grunt, Roland pulled his flask from the trench coat and took a swig from it. Mid-drink, his head turned toward Cedric walking by. "Hey, Cedric, come here."

His usual neutral expression on his face, Cedric changed course and joined Roland at his side. "What is it?"

Roland pointed his flask at the Aurora. "What's your stance on Rosette?" When Cedric's eyebrow rose, Roland elaborated. "Summoners go through some shit with a lot of people, and my priority isn't the corruption or Sybilla. It's keeping her safe. So far everyone else has shown they have no problems with what she is, except you. If we're going to be around you, I want to know what you think."

"I think I don't care," Cedric said.

Roland placed the stopper back in his flask then pushed it against Cedric's chest. "Well, I do."

Cedric remained unfazed, glancing from the flask to Roland's face. "What I mean is, I don't care because, as of now, there is no reason to be concerned. She is a child. At this point in her life, the chances of her summoning a Relinquished are exceedingly small. The concern will come when she is older and on her own and how life and those around her treat her. Life can be cruel, and the chances of her slipping through the years are never zero. But as of now, I'm not concerned." He turned and strolled off. "Satisfied?"

Roland huffed, his face a mixture of aggravation and relief. "He's not easy to talk to."

"I think he has the right idea though." Kyo grabbed his tome and pushed himself to his feet. "I'm going to walk around a bit.

"Go for it, kid."

The warm sea air brushed across Kyo's face. As he walked by other passengers, they wore smiles and laughed. They spoke of being away from corrupted people and having no worries while on the sea.

If only they knew what could happen in Oasis.

He paused when he spotted Krysta forming spikes of ice in her palm and firing them over the side of the ship and into the sea, while Marsh performed hand motions, using her body as a reference for healing spells.

"I guess you had the same idea, huh?" Kyo said.

"The fact we're heading to Oasis already puts us in danger. Even if we're with the Aurora, best to be prepared, though I still hope we don't have to do any more fighting." Krysta kept her gaze at the sea as she launched a fireball into the water. Marsh trailed his finger along her spine, making her shudder. "Watch where you're touching."

"My apologies," Marsh said, repeating the action without making physical contact. "We must prepare for the possibility that, even if we find Alden, it does not mean he will be alone. Our duty should be reconnaissance, leaving the rescue part to the Aurora."

"You're not wrong, but if he *is* alone, then it should be fine for us to rescue him ourselves. I guess we'll see when we find him." Kyo stepped back as Krysta turned.

She held her hands out toward the deck to construct a thick pillar of ice. Good thing no one else was around. Or maybe they'd all gravitated to one side of the ship to avoid her spellcasting.

Positioning herself so the pillar stood between her and the sea, Krysta built a ball of fire in her hand and launched it. She kept her hand out as it struck the ice, clenching her jaw. It melted its way through the pillar little by little, her arm shaking and low grunts escaping her throat. Finally, it burst through the other side and into the water, leaving her hunched over and gasping for breath.

"While you take a break, I'm going to use this to practice my own spell," Kyo said, rotating his shoulder.

"Oh no you don't." Krysta stood upright and inhaled deeply. "Your wind spells would launch ice shards all over the place. You'll hurt someone."

Kyo grumbled but couldn't disagree. "Fine."

He leaned his back against the taffrail, once more working to form the wind drill in his hand. They wouldn't reach Oasis that day, so he could exhaust himself while safe at sea.

"Your uncle probably has a lot at his disposal," Kyo said. "Powerful mages and stuff, right? I think I learned he has a royal guard or something that outranks the enforcers. Why not ask them to help?"

Krysta cocked a brow. "Look at you, knowing a thing or two about off-island stuff. I considered that but decided against it. A larger force might be a bad idea. If Sybilla and Blanq feel truly threatened, nothing will stop them from teleporting away, and we'll have no idea where to find them. They seem confident they can win with the current state of things. Strategically, that's where we want their mentality to stay so they don't do anything rash."

"More rash," Marsh corrected.

Krysta sighed and nodded. "Yes. More rash."

"Krysta, can I use that?" Rosette asked as she approached with Roland. "I'm sick of punching air. I need something to actually hit."

"You're not doing any fighting yourself, kiddo," Roland said.

Rosette huffed and crossed her arms over her chest. "I know. I can still train though. Everyone else is," she said with a frown. "I don't want to see the crazy lady again anyway."

"How about this instead?" Krysta created a new block of ice, not quite a pillar, but it reached her knees, with nearly the width of Rosette's arm span. "Here, you can beat up on this for a while." She pulled Rosette in for a one-armed hug. "Just be careful, okay?"

"I will." Rosette formed a fist, reared it back, and thrust it down. Cracks spread across the ice block. She released a deep breath then repeated her actions, chunks of ice flying off. After a third punch, the block shattered completely. "Can you make me another one?"

While everyone else's jaws slacked, Roland grinned with his arms folded. "Don't wear yourself out too much, okay? And don't wear Krysta out either. She has her own training to do."

"I won't," Rosette said. "I promise."

Roland wasn't kidding. She really was a little powerhouse. In fact, she might have been a more powerful mage than himself. And to think Krysta was worried about *his* spells sending ice shards everywhere. Kyo brushed a few from his hoodie. He nearly fell as the ship took a hard turn to port. The others gripped onto each other or the taffrail.

"What is that?" Marsh asked, his eyes wide and staring across the ship.

Even with the companionway blocking their view, Kyo could see something on the other end of the ship. Something massive.

He dashed with the others behind him then froze as he saw what drew everyone to gather at the starboard side. A few white pieces of a small boat floated past, and the reason why lay in the water, unmoving except for the small waves created by the breeze. Mostly submerged, a massive sea creature with a serpent-like body lay atop a significant portion of what used to be a boat. If it had been raised fully out of the sea, it would have been taller than the ship while laying on its side and long enough to fully wrap around it multiple times over. Kyo had never seen one before, as they were extremely rare in the sea between Kattelink and Terrorigo.

A Leviathan.

Its blue scales nearly matched the hue of the ocean. No wonder it had gone unnoticed until the ship had gotten closer. Those around Kyo smiled, and a few even cheered. He couldn't blame them—one less Leviathan meant a safer sea for travel. While they celebrated, he focused on the boat it had crushed. Could it have been the same boat Sybilla and Blanq stole? His eyes darted about, hope rising as he searched for their floating bodies.

The ship reached the creature's head. Its jaw hung open with multiple rows of sharp teeth, and the overall shape reminded Kyo of a dragon, with tendril-like protrusions. He squinted, leaning forward for a better look. Where the scales were fewer and its bare skin could be seen, dark green lines spread like webbed veins. Did they reach all the way to the tail under the scales?

"What happened to it?" Kyo asked himself but received an answer, nonetheless.

"It was poisoned."

Kyo turned to see Cedric standing next to him, again with his pupils smaller as his gaze ran over the Leviathan's body. Kyo turned back to the dead sea serpent, and his heart raced. "Sybilla."

With every passing day, she proved her power shouldn't be underestimated.

"I bet they teleported to shore after killing it," Kyo said. "But I didn't think their teleportation could reach that far."

"It's likely this occurred closer to Terrorigo and the currents swept the body and wreckage further away. But that's not the important thing." Cedric placed his hand on the taffrail, gripping it tight. "The important question is, how much magic did she drain from a creature like this to fill that accrue stone?"

A harsh chill ran through Kyo's body.

He gulped, staring hard at the massive creature. How many average humans would it take to equal the magical power within a Leviathan, creatures that could cause storms, maelstroms, and tidal waves? Even more concerning, if Sybilla did cause those people to turn into shades last night, how many could she turn with this much magic? Hundreds? Even the Aurora wouldn't be able to handle that by themselves.

"I'm really starting to think this trip was a bad idea." Roland wrapped his arm around Rosette, keeping her at his side. "I figured being alone with Rosette after Sybilla took a special interest in her could be dangerous, but maybe it would have been safer than this."

Marsh rubbed his eyes with his thumb and index finger. "Even if she used some of what she had stored within the stone to kill the Leviathan, what she would have gotten in return would have been more than worth it. It is no understatement to say Oasis is in extreme and immediate danger."

"I wonder if asking my uncle for reinforcements would be a good idea after all," Krysta muttered.

Kyo gripped the railing in front of him, trying to stop his body from shaking. With a Leviathan's power at their beck and call, Sybilla and Blanq would make what they did to Calmarock look like nothing. They could either kill the entire city, raise them as undead, or assuming their theory was correct, turn everyone into shades. An entire city's worth of monstrous creatures being let loose across the continent. And what could they accomplish with more than one accrue stone? In a snap, rescuing Alden had become about more than returning him home or even protecting a city. It may well be the key to protecting all of Feracael.

Chapter 22

Kyo stared with wide eyes at the desert city as the ship closed in on the harbor of Oasis. It stretched from the sea to a towering rockface with an overhang that kept the furthest buildings under the shade. Each building had glittering, multicolored sea gemstones decorating their roofs, sparkling in the sunlight. On either side, a fair distance from the port, were beach bungalows along their own docks and more still on tiny islands off the coast he'd heard were created through earth spells. His mind wandered for a moment. While he didn't remember exactly where it had happened, he was sure somewhere in his line of sight was where that boy had lost his life years ago. It had become about more than his memory alone. Layla, Ruby, and the people of Calmarock all combined with that boy to create a more solid foundation of his resolve to be like the Aurora and make sure nothing like that happened here.

Once the ship halted, Kyo wasted no time jumping off the ship and onto the dock, ignoring Krysta's lecturing cries. The salty sea air, crystal clear water, and warm weather all came together for a perfect environment of what a vacation destination should be. Restaurants and shops lined the port, strategically designed to be the first thing visitors saw to encourage the spending of cryst. Images came to mind of sitting in a chair drinking a fruity drink while the others played in the sand and sea. Though, once he took the time to examine his surroundings, he noticed something missing. The people.

He jumped when a pair of feet landed next to him. Rosette giggled and smiled at him. He smirked and patted her on the back.

"You truly have no sense of class or manners. And you're such a bad influence on Rosette," Krysta said, annoyance lacing her words as she and the others approached.

"What are you talking about?" Kyo asked. "We were going to reach the dock anyway — why bother taking it slow? We have important work to do."

Roland stood next to Rosette and placed his hand on her head. "Don't forget your manners, kiddo."

Huffing, she crossed her arms. "I'm not."

"There are far fewer people than is normal. The harbor and shopping area beyond are often packed with little exception," Marsh said.

At least Kyo wasn't alone in thinking the place seemed barren. Other than the occasional individual or group going about their business, it looked no different than Aquarin after the attacks. Between the corruption and the devastation Sybilla had caused, no wonder people would stick to their homes.

"They're afraid and rightfully so," Cedric said, coming up on the group. "Word of what happened in Calmarock and Aquarin would have spread quickly. Staying indoors is a wise decision."

"But not for long, nah." Garret patted Cedric hard on the back. "Things won't be like this forever, and once that terrible duo is taken care of, we'll celebrate. Maybe a few days on the beach. Rent a bungalow and feast on some freshly caught fish. You're in, right, Cedric?"

Cedric's lips tightened, and he gazed into the distance where the beaches were. "I suppose a short relaxation period would be nice. However, investigating the source of the corruption should not be delayed." He stiffened, returning his gaze to the city. "We will have to rendezvous with Estella. We should also visit the chancellor, though I don't want to waste any time in beginning the search for Sybilla and Blanq. Your Highness, since you have experience in meeting with leaders and officials, would you be willing to meet with Chancellor Bisca?"

Krysta nodded. "I'm sure I remember where her office is. I was going to suggest the same anyway. But if you have any leads on Alden, let us deal with that. Though, did Estella not speak to the chancellor since she's been here?"

"There wasn't a specific plan to, nah. I'm guessing she figured it wouldn't be necessary if she caught those two at the port. But assuming that boat under the Leviathan was theirs, I doubt that's happened." Garret stepped forward, pulling Cedric along by his arm. "But I agree Her Highness should be our emissary. She has some level of authority after all," he said with a smirk and a glare from Krysta. "Let's meet up with Estella and see what we can find. We'll leave the diplomacy to the kids." He briefly glanced at Roland. "Mostly kids. What could go wrong?"

Kyo shook his head. "He takes everything so lightly."

"Let's not waste time. Come on." Krysta walked on without checking if the others were following.

Kyo admired the beauty of the city up close. Something about sand that had drifted in from the desert gave it an exotic charm. Rosette pointed at one of the many canals stretching down a road, splitting it in half, and questioned if they were allowed to swim in them. Each canal had a stone archway at the edge, coated in more of the glittering sea stones. When Sybilla and Blanq were stopped and Alden was with him again, Kyo liked the idea of sticking around Oasis for a bit. It'd be a good place to let all his stress go before returning home. They could enjoy the beach, eat some delicious food, and explore the city.

Lost in thought, Kyo bumped into Marsh when they stopped in front of the chancellor's office. Unlike on Kattelink Island, this office had the look of a large beach bungalow, each story having a thatched straw roof. As they stepped inside, he admired the vacation-style décor: thin potted palm trees, the ceiling lined with thick straw, and various decorative items along the walls designed to look like shells and sea creatures.

Similar to Aquarin, Krysta introduced herself to the man on the lower floor. This time, she pulled something from the pouch at her side, some sort of medallion with a crest on it. The man nodded and escorted them up to the chancellor's main office. Kyo and the others didn't have to hide behind a door and eavesdrop. Behind a desk of black wood sat a middle-aged woman, fierce eyes staring down through long, graying black hair. If looks could kill, the papers on her desk would have ignited.

Chancellor Bisca glanced up from her work but didn't smile. "Your Highness, good to see you. Chancellor Ambers said there was a chance you'd be coming to Oasis."

While the two exchanged pleasantries, Kyo rocked on his feet, examining the office. Much of the furniture, from tables to bookshelves were composed of a different kind of wood than he'd ever seen. Instead of solid planks, they were long, wooden rods bent and cut to form the shapes needed. Behind the chancellor, a massive window allowed her to gaze upon some of the city. Shame the office didn't sit on higher ground, it'd be a killer view.

"So then, these are friends of yours?" Chancellor Bisca asked.

"Yes, they are." Krysta pointed to each, introducing them. "I'm sure you know why we've come to talk to you."

Chancellor Bisca stood, placing her hands behind her back. "If I were to guess, those two, Blanq and Sybilla, have made their way to Oasis. After all the news from Kattelink, I knew it'd only be a matter of time. I already have all enforcers out on patrol, looking for them. The chapel has also been advised to have all available clerics ready in case something happens." She slammed her fist on the desk. "I will not let what happened in Calmarock be repeated here."

"Sorry to say, your enforcers won't be enough to handle them. I haven't seen much of their power for myself, but these kids sure have," Roland said, motioning to all but Rosette. "And according to them, those two could stand their ground with the Aurora."

"In regard to having your enforcers looking for them, that may also prove difficult if not impossible," Marsh said. "Sybilla is quite skilled in alteration spells. She caught us by surprise while camouflaged. We had no idea she was nearby until she revealed herself. As for Blanq, I have heard she can use illusion spells?" He looked to Kyo for confirmation, who gave it with a nod. "However, the good news is there are three members of the Aurora in Oasis who are actively searching for them, one of whom uses impressive perception spells. Even so, they do have an entire city to search."

"Well then, those Aurora had best live up to their reputation. But relying fully on them would be disgraceful." The chancellor focused on Krysta. "Your Highness, is there any chance we could request aid from your uncle? I would feel much better if we had some of his royal guards here to help. Failing to stop those two here could cause it to become Alderdeem's problem soon enough."

Krysta cupped her chin. "Perhaps. I don't think it would be impossible to convince him. But even if you do, I have doubts they could arrive here in time to be of any help, unless Sybilla and Blanq plan to soak in the sun on the beach for a few days. Would you like me to use your com-orb to contact him?"

The chancellor shook her head. "I will do it myself. No offense to you, but I refuse to let someone else ask for help on my behalf." She paced behind her desk, using her thumb and index finger to rub her eyes. "Would you happen to know what they might be planning? Do they want to kill my people like they did in Calmarock?"

"I don't think so, but what Sybilla wants to do is probably worse." Kyo met the chancellor's worried gaze. "The night before we left Aquarin, there was an outbreak of shades. They all appeared in a condensed area, at least twenty of them. The Aurora took care of it, but the thing is, before I left the scene, I heard someone mention that a person who became a shade wasn't even corrupted to begin with. Which means they went right from being normal to being a full-fledged shade."

"What does that have to do with Sybilla?" Chancellor Bisca asked angrily.

"Look, at one point Sybilla told us she's not responsible for starting the corruption, which is probably true. But she and Blanq do have ways of manipulating it. I've seen Blanq cure people," Kyo said. The chancellor's hardening glare and tightening jaw convinced him to hurry with his explanation. "I talked this over with Garret of the Aurora, and we figure that, while Sybilla can't directly turn people into shades, because she is so skilled in alteration spells, she can actually make people more susceptible to it. So, our guess is she wants to turn as many people as possible into shades. Garret thinks what she did in Aquarin could have been a test run for what she wants to do in Oasis."

The chancellor slumped back in her chair, hands on her head. "To think someone has the ability to do such a thing. And if she's as powerful as you say, what can we do?"

"That's not the only transformation we have to worry about either." Krysta's body trembled with her fists by her sides. "While Sybilla may be eager to turn people into shades, Blanq prefers to raise those who have already passed as undead."

Chancellor Bisca looked up, her brow raised, and lip slightly twisted. "I'm sorry?"

"Blanq can take dead people's bodies and make them move again. Control them. Like...a puppet or something," Rosette said.

"Dead bodies? Are you referring to..." The chancellor snapped her fingers repeatedly. "What's it called?"

"It is referred to as necromancy," Marsh said.

"And you're sure? You've actually seen this happen yourselves?" Chancellor Bisca's eyes widened, and the color drained from her face. "What am I saying? Of course you have."

"Is there something—" Krysta's words cut off when the chancellor raised her hand for silence.

"What a disaster." Taking several deep, shaky breaths, the chancellor covered her mouth and looked out the bay windows at the city. "But what can be done?"

Krysta took the chancellor's hands into her own, staring into her eyes. "Chancellor, what is going on?"

The chancellor took several deep breaths. "Oasis has a long history, dating back to before it became the city everyone knows today." She pulled away from Krysta and stepped behind her desk, staring out the windows. "It has been well over two hundred years since the last attempts were made to colonize Morterra. It's no secret why every attempt to lay claim to the southern continent ended in disaster."

"Oh!" Rosette cried, raising her hand as if she were in a classroom. "It's because the ferals are too strong. There are dragons and all sorts of strong creatures down there."

"Yes, that's correct. No matter how many mages were sent down to protect the new towns being built, they simply weren't powerful enough to defend them before construction could be finished." The chancellor placed her hand and forehead against the window. "Many groups were sent to try to make colonization a success over a period of several decades before they finally decided to stop."

Roland grabbed his flask for a quick swig. "And where Oasis sits now was the launching point for ships to Morterra, right?"

"It was. Most believe that those who fell in the colonization attempts were left behind or abandoned, but that isn't true. Recovery parties were sent south to retrieve the bodies. There were too many to give each a proper burial, but the feeling was they didn't want to abandon them to that harsh land." The chancellor turned to face them, placing her hands on the desk. "All those many thousands of bodies were brought back and buried right underneath our feet. Oasis came much later, built upon the world's largest tomb."

Kyo's body grew cold, and he knew without having to look that the color had left his face. Could Blanq even raise bodies that had been dead for so long? So far, he'd only seen her do so to the recently deceased. Would she go so far? Considering she worked with a monster like Sybilla, he wouldn't put it past her.

"This is not good. At all." Marsh twiddled his fingers as his eyes darted around. "If so many potential undead rest beneath our feet, what of an evacuation?"

Chancellor Bisca shook her head. "To where? Desert to the east and west and to the north…we couldn't have an entire city's populace traverse a desert for days across the sand. The nearest destination would be the Infinite Farmstead, but it'd be far too risky."

"Now may be a good time to contact my uncle, Chancellor," Krysta said.

The chancellor made for the com-orb on one of the tables against the left wall. When everyone else left the room, Kyo followed, but it felt like his body moved on its own, all awareness focused on the possibilities swirling in his mind.

This could turn into a far greater disaster than he ever thought possible. If both Sybilla and Blanq unleashed their full potential upon Oasis, he wasn't sure if the Aurora would be enough. Especially with only three members within the city, it'd be too much ground to cover. And if they didn't help stop them, nothing would prevent the same from happening across the entire continent.

Chapter 23

Bursting from the chancellor's office, Kyo ran down the road behind the others, Marsh in the lead. The streets remained dead, which probably wasn't the best choice of words in the current situation.

"Why don't they evacuate the city?" Kyo asked. "Everyone could board ships and head to Kattelink Island."

"I seriously doubt the port has enough ships to evacuate the entire city, kid. Though they might try it anyway if they have no other options. But if those two notice the city emptying out, it might cause them to act sooner so they don't miss their chance." Roland held Rosette's hand as they ran. "We're dammed if we do and dammed if we don't. It's all up to the Aurora now, and it'd be a good idea to find any one of them. Quickly."

Kyo skidded to a stop and jumped onto the nearest rooftop. "Then I'm going to head to the western part of the city."

"By yourself?" Krysta asked.

"I can cross the city fastest, so better for me to search the parts farthest from here. They have to know about what the chancellor told us. And you can't forget that rescuing Alden is still a priority. If we can't stop those two here, we can at least keep them from getting more accrue stones. We'll cover more ground if we split up—they could be anywhere."

"Then I will head to the chapel," Marsh said. "The clerics should know what to expect and prepare should the worst come to pass."

Roland reaffirmed his grip on Rosette's hand. "Me and the kiddo will check the port. If things do take a turn for the worst, I can at least make sure Rosette can sail away from it."

"I'm not going to just run away!" Rosette said, scrunching her face in anger.

"No arguments," Roland said, pointing at her and narrowing his eyes.

"I suppose that leaves me with the east side. Be careful and stay out of danger," Krysta said before sprinting off.

Kyo ran across several connected rooftops then jumped to the shops on the next street over. Unlike the towns on Kattelink Island, Oasis had buildings of various sizes, including a dozen tall spires towering over the city. He also had a lot more space to cover this time. There had to be a way to narrow it down. At least with so few people on the streets, he wouldn't have to bother looking through crowds. His head darted back and forth, analyzing the few people he passed in hopes of seeing those green robes. "This is bad. This is very bad."

Since the spires were scattered around the city, using them as landmarks made the most sense. They probably had little purpose other than allowing people to get a memorable view. So, he headed for the nearest tower, keeping to the rooftops.

Upon reaching the spire, he stared up and nearly lost his balance, not expecting it to be so high up close. "Oh man. I am not climbing every one of these."

But he resigned himself to at least climbing this one. He entered the tower and found it nothing more than a set of spiral stairs that reached all the way to the top. With a groan, he got started. Despite all the action he'd seen recently, he still found himself out of breath once he reached the top, having run, or at least jogged, the entire way.

The view from the top gave him pause, the city like a sea of sparkling gemstones with the roads sectioning them off. He'd have to make it a point to come back up here, especially for some stargazing. Keeping his focus on the roads, he could make out the closest people and the color of their clothes but nothing matching the pale green robes of the Aurora. At least he had another reason for coming up here. The spire may have been too high for him to make use of, but it'd be perfect for someone like Cedric. He leaned forward and squinted but couldn't see anyone in the viewing areas of the closest three towers.

Traveling to different spires around the city and hoping to notice any of the three he sought would take far too long. What else could he do? Kyo placed his hands on the high railing. Having them take notice of him might be easier than the other way around, and the sand littering the streets would be perfect for that.

But first he had to get down. His heart leaped as an alternative to the stairs became the best option.

"Oh boy…" Rooftops were one thing, but he had to be a dozen stories up. "No time like the present, right?"

Before he could talk himself out of it, he hopped the railing.

"Shit!" he screamed at least halfway down.

The wind assaulted his face, tears escaping his eyes as the ground drew closer every second. Kyo thrust his hands down, and air burst from them and his feet to slow his descent. It worked, but he did so too high up. He reduced the power behind the spells, allowing himself to fall farther but still at a slower pace. After several more stop-and-go's, his feet touched the ground, and he released a heavy sigh, eyes wide as could be and pulse pounding in his head.

"Oh, wow. I did it. That was…" He glanced up at the spire he'd jumped from and couldn't stop the smile from forming as his heart pounded.

He'd have to do that again later.

All around him lay what he needed to be noticed. Oasis was a desert city after all; there could be no getting rid of all the sand and dirt that blew into the streets from beyond the city limits.

Kyo waved his hands, using wind to gather up sand from the road and rooftops. Guiding it down several streets like a pet and ordering it where to go, he added more air to the spell as the amount of sand he picked up grew. Once enough had been gathered to make his spell easily visible, he launched it into the air, a tall, swirling dust cloud bound to get the attention of any who looked this way. It may not have reached as high as the spire, but it still dwarfed any other buildings.

"Come on, someone notice," he muttered.

Maintaining the spell required minimal effort, but without knowing what was to come, he didn't want to waste too much magic. After several minutes, the sand cloud shrank back to the ground, leaving the sand in as neat a pile as he could manage in case he'd have to do it again. Kyo leaned against the side of the nearest building and relaxed. All he could do was wait and hope. This method had to be more effective than scouring the entire city.

Minutes felt like hours, but he couldn't tell for sure. He brought his fingers together and held his hand parallel to the horizon then raised it up several times. The sun had moved about two fingers, or thirty minutes.

He groaned, and his eyes flicked to the sand pile. "Okay, let's try it again."

"That won't be necessary" came a voice to his left. Cedric approached him, as plain-faced as ever. "Did you not think that trick of yours could lead Sybilla or Blanq to you?"

Kyo shrugged. "Had to take the chance. But I sure am glad to see you. How much do you know about what's going on?"

"I haven't been made aware of anything specific. Care to enlighten me?"

Kyo explained what the chancellor had told them, and her fear of the bodies underground being used against them. "I suppose with the accrue stone, Blanq could manage to do something like that."

"Well, that certainly is cause for concern. But knowing this does give me another avenue to search," Cedric said, rubbing his chin. "An evacuation could cause Sybilla to act in haste. So, the chancellor is relying on us to resolve this before anything happens. A risky bet."

"That's what I said." Kyo slapped Cedric's arm. "But can't avoid it now. Have you had any luck finding Alden?"

Cedric nodded. "Some."

Reaching into his chest pocket, he pulled out a folded sheet of paper. He unfolded it, revealing a large map of the city, setting it on the ground. Around the city were about twenty circles drawn in red ink, three of which had an X through them.

"It would make sense for them to conceal where they are hiding," Cedric said. "In this case, Blanq has taken it upon herself to cast an illusion over it to make wherever it is nondescript. The problem is, she seems to have prepared for someone like me. Each of these circles represents a building with a similar illusion cast upon it. They could be in any, or none, of these."

Studying the map, Kyo took a few seconds to stare at each circle. Alden could be in any one of them. He'd take it over having an entire city to search through.

"Let me help. I can make it from one location to another pretty quickly."

Cedric hesitated, staring into Kyo's eyes for a long moment, then picked up the map and handed it to him. "Very well. I made the map to remind myself which locations I've already checked, but if we're splitting the work, I won't need it anymore. But if you take notice of Sybilla or Blanq, do not engage them. Signal me like you just did again. I'll be looking for it. And stay hidden, as it will likely catch their attention too."

Folding and unfolding this huge map would be a pain—he had to stretch his arms out to hold it properly—but a small price to pay if it'd get him what he wanted. "I sure won't engage Sybilla. If I don't see that crazy woman again, that's fine by me."

Cedric turned to leave but paused and glanced over his shoulder. "Your parents would be proud of the young man you've become. Just don't go meeting them in the Flow too soon."

With that said, he took off.

"The Flow, huh?" There was no telling how long it took a soul to break down into the base energies that created it. Would their consciousness still exist when he died, or would it be too late?

Kyo shook his head. There were other things to focus on.

He examined the map. It took a minute or two to find his location then the nearest circle. The massive cliff to the north and the sea to the south made navigating the correct direction easy. Counting the city blocks, he'd need to travel south and west. He folded the map, jumped onto the nearest roof, and started running.

Whenever he knew a turn was coming, he'd travel in a straight line across other roofs to get to the correct road faster. Using this method, he reached the area encircled on the map in about five minutes. He checked the map again. The circle Cedric drew encompassed several buildings, likely not on purpose. Walking slowly down the road, Kyo kept his eyes on the shops he passed. Nothing seemed unusual about any of them. An alchemist shop sold herbs and potions that could restore magical energy and heal physical wounds. He wished he had the cryst to spare for one of those, though they were hardly affordable for the average person. Next to the alchemist shop was a store selling novelty items specific to Oasis and an ice cream shop.

How was he supposed to tell if one was an illusion?

"One at a time, I guess." He tried the alchemy shop first.

A bell rang when he opened the door. Herbs in pots lined the front window. Others sat on shelves and tables around the store. Bottles of different colored potions sat behind the exchange counter. He took a long whiff, inhaling the aroma of both herbs and dirt. Illusions couldn't affect smell, could they?

An old man came from the back room. "Hello there. Is there anything I can help you with?"

"Uh, no, thanks. I was just…looking for someone. But they're not here." Kyo turned to leave, closing the door behind him. "Maybe the next one."

He grabbed the door handle and pulled, but the door didn't budge. If it were locked, it'd at least move slightly, but this one wouldn't at all. Pulling harder, he placed a foot next to the door for extra force, but still nothing. He banged on the door with his fist but stopped after two bangs. Kyo leaned in close and lightly tapped on what should be a glass door but sounded like he knocked on wood. As he walked slowly to his right, he knocked on any surface that looked different until what should be stone sounded like glass.

"Well, no question here," he said. "Nice try, Blanq."

While building air around his right fist, Kyo took several steps back then thrust his hand forward. Glass shattered, and the whole two-story building seemed to wobble and distort until it no longer appeared as a novelty store but a partially burned, abandoned shop. A wooden board covered up what would be a doorway. The shattered remains of both glass and wood lay sprawled across the floor inside.

As he stepped through the window, he realized if Blanq or Sybilla were here, they would have heard what he'd done.

No one came.

Kyo searched the main room and the back room then headed upstairs. This used to be one of those shops where whoever owned it lived upstairs, the kitchen, living space and bedroom all on one level, not uncommon in Mistwell. After every room and closet and bit of open space had been thoroughly checked, he took out the map and did his best to use his fingernail to indent an X through the appropriate circle.

He studied the map and charted the way to his next destination. Now that he knew what to look for, he should be able to knock these out quickly. In truth, he hoped Cedric would be the one to find Alden. If he ran into Sybilla or Blanq, he'd have the best chance to successfully get Alden out.

Kyo made the mistake of assuming any building Blanq cast an illusion on would be unoccupied. Instead, an old man at his next location chased him off with a cane after he shattered the window to his home.

When he'd followed the map for about ten minutes, Kyo came across what appeared to be a souvenir shop. Through the window, he saw shelves of miniature statues of various sea creatures, clothing with Oasis's emblem on them, and toward the back, surf boards hanging from the wall. He double and triple checked the location on the map, took a deep breath, and while praying he wouldn't be intruding into someone's home again, shattered the window with a burst of air.

Once he stepped inside, the illusion faded for him. Bare cement floors, rolls of carpet piled against a wall, and a layer of dust over the only furniture in the large room, a single desk and chair. This place must have been undergoing renovations.

He froze when met by a familiar voice.

"Did you forget where the door was?"

Stepping out from the back room, Alden appeared.

Chapter 24

Staring wordlessly at Alden, who did the same, Kyo trembled and fought between wanting to hug and punch him. A week hadn't passed since Alden had gone missing, but Kyo had spent every moment worried about his safety, so it felt like months. At last, Alden stood before him, with his stupid bright red hair sticking up, holding the notebook he never went anywhere without, and not a trace of the corruption.

Decision made, Kyo rushed forward, wrapping his arms around his godfather, and burying his face in his shoulder. "About damn time," Kyo muttered to himself before pulling back, cupping Alden's cheeks. "Did they hurt you at all?"

Alden broke from his surprised trance and grabbed Kyo's wrists, pulling his hands away. "First, I'm supposed to be the doting parent here. Second, how on Feracael did you find me?"

"I had help. Cedric Felmont of the Aurora figured out where Blanq placed all her illusions. I just got lucky and found this one." Kyo leaned over to look behind Alden. "Are either of those two here?"

"No." Alden released Kyo's wrists, took a deep breath, and embraced Kyo tight. "You shouldn't be here.

You should be home, you idiot. But damn I'm glad to see you're okay."

Releasing a sigh and much of his body's tension with it, Kyo leaned into his godfather. Alden hadn't turned into a shade, Sybilla hadn't harmed him in some way, and he still lived. Seeing for himself did more for him than Blanq's assurances ever could. His body went a bit limp, and for the moment, all other concerns left him.

Alden was here and safe. The dream of returning home with him and picking up their lives again became a possibility again.

Alden broke the embrace, placing his hands on Kyo's shoulders. "Blanq's been keeping me updated on what's been going on. You've gone through some real trouble trying to follow me, huh? I'm sorry about that. Shades…and of course, Sybilla." The last word came out tainted in anger.

"Yeah, well, not like I'm going to let your dumb ass get hurt, even if you did let yourself get kidnapped. I guess I need to thank Blanq though. Kind of hard to believe someone who works with a woman like Sybilla, but it seems like everything she's told me is true." Kyo looked Alden over, grabbing his arm and forcing him to spin around. "So, did they cure you of the corruption that night?"

"Yeah, they did. Almost right away. Of course, they wouldn't let me go after that."

Kyo's eyes narrowed. "So, when did they make you take the accrue stone? Wait, never mind, you can tell me later. We have to get out of here while we can."

He grabbed Alden's hand and made for the door, but Alden didn't budge.

"Kyo, listen." Alden pulled his hand free, refusing to meet Kyo's gaze. "I'm so glad to see you and that you're safe. But I can't go with you. Not yet."

"What are you talking about? This can all end right now. I can take you out of here, and the Aurora can deal with Sybilla and Blanq." With wide eyes, Kyo motioned to the shattered window, impatiently hopping on his toes.

Alden shook his head. "There are still things that you don't know about this whole situation. I can't just leave. I want to come home with you, and I will…eventually." He placed a hand on Kyo's head, smiling. "I promise I'll return to you. But this has become far too important to ignore."

Kyo brushed Alden's hand off him and opened his mouth, but at first, no words came. How could he possibly not want to go home as soon as possible? Kyo glanced back at the broken window then to Alden again. Should he force him to come along? Groaning, he stomped his foot, fists tight by his sides.

"I do understand what's going on. I'm not some dumb kid, you know." He pushed his index finger against Alden's forehead. "I traveled across Kattelink Island, fought blobs, Sybilla, and shades. More than one of them. I found Ruby, who was scared and corrupted, and I tried my best to help her. But in the end, she turned into a shade I had to fight, and I had to watch her die, and I've been through some shit and—" Kyo tightened his jaw, clenched his teeth and fought hard to keep the tears at bay. Inhaling deeply through his nose, he ran his hands over his face. So much more bubbled up inside of him, the tip of the iceberg he'd let out not enough to be cathartic.

"Kyo, I'm sorry." Alden frowned. "I—"

Kyo shook his head. He had to focus. "I know what's going on, okay? I know about the accrue stone and that there are more of them. They needed you to get the first one from Mistwell, and they'll want to use you again to get the others. But we can't let that happen. I've seen for myself what Sybilla can do with one of them. If she gets more, I doubt even the Aurora could stand up to her."

Alden turned and placed his notebook on a nearby table then placed his hands upon it, staring down. "You're right. I agree with you completely. Sybilla is clearly the unstable one, but both of those girls are extremely dangerous." He sighed but didn't raise his head. "I have a confession to make. When we first came across them in Mistwell, that wasn't the first time I'd met them."

A chill ran through Kyo's entire body, like when he realized his parents were dead and was waiting for the words to leave Alden's lips. The anticipation of having terrible news confirmed. Whatever Alden wanted to say, Kyo already knew he'd be happier not knowing, but his curiosity wouldn't let him speak up.

"By then," Alden continued, "a plan had already been in place. They approached me weeks ago, knowing I knew where the accrue stone was. It became my job to retrieve the stone for them. The reason Sybilla told you to come back the next day was so I could have time to get the accrue stone and bring it back to them."

It was like Kyo's mind shattered, and he struggled to pick up the pieces again.

Here he thought Alden had been kidnapped against his will, kept prisoner, when in fact he had been part of a plan to steal the accrue stone from his own home.

"No. No way." Kyo's voice rose with each word, as did the heat of anger chasing the earlier chill away. "You can't tell me you're actually a part of their little group! And you agreed to do it?"

Alden raised his head but didn't look at Kyo. "Sybilla isn't the type you say no to. I didn't *want* to do it, but she had both you and the whole town of Mistwell as leverage. From what I hear, you saw what she did to Calmarock. She could have done that to Mistwell even without the stone. Blanq could have raised the entire population to use in her experiments, and Sybilla would've had free rein over the town to find the stone herself." He slammed his fist on the table, glaring so intensely Kyo thought he might burn a hole through it. "But they wanted to keep a low profile for a while longer."

Of course. Kyo should have realized they'd forced him to do what they wanted. Alden wouldn't have willingly helped them, knowing what they planned, or even if he didn't. "And…you becoming corrupted?"

Finally, Alden turned to look at him but only for a few seconds before staring at the table again. "Rotten luck. Or good luck, depending on how you look at it. Becoming corrupted while I was with the only two who could cure it — I guess it couldn't have happened at a better time. They fixed me right up, gave me time to rest, then off to do the job."

"And then left me behind," Kyo said, his voice monotone with a hint of accusation. "Like you planned to do."

"For the reasons I mentioned. To keep you safe. And…for your parents."

Kyo's brow rose. "What do they have to do with any of this?"

Alden pulled the chair from the desk and spun it around, sitting so he could face Kyo. "They died because they were betrayed by one of their own."

Kyo nodded. "His name was Zeshin." The name seeped through gritted teeth. "Cedric told me the other day. Now I have a name to go with my fantasy of beating the life out of him."

"Zeshin was planning something big, something that went against everything being an Aurora stood for. Kei and Iris were killed because they found out and tried to stop him." Alden closed his eyes for a second then stared at Kyo. "What he planned involved the accrue stones."

One shock to the system after another. Kyo didn't know if he could handle any more news like this. He gripped his hair, trying to process the newest information. The situation he found himself in was a continuation of the one that had killed his parents.

"Those accrue stones have to go," Kyo said.

Alden slapped his knees and stood. "Exactly! That's exactly it. As soon as I learned what Sybilla and Blanq were after, I knew I had to go along with it. Zeshin deserves all the blame in the world for what he did, but those stones are also a key reason Kei and Iris are dead. Yes, they were your parents, but they were also my best friends." He paced and shoved the chair to the ground. "This became my chance. I couldn't do anything about Zeshin, but I can do something about those damn stones. And I sure won't let them be the reason their son is killed."

To think the accrue stones had a connection to his parents. And Alden...how could Kyo be angry at the decisions he'd made? In the past six years, Kyo had hardly given any thought to how his parents' deaths may have affected him. Up to this minute, Kyo had selfishly thought that pain of loss was exclusive to him. What he'd said minutes ago couldn't have been more untrue — he was a stupid kid after all.

"Alden, I'm sorry," Kyo said. "I never considered enough how their deaths made you feel. I should have been there for you like you were for me."

Alden shook his head. "No, it's normal. You were a kid dealing with a huge loss. No one expects a child to have the maturity to think that way. But...thank you. You saying that shows you're growing up."

Kyo smiled then blinked hard, refocusing his thoughts. "Okay, so, you want to do something about the accrue stones. That's fine. I get it. So do it from home. Find out where they are then go deal with them and come back."

"I don't think it'll be that easy." Alden leaned against the desk. "Despite my reasoning, I still made the choice to help them. I stole something so important and powerful and willingly handed it over to someone I knew would use it for nefarious purposes."

"What, you think the enforcers and chancellors will see you as an accomplice? But you did it to protect Mistwell and me."

"Yes, I did. And as a result, Calmarock and Aquarin paid a price. And possibly Oasis. I can't imagine that's something they'll be willing to let go." Alden grabbed his notebook and flipped through a few pages. "If you look at it another way, they could have devastated Mistwell, taken the stone for themselves, and everything that followed may have still happened as it has, meaning my actions protected a town. But it might be hard to convince others."

"So, if you reveal yourself, you'll just be arrested with no guarantee they'll see it your way," Kyo said with a heavy sigh.

Once more, the dream of returning to their old life slipped away, so soon after he'd finally grasped it again. With so much death and destruction left in Sybilla and Blanq's wake, those in charge might not think rationally. The people who had suffered would want to see punishment.

As expected, Alden had thought this through to every detail.

"I'm not against facing whatever fate has in store for me," Alden said, "but it'll be after I find those stones and, if I can, destroy them. No more situations like this one or the one your parents had to deal with." Pushing from the desk, he approached Kyo and cupped his cheeks lightly. "You understand now, right? Why I can't go home with you yet? You're becoming more mature, but you're still a kid. Don't risk ruining your future — or worse, ending your life trying to solve the problems of stupid adults. I promise to do my best to meet you back home. I want to hear about these new friends of yours. Apparently one of them is a princess? Hard imagining you getting along with someone like that." Alden chuckled.

Kyo appreciated his attempt at lightening the mood, but no smile came this time. Still a kid—that was how Alden saw him, and he was right to do so. A sixteen-year-old couldn't be considered an adult. Kyo understood all too well why Alden had made the choices he had. But kids tended to be selfish by nature, and if Alden wanted him to be one, then damn everything else. This would be the last and most important time he acted like a selfish kid.

"I don't care," Kyo mumbled, gripping Alden's wrists tightly. "I'm willing to take that risk." Meeting Alden's eyes with fierce determination, he pulled him toward the shattered window. "I'll risk whether or not they let you off without punishment."

Alden tried to pull away, but Kyo held tight, the muscles in his arms flexing and his legs crouching as he struggled to pull his godfather to the window.

"If they hear you were forced to do it—if they hear you were protecting Mistwell and me, they'd have to listen, right?" Each time Kyo gained ground by forcing a few steps from Alden, he in turn found himself pulled back further into the shop. Back and forth they struggled.

"Kyo, I can't." Alden forced words out between grunts, digging his heels into the wooden floor. "This is too important. I know it's not fair to you, but it has to be this way."

"No, it doesn't. You have another option. You just won't give it a chance!" A voice in the back of Kyo's head told him how unreasonable he was. How many people Alden could save if he'd simply let go. He couldn't deny the logic, risking his own happiness to save so many others from the accrue stones being sought after and misused yet again.

But why did it have to be *his* happiness that would be sacrificed? Expecting a child to deal with losing two parents and come out of it a relatively happy person—ridiculous! Or it would have been if he hadn't had Alden there every step of the way.

But if he lost Alden now...

No, Kyo couldn't risk it. He didn't have the strength to deal with that alone.

Alden's foot slipped, kicking Kyo's and sending them both to the floor, landing hard on their sides. Alden tried to stand, but Kyo leaped on top of him, pinning his arms by his head. Gritting his teeth, Kyo mustered all his strength to keep him there. Little by little Alden strained, face turning red, and managed to lift his arms off the floor. What Kyo wouldn't give for Rosette's help. He was so focused on Alden's arms, he fell to the side when Alden rotated his body.

"You're...getting older, Kyo," Alden said, strained. "Stronger. You don't...need me anymore."

"Are you stupid? Of course I do. You're the only family I have left!" Despite putting all his effort into fighting off Alden, his godfather had the superior physical strength. "I don't want to be alone. I can't!"

Kyo thrust his knee into Alden's stomach, knocking the wind out of him.

As Alden fell to the side, Kyo lay on his back, panting.

Neither moved. At least he knew, whatever Sybilla and Blanq planned, they wouldn't let it harm Alden. They needed him too much. But that wouldn't matter if he could get Alden outside and signal Cedric.

"Just...come home. I swear I'll never skip studying again. I won't complain about helping you with your enchanting jobs again. In fact, I'll enjoy the crap out of it. We can pig out at the bakery, sleep in our own

beds. And I can help you with the accrue stone thing—
we can work at it together." Kyo grabbed Alden's hand,
holding it tight. "You can't tell me that doesn't sound
great. I know we can keep you out of Spellnix Hold if we
just explain the truth."

A tear trickled down his cheek.

Alden gripped Kyo's hand then sat up. "All of
that sounds damn good. Every bit of it." Releasing his
grip, he took the notebook from the floor and stuffed it
into the pouch at this side. "But I really can't leave."

He stood then extended a hand to Kyo, helping
him to his feet.

"No, you cannot." Blanq walked in from the back
room, hands cupped in front of her.

Chapter 25

Narrowing his eyes at Blanq, Kyo stepped between her and Alden. It was lucky she'd found them and not Sybilla, but that didn't stop his heart from racing. The last thing he wanted was to be turned into some undead puppet.

A sword appeared in his hand, and he pointed it at her. "I'm taking him home. I don't care what you want him for. He's *my* family, and we're going home together."

When Alden tried to move around him, Kyo grabbed his wrist and pulled him back. Kyo's eyes darted between the two, watching for any movement. What kind of rescue mission involved the victim not wanting to be rescued?

"Kyo. I know it's hard, and it's not fair to you. But Blanq is right—I can't leave yet." The second Alden's hand rested on his shoulder, Kyo gripped it with his own.

"You're wrong. The only reason you think so is because you're trying to protect me and keep me out of it. But I didn't leave home for nothing. I'll take you home and fight off anyone who tries to stop me." Even as the words left his lips, he knew that strategy wouldn't work. He'd already tried stabbing Blanq with a laughable result. However, he'd never forgive himself if he gave up and let Alden go.

Blanq took several steps forward, stopping a hair's breadth from the tip of Kyo's sword touching her throat. "It's admirable, seeing how fiercely you protect your family. I wish I'd been old and strong enough to protect my parents. I understand the pain. Even so, Alden's skills are too important."

Kyo met her eyes, but his hand wavered. Should he believe her words about her parents? Were the two of them similar, or was it a lie to lower his guard? She'd told the truth about Alden and his condition, but it still didn't excuse the things she'd done. He glared and bared his teeth, trying to show more confidence than he felt. Blanq was calling his bluff, certainly knowing he didn't have the strength to run her through. Was running an option with someone who didn't want to leave?

"Even if you return home together," Blanq said, "should Sybilla and I avoid capture, I have no doubt at least she would return to Mistwell. Do you want the fate of your home to mirror Calmarock? Or worse?"

Kyo released a dry laugh. "Weird question coming from a necromancer."

"Perhaps so. But it doesn't make my words any less true." Blanq's gaze fell to the floor.

Kyo glanced down as well and stiffened. A miniature skitter about the size of his foot crawled on top of his boot. Panting heavily, he stomped on his own foot to crush it, trying his best not to lose track of Blanq or Alden or lower his sword. When he pulled his boot away, the skitter continued to crawl as if nothing had happened, making its way up his bare leg. A tingling sensation on his arm stole his attention—another skitter, trying to crawl under the sleeve of his T-shirt. In a panic, he slapped his arm as hard as he could, but it wouldn't stop.

"Where did they come from? Get them off!" he yelled, dropping his sword, using both hands to brush his leg and arm.

More crawled across the floor, all coming right for him. With a yell, he blasted them with a burst of air that should have sent them flying against the wall, but it did nothing. He'd seen fire skitters before—could these be rock skitters? In the desert it would make sense, but given their size, they should still be light enough to blast away.

His chest hurt, every beat of his heart radiating throughout his body. Why skitters? Why not anything else? The sensations of little fuzzy legs on his skin were under his shirt and shorts. Frantically, he pulled his shirt over his head and tossed it to the floor, smacking himself anywhere he felt them crawling on him, all the while trying to keep himself from the others closing in.

"Alden! Do something, please," Kyo begged.

But Alden and Blanq simply stood there, watching with deadpan faces, the skitters passing them by as if they weren't there.

Kyo narrowed his eyes. Something was off, but he couldn't focus for more than a second without the terror of the skitters overtaking him. Backed into a corner, he tried wind spells again, stronger this time.

Yet the skitters advanced.

His hands and feet pressed against the wall as if hoping to climb it, for all the good that would do against such creatures. Tears streamed down his face. Why wouldn't Alden help him? Would they go so far just to get their way? He glanced at the shattered window, but the streets were filled with more skitters, crawling on the buildings.

Somehow the city had become infested.

More made contact with his boot. In a fit of hysteria, he summoned his sword back to him and stabbed down, barely beyond the toe. With his vision wavering, he missed and stabbed through the wooden floor. His sword and wind were useless, and going outside would make the situation worse. Kyo gripped his head, wind swirling around his body. Each pant and gasp of breath felt ineffective in filling his lungs. No matter how deeply he breathed, it wasn't enough.

A flash of white light filled his vision for a brief second. He had to squint and turn his head away. As the light faded, the skitters wavered, distorting and becoming transparent. As quickly as it happened, they regained their form.

A trick of the eyes? Was he losing his mind?

Realization struck him, and a little voice in his head called him stupid, growing louder and louder every fraction of a second.

"It's…not…real," he muttered, doing his best to ignore the sensation of those small fuzzy legs brushing against his bare skin. He repeated the words to himself, hoping to will the illusion away, but he couldn't stop himself from trying to brush off skitters that weren't there. This had to be the same as those spirits Blanq supposedly conjured during their last meeting. He gritted his teeth and muttered a curse. How could it have taken him this long to realize?

Clenching his eyes, he tried to focus on anything else, something strong—his parents, Alden, his new friends. But the legs were everywhere, brushing over his face, every inch of his body. Mental images did nothing. The illusion didn't only affect his sight—he swore he could actually feel them.

A story he'd read a few years ago popped into his mind, the hero finding herself in a similar situation. He placed the blade of this sword halfway up his left forearm, weakened its magic protection by shifting the energy elsewhere in his body, and ever so slowly dragged it across his skin. Blood trickled down his arm from a sharply stinging line. Sucking air through his clenched teeth, he dug the blade a bit deeper as it glided along the width of his arm. The pain became impossible to ignore, forcing a grunt from his throat, yet he kept going. As he held back a cry of pain and fresh tears, the sensation of the skitters lessened. No longer cutting deeper, he pulled the blade along the deep gash he'd created for the sole purpose of causing himself more pain without further injury. By the time the tip reached his arm, all other sensations had vanished.

Kyo opened his eyes and found himself alone.

No skitters. No Blanq.

No Alden.

His arms dropped as relief flooded over him, but his eyes and fists clenched at the wave of anger that quickly followed. Anger at Blanq, Alden, and himself. The sword vanished as he stumbled across the room, still trying to calm his racing heart. With a loud scream, he kicked the chair then banged on the table with his fists, each slam pulling another shout from him.

"You…idiot…" Kyo didn't know if his words were meant for Alden or himself. Probably both. Everyone, the entire situation was stupid, all because of those stones. That thought proved Alden's point, which added fuel to his anger. He kicked the table across the room then let his body slouch, taking deep breaths. Blood trickled down his arm and painted the floor.

He put his shirt on, tucked it under the hoodie tied at his waist, then stepped outside and jumped onto the roof with wobbly legs. The illusion over the building had vanished.

No sense in Cedric continuing his search for Alden. Once more, Kyo went through the process of gathering sand and dirt from the roof and road, creating another weak twister to signal him. After several minutes, he dispersed it and sat.

On occasion he twitched, swearing he still felt the skitters. He propped up his knees and curled in on himself. While everyone else worked to protect the city and its people, he'd failed in the most important task. It all relied on the Aurora to catch Sybilla and Blanq. Kyo had no idea how much time passed before a pair of feet landed on the roof and approached him, though he noticed the shadows of the surrounding buildings had shifted position.

"You found something?"

He didn't need to look up to recognize Cedric's always serious tone.

"I found Alden. Blanq showed up, and they got away." No way would he mention that Alden didn't want to be saved. That'd only hurt his chances of remaining free, should he be caught. "You should focus on searching for Blanq and Sybilla. Use those eyes of yours, find them, and stop them. It's what you do, right?"

"It is, and we will." After a brief pause, Cedric spoke again. "You're injured. That cleric friend should be able to deal with that."

Kyo waved him away. "It's not a big deal. Just a cut."

"Then you should get up and rejoin your friends." Cedric stepped next to him, overlooking the city. "Don't distress. I would like to say you should rest, but I imagine, should Blanq succeed in raising what lies beneath us, you won't hesitate to protect the people of this city. After all, you are your parent's son."

Using the rooftops, Cedric ran off toward the east, a faint black-and-purple glow under his feet.

Sweat trickled down Kyo's brow as the midday sun hung in the sky. The heat motivated him to move more than anything else. Cedric was right—he should rejoin the others. It'd make the most sense to head to the chapel first and hope Marsh hadn't left yet.

Kyo lightly slapped his face a few times. "Okay, come on. The Aurora can handle this. It's what they do."

He may not have been able to force Alden to go with him, but he bet Cedric could. And if it came to defending Alden from the law, he'd be the first to step up. Even so, his own failure and weakness weighed on his mind, hindering his focus. It took slow, heavy breaths and additional concentration to get his body to move how he wanted.

He realized he didn't know where to find the cleric chapel. A trip back to the chancellor's office might be in order. There he could find out where the chapel was and see if Garret or Estella had stopped by with any updates. For all he knew, they could have already caught Sybilla.

Kyo pictured his arrival by ship in his mind and the path they took to the chancellor's office. He ventured east, remembering the office lay in the northeastern section of the city, closer to the barren desert beyond.

The slightest of smiles crossed his lips when he thought back on his conversation with Alden. As frustrated, angry, and afraid as he'd been at the time, realizing Alden wouldn't be coming home with him, Kyo couldn't help but feel proud of his godfather for his determination to rid the world of the accrue stones. When Alden *did* return home, he'd have to more profusely apologize for hardly taking his feelings about the death of his friends into consideration.

Kyo paused, his brow raising when he noticed he wasn't the only person on a rooftop. Up ahead, a few children and even adults stood atop several homes, hands blocking the sun as they gazed toward the desert. On the road and along the canals, mutterings grew louder as people moved as one toward the east, while a few attempted to climb onto rooftops to get a better look. But a look at what? Kyo couldn't see anything interesting from where he stood.

Another of the tall spires sat two blocks away to the north, so he decided on a short detour.

When he got to the base, he sighed. "Keep it together, legs."

Once more he climbed the tall spiral stairs, taking slow, deep breaths when he made it to the top. He used his shirt to wipe the sweat from his face then gazed to the east.

A flash of light from the south drew his attention. A pillar of fire erupted into the air. Krysta and Rosette came to mind, but there had to be many in the city who could use fire magic. The question was, why? Kyo's heart raced, hoping his friends weren't in danger. But if the spell he'd seen got his attention from so far away, surely it would also be noticed by the Aurora, right?

Returning his gaze to the east, he blocked the sun with his hands and squinted. There were people out there, beyond the city. For whatever reason, they appeared to form a line. And their numbers were growing. Kyo focused on a single spot, and after a few seconds, he saw another climb out from under the ground like a burrowing worm.

With each passing second, more added to their numbers as they began marching toward the city. His breath caught in his throat. Though he couldn't see them in detail, there could be no other explanation.

Blanq had risen the dead from the tomb.

Chapter 26

For every few seconds that passed, the undead's numbers increased by the dozen. His eyes narrowed, and a slight smirk appeared on his lips. He didn't know what it would be like to fight them, but he would find out soon enough. Given how long ago they'd been buried, they had to be nothing but bones. Beating up on a bunch of them wouldn't make him feel as bad doing so to a freshly slain corpse.

This, he could do. A way he could be helpful and release some of his pent-up frustration in the process. Even so, finding any of the Aurora would be ideal in this situation, but he'd settle for the better chance of running into an enforcer.

Taking a long, deep breath, he jumped from the spire, the rush of air sending tears streaking from his eyes and blowing through his hair. If not for the hoodie tied around his waist, his shirt would have certainly lifted and covered his face. He expelled air from his hands and feet to slow his descent, gritting his teeth and trying to keep his arms from shaking. He landed harder than intended on the road. The shock sent ripples through his body, but his magic protected him from any real harm.

Kyo leaped onto the nearest roof and ran east, weaving around the few people who stood on the rooftops. He kept his eyes on the road, looking for any enforcers wearing the city's sand-colored robes. If he found one, they could get word to the others, but that wouldn't be so easy with so many leaving shops and homes to feed their curiosity.

Through his search, he couldn't get the pillar of fire out of his mind. There were countless reasons it could have been there. An amateur chef putting too much power behind attempting to cook or someone trying a new spell for the first time. Such things happened all the time. So why did his stomach churn at the thought of it?

At the easternmost part of town where the road led into the desert, a woman wearing enforcer's robes stared out at the oncoming horde. Kyo landed on the road and approached her, taking a few deep breaths to steady himself.

"Have the other enforcers seen this?" he asked.

The woman tore her gaze away from the approaching undead and focused on Kyo, her lips tight and eyes squinted. "You know what's coming?"

Kyo nodded. "Me and my friends spoke to the chancellor earlier about Sybilla and Blanq. We're way more involved than we'd like to be." He turned his attention to the desert. They were still too far away to make out any specific features, but that would change soon enough. "I think we should move people away from this part of the city, right?"

Wordlessly, the enforcer nodded, the oncoming threat certainly more important than questioning Kyo further. The woman cupped her chin, tapping her foot. "If you want to help, here." She took a circular metal object from her pouch and handed it to him. Kyo held it in the palm of his hand, examining the engraving—

multicolored dots surrounding a pool of water. The symbol of Oasis.

"Show this to people, and they'll know you're working with us. Tell people to head to the far western side of the city or the port." She pointed a finger at his chest. "But don't send everyone to the port, or it'll become overcrowded, and they may grow violent in a desperate attempt to claim a ship for themselves."

"But…that doesn't…" Kyo stammered.

"Sound fair? It's not." The enforcer sighed. "But we can't deal with two crises at once. There will be panic regardless, but if everyone panics in the same place, it'll be a disaster. Now get going." She turned and approached a group staring out at the desert, giving instructions and pointing toward the south.

"I guess I get the north, then." Kyo headed straight north along the border of the city, finding people closest to the edge. With each individual or group he came across, he showed them the enforcer badge and instructed them on where to go. When he came across another enforcer shouting instructions and knocking on doors, he shifted his direction further into the city.

Some he approached pushed for more information or outright refused to listen even when shown the badge. Kyo couldn't blame them, to them it happened so suddenly. He'd entered several shops and asked for everyone to come outside. When he explained the truth of the situation, an older man scoffed, accusing him of lying and having stolen the enforcer badge. His disbelief spread to those nearby, who waved him off or outright yelled at him. Groaning in frustration, he cast a spell under the man's feet and, despite his loud protests, raised him onto the roof and pointed east. He knew the man understood when his jaw fell and his eyes widened. After a moment's hesitation, the man confirmed the truth to the other citizens and asked to be helped to the ground. With the older man's support, the rest obeyed

Kyo's orders, though a few still mumbled words of uncertainty.

Kyo leaned against a building as more people marched down the road. At least he didn't have to speak to every individual in the city. When enough people learned of what was coming, word began to spread, and some took it upon themselves to flee and even peek into shops to inform others.

A flash of purple light guided his attention east. After several seconds, it happened again. Images of Estella launching her arrows in Aquarin came to mind. If that were the case, the undead must be close. Kyo jumped onto the nearest roof, turned east, and his entire body rippled with chills.

There were thousands of them, like swarming insects.

How could Blanq control so many at once, even with the accrue stone? Not only from a magic perspective, but Kyo couldn't fathom the amount of mental focus it must have taken.

As he ran across the rooftops, more purple light flashed in the distance. Far to the south, bolts of lightning surged every few seconds. It had to be Estella and Garret. Drawing closer to the conflict, he took notice of smaller spells — dirt and rock bursting from the ground, barriers here and there, and jets of water tearing through the undead ranks.

He stopped on a rooftop closest to the desert and could see the undead for what they were. Skeletons devoid of any flesh but with glowing blue eyes, staggered across the dirt. A group of undead were blasted by a water spell from an enforcer, bones flying about and strewn across the ground. Kyo's heart sank as he watched the bones roll across the dirt or hover through the air, remake the skeleton's form, then continue marching forward as if nothing happened. So that was the trick. A skeleton itself without muscle or flesh couldn't stand up too much, but if it could constantly reform, those defending the city would eventually fall due to fatigue.

Wide gaps separated the line of enforcers and clerics doing battle. He even spotted the occasional saber fighting alongside an enforcer, leaping between skeletons, using their claws and teeth to tear them apart. One drew in natural magic from its surroundings and released a bestial roar which created a shockwave, blasting skeletons apart. Kyo had to admit the speed of their organization was impressive. He jumped to the ground and joined Estella at her side, building air around his right hand and thrusting it toward the nearest skeleton, scattering the bones that made up its body.

"How are we supposed to handle this?" he asked.

Estella spared him a momentary glance before focusing her gaze on the oncoming horde again. "You shouldn't be here."

"There's nowhere else I should be more than here." Kyo summoned his swords in both hands. Close combat with a bunch of bones shouldn't be too bad. He couldn't imagine this finishing quickly, so preserving his magic would be best. The last thing he wanted was to be overwhelmed after he'd exhausted himself. "My parents would be standing right here beside you. So will I."

Estella raised her glowing purple bow, pulled her hand back as an arrow appeared, then let it fly. It tore a long line through the undead's ranks, incinerating any bones it came in contact with before vanishing. "You really are a stubborn kid, aren't you?" she asked, offering a brief warm smile. "If you insist, then be sure to pace yourself. We don't need to destroy them all, only buy time for Cedric to find Blanq and put a stop to her spell. Though even for him, it will take time when he has an entire city and its catacombs to search. I hope you're up to the task."

"Watch me." Kyo put some distance between himself and Estella, then marched forward.

Moving skeletons with glowing eyes were a frightening sight, enough to give him pause and make his legs shake, but he tried to think of it logically. Weak, brittle old bones, no muscle, or weapons. He could probably knock one over with a fart. Not that he'd waste time putting that to the test—his swords would suffice.

Once within striking range of the nearest skeleton, he swung his sword toward its neck, not even a full-strength strike, yet it fell easily. It grasped at his ankle, trying to pull itself up or him down—he couldn't tell with how little strength was behind the effort.

"Get off," Kyo said, thrusting his boot into its skull. It split open, and the body went limp, the faintest hint of blue-hued magic escaping then vanishing.

Seconds passed, yet it didn't move again. Krysta's words about damaging the head came to mind, something she'd read in a story.

Kyo stumbled back as two skeletons clung to him, taking advantage of his lapse in focus. He kept his footing, and his swords vanished so he could grip their wrists and pry them off. One attempted to dig its teeth into his arm, but he pushed it away before it could do any damage, assuming it could get through his magic in the first place.

"Are you seriously trying to eat me?" He placed a hand on each of the skeleton's rib cages and blasted them back into the crowd of undead then turned to dash toward Estella.

"Have you noticed they don't get back up if you destroy their skulls?" Kyo asked.

"The word has been spread. Sorry, I should have mentioned it earlier." Estella fired another arrow, obliterating two skeleton's skulls among the dozen that were struck. "At this rate, we won't be able to keep them from entering the city," she said, gritting her teeth.

Kyo raised his voice to be better heard among the booms of spells, the rattle of bones, and occasional shouts of the enforcers. "That's fine though, right? So long as we can keep them from getting past us. My main concern is, while we're all here, where's Sybilla?"

"Cedric is certainly keeping his eye out for her too, though Blanq is his primary focus. I fear what might happen here if Garret or I leave to go search, and even if we did, two people are unlikely to find her in a city this size." Estella's bow vanished, and in its place appeared a sword with a blade as tall as her. Dashing several steps forward, she slashed at the nearest skeletons, slicing through no fewer than four skulls at once. "All we can do right now is protect the people and trust in Cedric."

Kyo sighed, unable to think of an alternative. Of course protecting the people should be a priority, but he wondered which of their enemies truly posed the biggest threat. An army of skeletons was frightening but weak. The idea Sybilla could cast her spell and turn the defenders into shades without a moment's notice Frightened him far more. But Estella was right. Even if he left now to begin a search, he had no idea where to start, and it might not matter. With her ability to camouflage herself, he could stare right at her and not notice. All he could do was fight the enemy in front of him.

Swords back in his hands, he ran toward the nearest skeleton and kicked it in the ribs, sending it to the ground then stabbing through its brittle skull. Like before, the glow in its eyes faded.

"Okay. We can do this." He got into a rhythm of focusing on those that weren't too clumped together, getting them onto the ground, and piercing their skulls. Five, ten, fifteen down out of several thousand. Even if he were to take out his 'fair share', that left so many for him to destroy alone, and he didn't even know if all of

the skeletons had been risen yet. Forget magic stamina—
he doubted he had the physical stamina for that.

"Hurry up Cedric," he muttered.

Kyo turned just in time to raise his swords in
defense, crossing them like an X above his head to stop
another blade from striking him. Pushing the blade
away, he thrust his own through its skull, the skeleton
and rusty blade dropping to the ground.

The impact was weak, but his breath still caught
in his throat at realizing that some of the undead did
wield weapons after all, even if sloppily.

A weak mage or non-magic user could easily
have been killed by one of these. Even more reason to
keep these things as far from the people as possible. As
the minutes ticked by, the closer the defenders were
pushed toward the city limits. Kyo spared a second to
wipe the sweat from his face with his shirt then returned
to battle. For every skeleton he struck down, he found
himself having to take several steps backward before
attacking another as they grouped closer together. If he
wasn't careful several could bring him to the ground.

To his left, several skeletons leaked through the
defensive line. Kyo ran toward them, jumping and
landing upon two before destroying the skulls, then used
the back of his blade to knock another off its spine,
crushing it under his boot. He glanced back to where
he'd been a moment ago, finding the same situation.
And not only around him. While Estella held the line
well, the enforcers struggled. There simply weren't
enough defenders.

As he ran back to his original spot, someone else
had the same idea. A woman with sun-kissed skin in a
white sundress dashed at a skeleton and swung a shovel
into its ribs, sending it to the ground.

"You shouldn't be here— this is too dangerous."
Kyo cringed a bit at how his words mirrored Estella's.

"I am not afraid of some moving bones, nah!" the woman cried out, arching her shovel down, crushing the skeleton's ribs. "I don't know what's happening, but I will defend my home and my family. Besides, you're no enforcer. If you can fight, so can I."

Kyo dashed into a skeleton, ramming it with his shoulder, then stabbed its skull after it fell. No point in pulling out the temporary enforcer badge. "Fair enough, just be careful. Watch your back. And aim for the head so they don't get back up."

"Noted. And don't worry, I wasn't the only one who decided to come and help, nah." The woman brought her shovel down, splitting an undead's skull, then brushed some of her long, raven hair from her face before rushing to attack another.

Citizens emerged from between the buildings, some wielding weapons, others with spells ready in their hands, whether a glowing light or one of the more common elements. Old, young, though thankfully no children, and though they were only a small fraction of those who fled, seeing the extra help brought a smile to Kyo's lips and a sigh of relief. He wondered if Krysta had this same experience in Calmarock when its people dealt with the shade.

A slow old man with wrinkles covering every bit of his face slammed his cane into the ground. Sand and dust came out in little bursts in a line toward the undead. Then from within their ranks, jagged spikes of rock ruptured from below. Some skeletons were raised off the ground, pointy rocks weaving through the gaps in their bones. Others were broken apart, though the bones reconnected seconds later.

"Destroy the skulls, and they will no longer reform," Estella said in a loud, booming voice that echoed across the battlefield.

With a confident grin, Kyo resumed his pattern of getting skeletons onto the ground and stabbing them through their skulls. Another wielding a sword approached the woman with the shovel, but its slow, sloppy movements gave her more than enough of an opening to take it out first.

The battle raged on, shadows stretching further along the ground, showing the passage of time. Skeletons stumbled over their fallen brethren, becoming easy prey for anyone with a weapon to dispatch them. Kyo hadn't noticed a single one making it through the line and into the city. He hoped Cedric would find Blanq and put an end to this. With additional defenders, some could take breaks to regain their strength, allowing others to fight in the meantime. Though their contributions couldn't be missed for long.

Soaked in sweat from the desert sun, Kyo took an orb of water a man had formed with a spell and drank it down. The mage didn't fight, doing his best to stay out of danger while passing out water to any who could spare a few seconds. Gripping the hilts of his swords tight, Kyo marched to rejoin the fight again but paused as a rumbling assaulted his ears.

The bones of fallen skeletons shook and shifted then rose into the air. Though no one could stop fighting without risk of being hurt, everyone's attention had been drawn to the spectacle before them. The bones came together and fused, built on top of each other to form a monstrosity like he'd never seen before.

At least two stories tall, this new creature stood on four thick legs like a beast, had a wide, human-like torso with arms, and three large skulls atop its head. And down the line, similar creatures took form and marched toward the city.

Chapter 27

Blanq's grotesque creation stomped forward, Kyo and those around him scattering to avoid being crushed. The woman to his right gripped her shovel tight, holding it close to her chest as she backed away like a saber with its tail between its legs. For a moment, Kyo couldn't move. Why couldn't it have stayed human-sized skeletons he could knock down with a single kick? Down the line from the cliffs overlooking the city to the sea, there were about a dozen of these creatures, all with varying extremities—numerous limbs, whipping tails, one even with wings of bone.

"Don't be afraid! Stand strong, protect your city and the people you love. They're counting on you!" Estella's voice echoed again and carried with the wind.

As everyone continued to backpedal, a massive hammer, glowing purple like her other spells, formed and floated in the air. Though she held nothing in her hands, she mimed a heavy swing, and the hammer followed her movements, striking the giant hard and sending it toppling onto the dirt.

Without thinking, Kyo rushed forward and leaped atop its clavicle, thrusting his blades at one of its three heads. He couldn't so much as crack the thick bone. Kyo crouched, gripping the bone he stood upon as it shook beneath him, attempting to right itself. Dismissing his swords, Kyo opened his palm and formed the wind drill he'd been practicing, thrusting it into the side of a skull.

He grunted as he pushed with all the strength that arm could muster while the other hand gripped the space between eye sockets for support. A deep crack formed before the spell vanished.

Another failure, but it'd be enough. His sword appeared again, and he stabbed through the crack, easily breaking through.

The blue glow within the eye sockets faded, and the skull went limp.

Kyo jumped and landed on the ground as the creature stood. "One down, two to go."

Cheers rang out for his and Estella's joint effort, though all the while the smaller skeletons had not ceased their advance. Some were entering the city proper, and if pushed back into the streets, those fighting would be separated by the buildings. They had to keep that from happening.

The two remaining skulls turned, as if focused on Kyo specifically. But were they? So far, he hadn't seen any undead—skeletal or otherwise—show specific attention to anyone other than whoever was nearest to them. The giant before him seemed almost angry at what he'd done. Angry…or at least interested.

Turning toward the city, Kyo ran a few steps into a road and worked to take out several undead that had broken through the line. They were easy enough to dispatch, and from the desert, a man wielded a stream of water like a whip, sending limbs and skulls flying and rolling onto the ground. Kyo took the chance to stab or stomp any skulls he came across on his way back.

A woman shrieked as the monstrous skeleton gripped her in its hand. She beat a finger with her shovel to no effect. The creature raised its arm up and back, like it planned to throw her across the city.

"Dammit!" Kyo crouched, ready to leap to her aid.

Before the giant's motion could complete, a huge purple javelin pierced the creature's center skull through an eye socket and out the back. The loss of another head caused it to stumble, and Kyo dove away before it crushed him. Its grip loosened, and the woman screamed as she fell. He scrambled to his feet, every muscle clenched as he watched her near the ground, but before he could make a move, a pillar of water rose from beneath her, softening the fall. It shrank until she could safely step onto solid ground.

"Nice catch," Kyo said before thrusting through the skull of a skeleton nearly on top of them.

"Save the thanks for later. Watch your back," the man replied, shooting a jet of water past Kyo's head to knock down another undead.

Though their section did a good job of keeping the skeletons out of the city, others weren't so lucky. To the north, enforcers and citizens alike fought hard with spells and weapons, but they didn't have an Aurora with them to help deal with the giants. Others ran away as it approached.

To Estella's credit, another javelin shattered the final skull, causing the massive skeleton to drop where it stood. Before it even slumped forward, she ran toward the north, Kyo assumed to help deal with another.

"All right, we only have to worry about the little ones now," the man using water spells cried out. He shot bursts of water at the oncoming horde, a few lucky and knocking skulls off bodies, though most did little more than send them tumbling backward, only for them to rise again seconds later.

The woman in the sundress took the opportunity to grab her shovel again and continue her assault. Others rallied as well, pushing forward, their morale boosted by the defeat of the giant, demonstrated by their roars and cheers as they struck down their enemies. If only one could spare a moment to blast Kyo with some water, he'd appreciate it. Already drenched in sweat, he wouldn't look any different.

Once again, bones shifted and swirled across the ground, fused, then rose into the air.

"Oh, please no," Kyo muttered. But he knew what it meant.

The bones shaped into new skulls, their eyes glowing and the giant rising to its feet once more.

"Of course she can. Dammit Blanq!" Kyo shouted in frustration, gripping the hilt of his blades so tight his knuckles turned white.

The trio of skulls shifted, once again looking directly at Kyo. It couldn't be a coincidence. Could Blanq be watching the battle through the giant's eyes? After all he'd seen her do, he had no reason to doubt she could.

He pointed his sword at the one towering over him. "We're not going to let you get your way, got it?"

In response, the giant raised its fist into the air then swung it down hard. The impact sent Kyo and several others tumbling backward across the sand.

"You know, you're a lot more temperamental while hiding behind your undead. What happened to that calm girl I met in Aquarin, huh?" Kyo jumped onto the nearest rooftop closest to the desert to be closer to eye level with the creature. If he could keep it — or her — focused on him, then the others could deal with the smaller skeletons. Even as he thought this, he noticed more leaking into the city streets, and the oncoming horde grew thicker with their number. There weren't enough people fighting to hold them back.

Kyo kept his grip tight on the hilts, knowing if he didn't, he'd be trembling while staring down such an enormous enemy. Though nothing could stop his breathing from coming out shaky. He didn't know how much his magic would protect him if that huge fist came crashing down on him.

The giant reared its hand back then swung, attempting to swipe Kyo clean off the roof. Its large size meant slower speed, allowing him to easily jump over its hand with help from wind from his feet.

As soon as he landed, Kyo leaped from the roof onto the creature's collarbone. When it reached for him, he slipped through a gap between two skulls, and the hand stopped. So far, his theory has proved correct. None of the other undead had cared about damaging themselves in their attempts to attack.

This one, and maybe the other giants, had some intellect behind them.

With his eyes fixed on the giant hand, Kyo carefully slipped back between the skulls and peered into one of the glowing eyes.

"You're actually there, aren't you? Watching through this thing? No point in hiding it now." After a few seconds pause, the skull gave a slow nod. "Well, let me make this clear. I know Sybilla wants to turn people into shades and you want more undead. We're not going to let either of those things happen. You've done far more than enough damage on Kattelink Island, and too many people have lost their lives because of you."

His teeth clenched and his eyes narrowed. Confronting her this way allowed his pent-up anger to start flowing out.

"You're not special, and people who do the things you do don't get their way because you feel like it. Like my parents would have, I'll stand here with everyone else and not stop until you've run out of magic. Then we'll hunt you down. There's no getting out of this. And when it's done, I'll take Alden back." He slammed his fist against the hard bone between the eye sockets. "I lost my parents just like you, but you don't see me trying to kill everyone. Maybe you'll have time to think things over in Spellnix Hold."

Out of the corner of his eye, he noticed the giant's fingers too late. They gripped him tight, lifting him into the air. He struggled to break from its boney grip, but his arms were pinned tight to his sides. A few mages had turned their attention and spells to the giant. Though it shook and stumbled, its grip didn't loosen. It fixed its glowing blue eyes on him and stared for a few seconds.

The giant reared its arm back and threw Kyo far across the battle and beyond it toward the north. Kyo screamed, dismissing his swords, limbs flailing as he flew parallel to the city and the cliff overlooking it. Air rushed against his face, and tears streamed from the corners of his eyes—he'd never traveled so fast before.

He thrust his arms in front of him, blasting wind from his palms, hoping to slow himself down.

"Come on, come on," he muttered.

His speed declined but not enough. He hit the ground hard, pain rippling through his left side, bouncing across the dirt and rolling until he came to a stop.

For a minute, he didn't move. For what it was worth, he could feel his limbs, relieving him of the worry the impact could have caused some immediate and severe damage. Forcing himself to sit up, he checked his arms and legs more thoroughly. A few scrapes, bruises, and droplets of blood, but his magic had done its natural job in protecting him. His clothes were coated in dirt with a few tears. Attempting to brush some off his shirt sent a puff of dust into his face, drawing a few coughs from him.

The sounds of battle were faint. Those participating looked like insects. How had that thing found the strength to throw him so far? He rose to his feet, brushing some dirt off his shorts, then stretched his limbs to work out the aches as best he could. "Dammit, I hope Cedric gives her a good beatdown when he finds her."

A voice echoed in the air.

He had to strain his ears to hear it, but he'd heard the words before.

"Altruist Guardian, I seek thine aid. In these darkest of times, when all hope fades. To protect the life which thine hath laid. In this time of need, I call you by name. Tutelvus!" A bright light shimmered against the orange sky to the west atop the cliff overlooking the city. It could have been another summoner, but it sounded like a young girl.

Roland had to be with Rosette and, if he had to guess, Marsh and Krysta too. If they weren't taking part in the battle against Blanq's forces, then that left one possibility. After repeating the point of avoiding it, they must have been fighting with Sybilla. Kyo glanced between the two battles.

Abandoning either group could be devastating, but when he thought of his friends beaten—their bodies strewn across the ground, lifeless—a sharp pain struck his chest. They hadn't known each other long, but he couldn't bear the idea of discovering they'd been killed. The thought alone made him want to wretch. His body grew cold as the image refused to leave, Sybilla standing above their broken bodies as if his mind were trying to convince him which course of action to take.

How would his parents have handled this? The people always came first to the Aurora. Above anything else, they had to be protected. Yet he couldn't bring himself to take a single step in the direction of Oasis. Asking what his parents would do had always helped him make good decisions, the right decisions. This time, he wanted to do anything but that.

'Being inspired by them is great and all, but don't try so hard to be like them that you stop being you.' Roland's

words repeated in his mind, each time pushing the idea of rejoining the fight against the undead away.

Kyo already knew what he wanted to do. All that remained was to let himself have it.

Besides, stopping Sybilla was as important, if not more so, as stopping Blanq. Even that reasoning came second ahead of wanting to protect the others. Eyes focused on where he'd seen the light from Rosette's summoning, he ran with all his might.

Nobody could save everyone, but at the very least, he'd protect them.

Chapter 28

Multiple indistinguishable shapes leaped around in the distance as Kyo ran toward the conflict. Flame burst to life every few seconds, and the shimmer of a barrier vanished seconds after appearing. A cloud of green gas swirled into existence, sending all but one scattering. He could make out the red and black of Sybilla's dress and didn't let her out of his sight. Wind pushed at his back with such force he leaped more than ran, desperate to make every second count.

Sybilla had her back to him, her attention on the other four.

Kyo launched himself forward, summoning his swords as he skidded to a halt at her side and slashed across her abdomen. Her eyes widened, her breath catching. The swords vanished, wind building around his hands as he thrust them against her, launching her into the air and tumbling across the ground. She righted herself mid-tumble, dragging her feet and hands across the dirt. A cloud of dust kicked up as she stopped right before tumbling off the edge of the cliff and down into the city.

"You little brat!" Sybilla said, rubbing where the blades had slashed against her skin. Two red lines gleamed from beneath the gash in her dress, though they were too faint to be fresh blood but aggravation of the skin.

"Yay! Kyo's okay," Rosette cried, thrusting her fists into the air. Beside her on the ground, barely reaching her knees, sat what looked like a semi-transparent dodecahedron with eyes. Could that thing actually be an Altruist?

Kyo glanced between his four friends. Sweaty, a bruise here, a cut there, and plenty of dirt on their clothes. Blood soaked much of Krysta's left sleeve. Even Rosette had a few small, bloodied abrasions on her legs and arms.

"Nice of you to join us, kid. Though, it may have been in your best interest to stay away," Roland said, his gaze falling to Sybilla.

"Yeah, well, I got tired of playing with Blanq's puppets, so I figured I'd look for something else to do." Kyo approached them, not taking his eyes off Sybilla. "I thought you weren't going to let Rosette get involved again."

Roland grumbled. "When she focuses her magic into her legs, she's too fast for me to catch."

"Aw look, the gang's all here. Do you really think your presence will make a difference?" Sybilla asked, tilting her head, her neck releasing a slight crack.

"I wouldn't act so high and mighty right now," Kyo said.

Krysta stared down the cliff and into the distance at the countless dots littering the desert. Flashes of spells streaked across the battlefield. "How is it down there?"

"Manageable, I guess. It's a matter of buying time until Cedric—" When Kyo noticed Sybilla staring down at the city with her hand raised, he thrust his own forward, hitting her with enough air to make her stumble forward. She turned around and glared at him. "I'll tell you later. What happened to avoiding her?"

Marsh narrowed his eyes at Sybilla. "After we regrouped, we ran into her near the chapel. When she took off, what choice did we have but to follow? We did not know where to find any of the Aurora."

"So, Little Miss Crazy, you were able to turn people in Aquarin into shades and figured you'd do the same here. That about sum it up?" Kyo asked.

Sybilla traced her finger over the lines Kyo created on her side, examined it, then shrugged. "Incorrect, if only due to a technicality. I can't actually turn people into shades. It's like I told you before, I have nothing to do with causing this corruption. However, as a rather gifted alteration mage"—she bowed low then stood upright again—"I did figure out how to make others more susceptible to it. I have to admit it worked better than I thought it would." She turned her eyes to the battle in the distance, and a grin crept over her lips. "Blanq did a good job keeping them distracted. It's a bit much, but I think I can manage."

So, their theory was correct after all.

"Yeah, we're not going to let that happen." Kyo exhaled hard, hoping he kept the wavering from his voice. Seeing her in person again made his body tremble more than the giant skeletons. Could they last long enough to have Cedric find Blanq then have any of the Aurora come and take over this fight?

Sybilla bared her teeth. "Oh? You'll stand together with your friends and stop the big bad mage? Put it all on the line? You really do disgust me. Bringing back distasteful memories." She visibly shook, her face swapping between utter rage and a maniacal grin. "I don't think playing with you will be fun anymore, so I'll gladly put an end to your miserable lives."

"Oh, yeah? You might find it harder without that precious accrue stone of yours." Kyo looked at his friends. "There's no way Blanq could do all of that without the stone and all that magic from the Leviathan."

"You saw my handiwork? I'm flattered," Sybilla said, a hand gently resting on her chest. A grin stretched across her lips, as if she had trouble containing her glee. "But once again, I must prove you wrong."

She reached into the pouch at her side, and when she removed her hand, her fingers tightly gripped the accrue stone.

Kyo's eyes widened, unable to look away from the stone and the energies swirling within. Seeing it was enough to put the others on guard, spells building in their hands, or taking a step backward.

"There's no way." Kyo stared down the cliff at the massive army of skeletons, all moving, reforming, and fusing into larger monstrosities. "There's no way Blanq could be powerful enough to do all that on her own. You're bluffing! It has to be a fake."

"Oh, it's real." Sybilla placed her free hand above it, allowing the magical energy to seep from it, swirl around her fingers, then return to the stone. "The one we took from Mistwell needed magic, so we drained it from whatever suckers we could. But it didn't amount to much, even in Calmarock. Not until luck granted us that Leviathan. Your mistake was assuming we didn't already have a stone before then." She slipped the stone back into the pouch. "Not that I need it to take care of you."

A maelstrom raged in Kyo's mind, running through all the pieces of this situation, trying to make sense of it. He gulped hard, his body racked with chills. "But the stones are protected by enchantments and other spells, right? That's why you need someone like Alden."

"So many assumptions. He helped us get that first stone too. Months ago. Though, he probably told you he had a job to attend to somewhere far away."

Sybilla's chest shook from trying to suppress her giggles. "You should see your face right now."

"So, he knew about you for months and didn't say anything to anyone?" Krysta asked.

Kyo dared glance her way as she glared daggers at him. "He didn't have a choice. Sybilla would have done to Mistwell what she did to Calmarock if he tried anything."

"Did he even try? Wasn't he your parents' best friend? Surely, he knew of a way to find the Aurora and warn them," Krysta shouted, clenching her fists.

Sybilla burst out laughing, wrapping her arms around her stomach, bent forward. "Please, please, stop. I can't take it. Seeing you two like this is just so wonderful. It serves you better than trying to play hero, as if you're such great and amazing people."

"We're a lot better people than you. You're terrible," Rosette yelled. The creature by her feet chirped and wobbled.

Raising both hands to her lips, Sybilla kissed the back of the two golden rings she wore. "We will not fall without putting up the fight of our lives. No surrender. Do what it takes to survive." She lowered her hands, clenching them into fists. "You think you're so great? You're nothing but monsters. Monsters! Just like everyone else—deceptive, vile, selfish creatures!"

"That's a load of crap! I was down there," Kyo said, pointing to the battle below. "People are scared but are still standing up to protect themselves and each other. They're putting their lives on the line to help one another."

"For their own selfish gain. To make themselves feel good and to fight away any guilt that may come from doing nothing. They don't care about the lives of others. This is why you make me so sick. You're just like I used to be," Sybilla shouted. She raised her hands above her head, green toxic gas swirling around them.

When she thrust her hands forward, the gas tore through the air.

Kyo shoved his own hands forward and dug his feet into the ground, blasting wind at the oncoming miasma. The others huddled behind and pushed against him as the gas forced him to slide back across the dirt. He grunted, arms trembling as he strained to keep the cloud of death from reaching them. If this kept up for too long, he would drain every last bit of magic he had holding back this single spell.

"I had my group, just like you. There were four of us, and we actually enjoyed using our magic to help others," Sybilla shouted over the roar of the spells. "We came across a small town, constantly besieged by a group who blackmailed them for anything they wanted. So, we helped them. We stayed for months, fighting them back each and every time they tried something, putting our lives on the line for them time and again."

Kyo gasped as the gas vanished, putting an end to his own spell, to see Sybilla building up another.

"Those. Miserable. Wretches," Sybilla cried, thrusting her hand forward again.

This time she released a thick white mist. As it traveled across the ground, even the dirt and rock condensed, dried, and withered away into dust. A barrier encircled them and closed at the top, creating a dome. The shield vibrated as the white mist slammed into it.

"Thanks, Tutelvus," Rosette said, picking up the Altruist in her arms.

Sybilla screamed, her right hand taking on a metallic sheen ending in a sharp point at the fingertips. She thrust her new claws into the barrier repeatedly, creating small cracks. "Those people…they struck a deal with the bandits. If they handed us over, they'd leave the town alone forever. They actually did it, after all we'd done for them!"

Each strike widened the cracks. Marsh placed his hands against the barrier, attempting to strengthen it with his own magic while Roland stepped forward, putting himself between Sybilla and the rest of them. Kyo couldn't look away from Sybilla, her grin wide and wild, messy hair clinging to her face, which she pushed against the barrier.

She was the image of utter madness.

Kyo's whole body trembled as he imagined how she would slice deep into them with those claws or force her withering gas down their throats.

"They tricked us. We were their heroes, their friends, and they sacrificed us!" More shouts, each sounding as though they'd tear her voice apart. Both hands sought to claw and smash through the barrier. "Right there in the middle of town, those people watched as my friends were killed, one by one."

Tears streamed down Sybilla's face, dripping onto the withered dirt.

"I had to watch as they. Executed. My. Husband!" she screeched as the barrier shattered, sparkles of what remained raining down upon them.

Kyo crouched, gripping the hilts of his swords tight. Roland thrust his polearm forward, a blast of raw magical energy shooting into Sybilla's stomach. The force pushed her back but not enough. She leaped for him, wrapping her metallic hands around his throat and squeezing. Krysta grabbed one of Sybilla's arms, icing the skin over. Sybilla cringed but wouldn't release her grip on Roland, whose eyes rolled back in his head.

Rosette reared her fist back and punched Sybilla in the ribs, sending her tumbling to the ground. Roland collapsed, gasping for air while Rosette knelt by his side.

Panting heavily and hunched over, Sybilla pointed to the battle going on in the distance. "That is the true nature of humanity. Selfish, greedy monsters. So why not help this corruption along and let them all become on the outside what they truly are on the inside."

She pulled the accrue stone from her pouch. Magical energy seeped from it, swirling in the air and wrapping around her hand.

"Oasis will be the first of many," she said.

Kyo ran toward her, building a spell in his right hand. The air circulated then condensed, kicking up dirt all around him. "Marsh, use that shadow spell!"

Of all the times this spell had turned into nothing but a dud, this couldn't be one of them. If he got it right once in his entire life, let it be here, for the sake of his friends and everyone in the city.

The circulating air altered its shape into that of a drill rotating in the palm of his hand.

Sybilla extended her hand toward him. Then everything went black. Kyo couldn't see anything through the blanket of darkness. For all he knew, he'd run right off the cliff. But this was the best chance he'd have.

"Kyo! Right, twenty degrees," Marsh shouted.

Sybilla must have shifted her position. Twenty degrees, how much of a correction did that require? Kyo didn't suck at math but needing to do this on the spot, all he could do was estimate. He made what he assumed to be a proper adjustment then launched himself forward with wind from his feet, in case Sybilla still planned to cast a spell.

Kyo's air drill came into contact with something.

The second it did, the shadows vanished. His spell pushed against Sybilla's chest, and while it rotated and dug against her with great force, it couldn't so much as break the skin.

She grinned and puffed out her chest, as if challenging him to keep trying. He followed the trail of magical energy swirling around her back to the stone. Not knowing how it worked, he threw caution to the wind and grabbed it with his free hand. To his surprise, pulling magic from it came as easily as doing so from his own body, as if it belonged to him.

Sybilla tried to pull the stone away, but he gripped it tight.

"Get off! This isn't yours," she cried.

Every bit of magic he pulled from the stone, he redistributed into his spell. Sybilla grunted, face contorting in pain. Through the hole in her dress, he could see her skin attempting to turn into rock but couldn't cover the spot where his spell pushed. Then she tried metal with the same result, the magic he poured into the spell at least matching her own.

With a loud yell, he pushed the wind drill as hard as he could against her chest.

It tore at the skin, droplets of blood spilling out and launching into the air. The spell condensed, like someone pressing a balloon together, then exploded with all the force pushing out from his hand.

Sybilla flew through the air like a ragdoll and hit the ground hard. Her body bounced several times on the hard dirt, rolling, then stopped.

Kyo fell to his knees, hands on the ground, panting hard. He clenched his eyes shut for a few seconds, trying to stop his body from shaking. Though his hand trembled, he smiled. He'd hoped to send her tumbling off the cliff and crashing to the ground far below, but he'd settle for unconsciousness.

"Kyo!" Marsh rushed to his side with the others behind him, Roland rubbing at his throat.

"Good job," Kyo said with a weak smile.

"That was impressive. No wonder you have been working on that spell. How do you feel?" Marsh asked.

Kyo wobbled as he stood, and Roland offered him an arm to steady himself, which he gladly took.

"Like crap, honestly. All that power from the accrue stone…it was intense. It didn't feel any different from pulling magic out of my own body though." For the first time, he noticed a dark red burn mark across Marsh's forehead. "How do *you* feel? That burn looks nasty."

Marsh grazed his fingers across it, cringing as he did. "I will deal with it shortly. For now, I can bear it."

"Where is the accrue stone?" Krysta asked.

Kyo stared at his hand. "I tried to keep a grip on it when she went flying, but I couldn't. It should be around here somewhere."

After a few seconds of examining the area, Marsh pointed. "There."

The accrue stone lay in the dirt, a few short steps from Sybilla's unmoving body.

Kyo took a deep breath then trudged forward. "Yeah, I got it. One of you should head down and get Estella or Garret. With their flashy spells, they shouldn't be hard to find."

Sybilla leaped to her feet, making a dash for the stone. Kyo's body tensed as he dove for it, but she snatched it from the ground first then stomped on the back of his head, digging his face into the dirt.

"Kyo!" Krysta shouted.

"You sure are full of yourself, aren't you? Daring to touch *my* accrue stone? To use *my* magic?" She kicked his forehead, and pain vibrated through his head from the steel sole. Blood trickled down his forehead and into his eyes. He held his head tight with both hands and rolled onto his back, crying out.

Sybilla leaned down to grab Kyo by the throat. "This must be déjà vu for you, isn't it? Except this time, Blanq's not here to stop me from draining you dry."

He kicked his feet, grabbed her wrist, and tried to pull her away. "He'd never…agree to…get the stones…if you…kill me."

"I'm willing to take that risk." Sybilla tightened her grip, not allowing a bit of air to reach his lungs. "Now, give back what you stole."

Thrashing wildly, he pulled at her to allow even a single breath through, but he couldn't. His vision began to fade. Magical energy flowed through his body. It felt similar to when he cast a spell, except it traveled to his throat and then down Sybilla's arm.

Chapter 29

With every second that passed, it took more effort for Kyo to move his limbs. His grip around her wrist loosened, and he could do no more than lie there as the world faded away. An emptiness grew within him, like a well being drained. His heart pounded as if trying to escape, knowing he didn't have enough magic left to protect him from a fatal blow. As darkness seeped into his vision, a bright light fought it back.

Sybilla's hand loosened, and he gasped desperately for air.

Growling, she changed her hand to metal again, thrusting her sharpened fingers for Kyo's face, but they struck a barrier coating his body.

She looked up as Rosette's tiny fist punched her, sending her tumbling across the ground.

Marsh couldn't create a barrier like this as far as Kyo knew—it had to be Tutelvus's. The barrier faded. Kyo tried to stand, but his body wobbled from the lack of magic. Last time, it had taken well over a day for his strength to recover. But he only had seconds before he'd have to defend himself again. Sybilla already rose to her feet. With hardly the strength to stand, he crawled backward, desperate for as much distance from her as possible.

"You all right, kid?" Roland asked, hoisting Kyo to his feet.

The world spun for a second before righting itself.

"I'm alive. I can't really say more than that." Kyo said in a shaky voice.

"Do you still have magic left?" Marsh asked.

Kyo flexed his fingers, rotated his arms, whatever he could to fight off the fatigue. "A little bit." His gaze fell on Sybilla, who stood upright and turned to face them. "Definitely not enough."

Krysta stepped in front of him. "Then you should stay back while you recover and leave this to us for now. For everyone else, the goal is that accrue stone. Get it away from her any way you can. And do not let her get any spells off."

Sybilla reared her hand back, toxic gas building around it. Krysta thrust both hands forward, waves of flame engulfing Sybilla while Roland jumped into the air, throwing his polearm at her. She smacked the weapon away with her metallic hand and used the other arm to shield herself from the flame.

Landing in a crouch, Roland extended his hand to his side, the polearm vanishing and reappearing. He dashed toward Sybilla, Rosette joining him at his side.

"Launch time, kiddo," he said.

Rosette nodded and jumped, landing on his polearm, which he swung to send her flying forward. Her punch met Sybilla's own metallic fist. Rosette took the brief second of the impact to try to snatch the pouch with the accrue stone, but despite the girl's superior strength, Sybilla sent her to the ground before reaching it.

Marsh's golden rope wrapped around Rosette, pulling her back. "Are you hurt?"

"I'm okay. Punching metal makes my arm vibrate though," Rosette said, shaking her arm.

Sybilla placed her hand on the ground, and white, withering gas spread across the dirt. Krysta countered with her own spell, stomping her foot, a thick sheet of ice spreading out. The second it reached Sybilla, she slipped and fell, sliding toward the edge of the cliff.

She dragged her metal claws into the ice to stop herself and crawled her way back to dry dirt.

"Dammit," Kyo mumbled under his breath.

If he had been fighting with them, he could have blasted her clear off the edge. While he doubted the fall would have killed her, it could have at least injured her or maybe gotten the attention of an Aurora. Instead, he stood alone, holding his breath as he watched the others fight. There had to be something he could do to help.

Looking back, he saw Tutelvus sitting on the ground like a rock. He picked it up, finding it lighter than he expected. The little Altruist trembled in his arms.

"Use up too much magic too?" Kyo asked.

It answered with a weak squeal.

As Sybilla rose to her feet, Marsh created a barrier and pushed it forward, knocking her back onto her butt.

"You're all really getting on my nerves!" she cried out, slamming her fists into the ground several times like a child throwing tantrum.

An idea struck Kyo, and his heart raced with hope. He didn't know if a summoned Altruist would listen to anyone other than its summoner, but it was worth a try.

"Tutelvus, could you make a dome barrier around Sybilla?" Kyo asked.

It squealed, and to his relief, it obeyed. The barrier appeared, too small to allow her to stand.

"Open a gap near Krysta."

Once more, it obeyed.

"Krysta, light her up!"

Before Sybilla could crawl out of the gap, Krysta raised her hands above her head, fire igniting around them, then let it loose in an intense wave into the barrier. Sybilla screamed, and even from this distance, Kyo could see the barrier shaking, both from her attempts to destroy it from within and the intensity of the flame. The others stepped back, Roland tucking Rosette in his trench coat to shield her from the heat.

"Keep that barrier intact as long as you can," Kyo said.

With each passing second, the Altruist trembled more violently but, to its credit, kept the barrier in one piece.

"That's it, you can do it," Kyo encouraged.

A few seconds later, the barrier shattered. As it did, Tutelvus dissolved, the sparkling ashes rising into the air.

Krysta ceased her attack, the others peeking from behind their arms shielding them from the heat. Everyone stared at where Sybilla should have been, but the remaining fire hid her from view. Seconds passed, and though Kyo knew the attack wouldn't put an end to the fight, he clenched his fists, hoping Krysta's attack had done some damage.

"That…was a nice strategy," Sybilla said, rising amongst the flames.

Her body hadn't even taken on a metallic or rocky coating. It didn't need to. In her right hand, she held the accrue stone, draining magic from it and into her body, enough to mitigate any damage Krysta's spell may have caused.

Kyo trembled as he stared hard at the stone. So long as she had it, defeating her was impossible. Their own magic reserves would certainly drain long before the stone's. He stared down the cliff and into the distance, the battle against Blanq's skeletal army still waging. For all he knew, it could take Cedric well into the night to find Blanq and put a stop to that.

They were on their own.

Marsh hurled the golden rope at Sybilla, nearly reaching the accrue stone before she grabbed it with her hand. Toxic gas traveled down the length of the rope and erupted in the cleric's face. The rope vanished, and Marsh coughed and hacked, stumbling backward.

Kyo lumbered toward him. The cleric had his own glowing hands around his throat as he lay on the ground. Krysta ran for Marsh, but Sybilla met her partway. She thrust her fingers into Krysta's stomach.

Krysta hunched over, body shaking and mouth hanging open, but no sound came.

Another thrust of Sybilla's fingers into her back, and Krysta fell to the ground. Finally, a scream released from her throat, her body trembling.

"Krysta!" Kyo cried out.

Sybilla dealt devastating blows, and Kyo couldn't do anything about it. Even so, he tensed his leg muscles in preparation to run to her defense. Before he could act, Roland dashed forward and thrust his polearm against Sybilla's side.

It didn't even break her skin. She grabbed his weapon and kicked him in the chest. While he was dazed, she slashed him across the face with her metallic hands, blood immediately seeping from the wound. Another slash across the chest then his back. He fell to his knees, glaring up at her. Kyo's stomach clenched as blood stained Roland's coat.

Before Sybilla could deliver another blow, Rosette kicked her leg from behind, forcing her to one knee. The young girl reared her fist back for a punch, but Sybilla backhanded her in the face then grabbed her head and slammed it hard into the ground. Rosette pushed against the dirt, fighting against her.

"You summoners really are something else," she growled.

Roland raised his weapon but froze when Sybilla brought Rosette in front of her like a shield. Sybilla threw Rosette into Roland, who caught her in his arms. Altering her arm from metallic to heavy stone, Sybilla brought it down hard upon both of them several times. Roland wrapped his arms around Rosette, shielding her with his body.

Kyo reached Marsh, who struggled to breathe and focus his magic to not succumb to the poison.

"Come on. Keep at it. You can get rid of the poison, no problem." Kyo certainly hoped that would be the case. Sybilla's vicious attack made him cringe and curse under his breath. He could almost feel her metallic claw tear through his gut in his weakened state.

Sybilla tore Rosette from Roland's arms by the collar of her sundress and carried her toward the edge of the cliff. "You may have a lot of magic, little girl, but not enough. Oh, don't worry. I'm not going to toss you over the edge or anything. No, all five of you tried so hard to stop me from revealing the true faces of those people down there. It's only fitting you be here to watch when it finally happens."

Roland struggled to push himself up but collapsed in a panting heap.

"True faces, my ass!" Kyo called out.

With nothing he could do for Marsh, he dared step closer to Sybilla, a sword appearing in his right hand. His own safety be damned. He wouldn't put more than a few steps between himself and Marsh, but if he had to fight again, he'd rather keep it away from him.

"Don't give us that crap," Kyo continued. "You had a bad experience with a bunch of people desperate for safety, so suddenly everyone in the world is some horrible person? I'll admit what they did was awful, but that doesn't reflect on everyone else."

Sybilla turned to him, glaring daggers through the sweaty hair matted to her face. "What would a brat like you possibly know about it?"

Kyo pointed to the battle down below, shifting his gaze between Sybilla and Marsh, who still hacked and choked trying to remove the poison from his lungs. "I know those people are fighting hard, for themselves and each other. And we're trying to stop you from doing something terrible. You think we'd be putting ourselves through all this if we were monsters who didn't care about other people? Just as you said, you used to think the same way."

"Yes, *used* to. Until my eyes were opened. A child like you couldn't possibly know what you're talking about. You've lived secluded in your little island town your entire life, not having a clue about how the world really is." She motioned with a nod toward the battle below. "For every person standing up to fight, how many more are running away, fleeing to protect themselves, sacrificing others for their own safety? I guarantee if no one else was watching, so many of them would push another in the way of those undead so they could escape." For a moment, her scowl shifted into a twisted grin as she dug her fingernails along her right cheek. "Don't try to reason with me. I know what I am. A murderous, vengeful woman who will gladly watch every man, woman, and child turn into raging shades. And I would rather be turned into one of Blanq's blasted undead and be trapped in this miserable world forever before I ever pretend otherwise again!"

Her words echoed into the desert.

Rosette grasped Sybilla's arm, but she thrust her knee into the girl's stomach. Rosette's body went limp, though her eyes remained open.

"Stupid brat." She turned her attention back to Kyo. "And you're forgetting one thing. My husband, who worked so hard to protect those people, who showed me every single day what love and devotion truly meant, and how those people watched silently as he was killed right in the town's public square." Her face contorted, swapping between pure rage and maniacal laughter. "Which is why that town and its people no longer exist. I saw to that, and it was the greatest feeling in the world."

"By your own logic about people all being monsters, doesn't that mean your husband was also a monster and you just hadn't noticed yet?" Kyo asked. As soon as he finished his sentence, he clenched his jaw, wishing he could take it back.

Sybilla's eyes widened as if trying to destroy him without touching him.

"He was perfect!" she screamed, clutching a fist against her chest. "The last perfect person in this world. You know nothing. Nothing. *Nothing!*" A black shroud enveloped her and Rosette. Deep gasps and stuttering giggles escaped her lips. "But that won't matter in a moment. I wonder how many will become shades instantly. One hundred? Five hundred?"

She held the accrue stone up, its magic trailing up her arm as she absorbed it. Extending her arm with her grip firmly on Rosette's dress, Sybilla held her over the cliff, facing the city below.

As her laughter reached a crescendo, Rosette thrust her arm out, sending the accrue stone flying from Sybilla's hand and rolling across the ground.

"You little cretin," Sybilla screeched. "Forget what I said before. I'm sending you to your death right now!"

Roland swung the ax blade of his polearm across Sybilla's back, leaving a deep gash in her skin. She cried out as her body shook and she lost her grip on Rosette. The young girl landed hard and crawled behind Roland, who held the accrue stone in his left hand, magic trailing up his arm and down into his weapon.

"Get back, Rosette!" Roland ordered. She ran to Kyo's side, gripping the hoodie around his waist as Roland faced off against Sybilla.

Kyo sucked in a breath, his entire body clenching. If Roland could keep the stone away from her, there was hope they could get out of this alive.

"Kick her ass," he mumbled mostly to himself, not wanting to cause a distraction.

"Give. That. Back!" Sybilla shrieked, reaching wildly for the stone.

Roland jumped back and swung his polearm again. The spear barely missed her face, but the magical energy that left the tip in an arch did not. It nearly knocked her to the ground, but she caught herself, glaring through disheveled locks of red hair.

"That's mine!" she yelled, her skin turning to stone as she barreled forward.

Roland thrust his weapon into the ground, causing it to shake and break apart. Sybilla stumbled but managed to tackle Roland to the ground. The stone flew from his hand, rolling across the dirt past Kyo's feet.

"Marsh, on your right," Kyo shouted.

Still struggling for each breath, Marsh reached out, wrapping his fingers around the accrue stone and draining magic into himself. With each passing second, his chest heaved more noticeably. Like pulling a struggling worm from a hole in the ground, he raised his hand, and the poison gas left his throat with a loud gasp and dispersed in the air.

"How dare you touch it! Give it back now," Sybilla shouted, attempting to crawl over Roland, who held firmly to her legs.

Marsh kept the stone in one hand and dashed to Krysta, casting a spell to ease the pain that left her shivering. Her body shifted, limbs stretching out, her face still scrunched.

"Kyo was right," Marsh said. "It truly is like drawing on your own magic."

"I've never…felt worse pain…in my life," Krysta gasped. "Like she hit my nerves directly."

Sybilla beat Roland over the head with her stone arm until his grip loosened enough for her to escape. She ran forward, but Krysta was already on her feet. Marsh pulled her behind him then erected a barrier. Sybilla shifted right then left, but the barrier moved with her, blocking her advancement. Thrashing against it with stone hands, then metal, a few small cracks formed, but it held strong.

"Give me that, or I'll make sure your body withers away into nothing," she screamed.

Kyo's eyes remained on the stone. Marsh wouldn't be able to use it for an offensive spell, but with Sybilla's focus more on the stone than whoever held it…

"Marsh, toss it here!" Kyo called.

Shedding any alteration of her body, Sybilla jumped, grabbed the top of the head-high barrier, and leaped over it. Marsh and Krysta ran in opposite directions, and once around the barrier, he threw the stone.

Kyo and Rosette ran for it, but the young girl reached the stone first.

Sybilla completely ignored Marsh, running past him, her skin once again taking on a rocky texture. A ball of white, withering mist appeared in her hand, and she threw it at Rosette, who dove out of the way before it hit the ground, turning the dirt black and decayed.

From a crouch, Rosette launched herself at Sybilla, landing a solid punch that sent cracks spreading across the woman's rocky skin. While Sybilla stumbled, Rosette jumped and kicked down at her chest. Sybilla landed hard, mouth open in a silent cry, shards of rock flying from her body. As Rosette approached her, Sybilla caught the girl's legs within her own and sent her to the ground. Rosette pressed her feet against her chest to keep Sybilla barely out of reach of the stone, holding it above her head.

"Rosette, behind you!" Krysta called.

Rosette tossed the stone back, and Krysta caught it, pulling its magic into herself. Sybilla abandoned Rosette, chasing the stone like she needed it to breathe.

"This is for all the people you killed." Flame erupted from Krysta's hand, fiercer and wilder than ever. "For Calmarock. And especially for Layla!"

Sybilla screamed, running this way and that, trying to escape it.

Kyo raised his arms to shield himself from the heat, but his exposed skin burned even when out of reach. He untied his hoodie from around his waist and used it to protect himself. Through gaps in the flame, Sybilla's skin changed into various forms that might protect her from the fire. Whatever she coated herself with, be it rock or metal, shed off her like a snake's skin. Krysta didn't let up, her flame fighting to rid Sybilla of any protection, while Sybilla fought to maintain it through Krysta's attack.

Toxic gas erupted like geysers from the ground in a trail leading to Krysta. She ran and dove to avoid them. By the time Krysta turned her head, Sybilla was nearly on top of her.

"Krysta, here!" Kyo called.

But her toss went wild as Sybilla tackled her.

Using what little magic he had left, Kyo cast a spell not to blow the stone away but draw it toward him. He caught it and worked to regain the magic he'd lost by pulling it from the stone. Within seconds, he moved more easily, energy flowing through every bit of his body.

"I swear I'll kill you all! Every one of you," Sybilla shrieked.

Krysta wrapped her arms and legs around Sybilla to keep her in place, but the threat of a poison spell to the face forced her to release her grip.

Kyo eyed the cliff then Sybilla, shifting himself so she'd be between him and the city below.

"You're not killing anyone else." With the accrue stone in his left hand, he circulated air above his right palm, forming into his wind drill spell. "In a way, I guess this is like letting anyone you killed get their licks in, huh?"

He let Sybilla get closer, using every spare second he had to absorb as much magic as possible. Then, he launched himself with wind from his feet and thrust his spell into her chest.

This time, he kept the stone out of her reach.

Like before, she tried to coat her skin in stone, but it couldn't cover where his spell made contact. With so much magic behind the wind from his feet, they flew through the air and over the cliff with the city far below. His arm quaked against his own spell as his body tensed to steady himself, while struggling to pull as much magic as he spent. The drill rotated rapidly, squishing against her.

She could do nothing but let her mouth hang open in a silent scream. Kyo swore he saw fear in her wide eyes.

The spell exploded, sending Sybilla hurling toward the ground far below. Kyo fell from a height far above the city's spires with little magic left. Sybilla reached the ground in seconds, crashing through the wall of a building and out the other side. His heart raced as the city grew closer.

Pulling more magic into himself, he slowed his descent with air from his hand and feet. "Come on. You've done this before. Slow down already!"

His heart pounded against his chest. Every bit of magic that he drained went into his spells, leaving almost none remaining in his body to protect it if he landed too hard. His vision blurred, exhaustion catching up to him. If he didn't keep it together for a few more seconds, his body would be a broken heap on someone's roof. Each muscle tensed as he focused on the spells. The air around him calmed, and he slowed to a comfortable pace. Once his feet touched the roof of a home, he collapsed, panting and keeping a firm grip on the stone.

Kyo's body screamed for rest, to lie there, maybe even fall asleep and forget everything. Leave anything else to anyone else.

But a nagging voice in the back of his head wouldn't let him, not yet.

He crawled to the edge of the rooftop and peered over. On the road lay Sybilla, unmoving. Was she faking again? Kyo stared at her as the minutes ticked by and the light in the sky dimmed. And yet she didn't move. Unconscious or dead, he didn't know. He hoped for the latter, but he had his doubts. If she had enough magic left in her, she could have survived.

"Whatever," he mumbled, using the last of his energy to slide the stone into his pouch, then let his eyes close and his consciousness fade.

Chapter 30

A full day had passed since the battle ended, and Kyo couldn't think of any better way to calm his mind than staring up at the sparkling stars in the night sky. Though, even his favorite pastime's effects were limited. Chills ran through his body any time he thought about Blanq's skeletal army and Sybilla. After what they'd done, he'd be glad to never see their faces again.

Any sight would be preferable to the desert, which remained littered with countless bones, but the sky by far held the most appeal to him. If only he were close enough to the sea to hear the waves break, he could close his eyes and feel like he was home.

A muttering of voices came from below. No one had protested when he'd gone to the roof of the chancellor's office. He couldn't stand around waiting for the other chancellors to arrive, so he'd been stargazing for the past two hours or so. While the others had genuine smiles knowing they'd survived, Sybilla and Blanq had been taken into custody, and the people hadn't been turned into shades, he could barely force one on his own lips.

Alden was nowhere to be found, so Kyo couldn't consider this a full victory, at least for himself. Not to mention the annoyance of learning that the others saw the skeletal army fall where they stood ten minutes after their battle with Sybilla ended. The memory of being told still made him pull at his own hair. If Cedric had thought to look for her below the city in the catacombs sooner, they wouldn't have nearly died.

"Kyo, they have arrived," Marsh called from the open window.

Stretching his arms above his head and twisting his back, Kyo cringed as aches racked his body. Estella and other clerics managed to heal their wounds after the battle, but their bodies had to do some of the work themselves. His shoulders throbbed, his ribs stung when he moved certain ways, and he walked carefully to keep the pain in his right leg at bay as he lowered himself to the window and slipped inside.

Aside from his friends, the Aurora remained near the door of the chancellor's office, and the chancellors of Aquarin, Mistwell, and he assumed Calmarock stood beside each other against the far wall. After reflecting on the previous day while on the roof, Kyo released the tension in his body, feeling safer in such company than he had since leaving Mistwell.

"Hey, old man Chancellor," Kyo said. "It's been a while."

Krysta pinched the bridge of her nose and shook her head. "Is it really impossible for you to show respect?"

Chancellor Demaskus chuckled, stroking his long white beard. "I see you haven't changed much. But I'm glad to see you're still in one piece," he said in his slightly strained voice. Stepping forward, he slapped Kyo upside the head. "Reckless as you may be, at least you've come out of this alive."

"Hey, take it easy. Not like I asked for any of this." Kyo rubbed his head and took a step back. He briefly eyed Marsh, who kept his eyes on the floor.

"None of us asked for this." Chancellor Bisca remained behind her desk, pacing. "And far too many lives were lost before it finally came to an end, thanks primarily to your efforts. The eight of you have done more for us and Feracael than I'm sure even you can guess."

Estella nodded. "It is the purpose of the Aurora to protect Feracael in any way we can. I'm only sorry we couldn't have put an end to this sooner."

"But let's be honest. We would have failed if not for the kids over there, yah." Garret smiled like a giddy child. "To think they were able to defeat someone like Sybilla. I wish I were there to see it. You'll have to tell me every detail."

"Don't make them recount what was almost their demise," Estella said sternly, shoving her elbow into Garret's stomach.

"Aquarin Port certainly has your thanks as well. Without your efforts, things could have been far worse." Chancellor Ambers frowned, approaching them with outstretched arms, before being pulled back by Chancellor Demaskus. "You poor dears, dealing with all of that. You're far too young to be involved in such situations."

Krysta chuckled. "What's done is done. I think we can all do with a good rest at this point. And Chancellor Barion, I will speak to my uncle about giving aid to Calmarock as soon as possible."

The middle-aged chancellor bowed his head. "We greatly appreciate it, Your Highness. Losing half our population in one fell swoop, not a single citizen escaped untouched. They are still coming to grips with the reality of the situation. The effects have sent ripples through every facet of our beloved home."

"Aquarin will give what help we can as well." Chancellor Ambers put her arm around Chancellor

Barion. The man showed little emotion, his face neutral, but his body trembled like he held back a flood of tears.

"If I may ask — I know it is a sensitive topic — but how many were lost here in Oasis?" Marsh asked. "And were any clerics lost?"

Kyo frowned. Since becoming a cleric, Oasis had been Marsh's home. He looked to Chancellor Bisca, fearing the worst.

But to his surprise, she smiled. "After such an event, we could hardly expect there to be none. A poor old man's heart couldn't take the sight of the undead, according to his wife. Others were trampled or drowned in the frantic attempt to board ships at the port. It'll take time to gather the bodies and get an accurate count." She shook her head. "However, the miraculous news is that no one seemed to have been killed by Blanq's undead, though we're still working to confirm this."

"None at all? That is truly incredible. But one can't help but wonder how that's even possible," Chancellor Demaskus said.

"My assumption is Blanq's army was intended to be nothing more than a distraction, primarily for us Aurora," Cedric said, his arms crossed over his chest. "They knew the best way to keep us rooted to the spot and away from Sybilla. We couldn't very well abandon the people in danger to go looking for her."

"Not just that." Roland rested a hand on Rosette's back, keeping her close against him. "I figure Blanq never intended to kill anyone in the first place. It would run contrary to their overall goal. Each dead citizen is one less to turn into a shade."

Rosette thrust a fist into her open palm. "They tried to keep everyone from that crazy lady, but we kicked her butt anyway! I don't even care if other people don't like it anymore. I'll keep summoning the Altruists to help people."

A few chuckles rang out from Rosette's innocent view of things. Kyo couldn't help but admire her. So young, yet she seemed to have come out of such a terrible experience unchanged.

"Yeah, who cares what they think?" Kyo said. "I guess you aren't afraid of Sybilla anymore, huh?"

Rosette shook her head. "Nuh uh, I was more angry than scared, so I chased her."

Discussions continued, giving explanations about Sybilla's plan and their use for Alden, who remained missing. Opinions were split about him and whether they considered him a victim or an accomplice, Krysta having been quite vocal about her thoughts. It took a rare glare from Marsh for her to put the topic to rest.

When talks shifted into politics, Chancellor Demaskus interrupted. "I believe we chancellors can take it from here. Why don't you all go and get some rest?"

"Yes, please do," Chancellor Bisca said, wearing a gentle smile. "You will not have to worry about paying for food or board while you are here, so don't let cryst weigh on your minds."

After saying goodbye to the chancellors, they left the office and sauntered toward the inn they'd stayed at the previous evening after the battle, keeping the pace slow so as not to aggravate anyone's lingering pain. The night air was cool and dry, accompanied by an occasional breeze from the sea. Kyo unwrapped his hoodie from around his waist and put it on. Such dramatic shifts in desert temperature would take some getting used to.

"Are you sure it's a good idea not to mention the other accrue stones?" Roland asked.

"The fewer people who know about them, the better. That includes chancellors. Power like that should be left out of everyone's hands," Cedric said.

"By the way, you could have found Blanq a little faster. Having to deal with Sybilla all by ourselves was insane." Kyo shoved his hands into his pockets, grumbling.

"Come on, I'm sure he did the best he could. He had to search a whole city!" Rosette frowned at Kyo and extended her arms as if to show off the size.

"You all managed to pull it off though, yah?" Garret slapped Kyo's back. "All's well that ends well."

Kyo wanted to lecture them, tell them it could have ended sooner if they'd left the people to the enforcers long enough to handle Sybilla on their own. But he knew more than anyone that the Aurora wouldn't do that.

"Blanq gave up quite easily and didn't put up a fuss when I took her into custody," Cedric said.

Estella shrugged. "Even Sybilla didn't put up much of a fight after she came to, though I suppose she didn't have much magic left to fight with. Either way, off to Spellnix Hold they go. I'm sure not even they would entertain thoughts of escape from a prison on a floating island off the coast of the most dangerous land in the world. How are you holding up, Cedric? You escorted them and came right back. Did you get any sleep?"

"A little. I could use more, honestly. I had a bit of work to do and also spoke to the warden. We want to set up a system where any corrupted people can be brought to Spellnix Hold and be cured. Sybilla, of course, refused to take part. Blanq didn't object though. I'm glad for that, but it creates another complication," Cedric said, sighing.

Krysta raised a brow. "What do you mean?"

"The last thing we want is for Blanq to change her mind. Curing the corrupted must be priority one. But that means our options are extremely limited when it comes to interrogating her on what she was doing with those she raised into undeath and where they might be.

Whether this was a calculated move on her part, I can't say."

"I imagine you would also want information on where they acquired their knowledge. Draining magic, making others more susceptible to the corruption, teleportation…the first two strongly hint they may know the source of the corruption." Marsh stroked his chin. "I would be very interested in how they learned these abilities."

Garret grunted in agreement. "You're right, and we'll be doing our best to get that information from Sybilla at least, yah."

"What of the accrue stones?" Marsh asked.

"For the moment, we're holding on to them, yah. Until we figure out what to do with them. Turns out, destroying them isn't as easy as we hoped." Garret slapped Cedric on the back. "Even this guy couldn't put a dent in them, nah."

They stopped upon reaching the front door of the inn.

"We already have rooms at a different place. Please take good care of yourselves, okay?" Estella said with a smile.

"What are you three going to do now?" Kyo asked.

Garret put his arm around Cedric's shoulders, pulling him closer. "Well, I promised this yolk a dessert or drink of his choice when this was over. I plan on making good on that, yah. I'm ready for something delicious."

Cedric's face was stern, but like before, he didn't argue or pull away.

"Besides that, we need a bit of a break. But not for too long. We need to continue our investigation of the corruption and hopefully find a source or maybe a cure aside from what Blanq can offer." Estella cupped her chin, narrowing her eyes. "We have a few theories but nothing solid. Regardless, you shouldn't concern yourselves with it. You've done more than enough." She approached each of them, embracing them and adding a kiss to the top of Rosette's head. "Keep yourselves safe."

The Aurora continued down the street while Kyo and the others headed inside the inn. They entered a room, Rosette pulling Roland to follow the others instead of entering their separate space. One by one, they found a spot to sit or lie on a bed and relax, a collection of sighs ringing out.

"I forgot to ask, how did the four of you end up together to chase down Sybilla?" Kyo asked.

"Once the people realized what was happening, I made my way to the port to attempt to keep people calm and assist them in boarding ships in an organized manner." Krysta sighed, staring down at the bed she sat on. "It did not go as well as I hoped."

Marsh nodded. "Unfortunately so. The cleric chapel is close to the port, so I was nearby."

"And you remember Rosette and me were already there, where she was *supposed* to stay away from the danger," Roland said in a firm tone, glaring at Rosette, who shrank in on herself.

"I'm sorry. I did get to punch her really hard a few times though. Isn't that good?" Rosette asked, wide eyes glancing up at Roland.

Sighing, Roland pinched the bridge of his nose with one hand and ruffled Rosette's hair with the other. "Yeah, I hate to admit it, but we wouldn't have won if you weren't there, kiddo."

Rosette giggled and leaned into his hand.

"Sybilla purposefully made herself known to us. Her idea of taunting, I suppose. In the end, her hubris is what resulted in her defeat," Marsh said, stifling a yawn.

"Lucky us," Kyo murmured. "You know, *Your Highness*, I'm surprised your uncle didn't come to take you home after all this."

"About that, I've been thinking about it. I'm ready to return home at this point." Krysta pulled her hair tie out, letting her emerald tresses fall free. "The royal guard he sent have arrived in the city, so my escort is already here."

Marsh covered his mouth, stifling a yawn. "Does this mean you have changed your mind about being a princess?"

"Absolutely not. I still have no intention of being told what to do and how to do it every minute of the day. But I do miss my family. I really want to see them." A moment of silence lingered, Krysta shifting uneasily. "You know, a lot has happened. I wouldn't be against you all coming too. You could see all the beauty Alderdeem has to offer, and there is plenty of room in the palace. You would love seeing The Ancient up close."

The famous tree so massive a city had been built around it—that would be a sight to see.

Kyo raised his brow, looking at her from over the pillow he hugged to his chest. "You're actually inviting us to come with you?"

"Yes." Krysta's lips tightened in a thin line. "Even you."

"Really? We get to live in a palace?" Rosette asked, bouncing up and down on the bed.

"Easy, kiddo. We're just visiting. But can't say no to a roof over our heads for a while. So, I don't see why not. It's appreciated." Roland placed a hand on Rosette's shoulder in a fruitless attempt to keep her still.

A smile crept over Krysta's lips. "Well, I could certainly talk to my uncle about finding the two of you a home in Alderdeem. After all you've done and helping me in the process, I think it's quite doable. And we'll make sure you are not mistreated for being a summoner."

"W-wait, really?" Roland asked. "You mean, an actual home?"

Krysta nodded, and Rosette turned to Roland with tears in her eyes.

"We can have a real home we won't have to leave?" She looked between the two then settled on pulling them both in for a close hug. "I can't believe it, this is great," she said, burying her face into Roland's chest. He kept his head low, trying to hide his tears of joy. "When we're at the palace, can I wear a tiara?"

Chuckling, Krysta ruffled Rosette's hair. "Of course. You'd make a great little princess."

Roland embraced Rosette and gently ran his fingers through her hair. "Well…I suppose we can give living in a single place another try. But we'll have to talk about rules and precautions, okay?"

Kyo couldn't help but smile, happy for the two of them. He sincerely hoped they'd be happy in Alderdeem. Having a good relationship with the princess was sure to give them plenty of benefits.

"I guess it's not a bad idea. If I'm being honest, I'm not really ready to head home yet." In truth, home sounded wonderful. But not without Alden. Who knew how long he'd be gone and what might happen to him once he returned. Kyo could use the distraction. "Count me in. I just hope I can stomach that fancy royal food."

Marsh shook his head. "I appreciate the invitation, but I believe I should decline. Even with so few casualties, I feel my place is here in Oasis. Many will seek out clerics for some sort of aid in such a trying time."

"If that's really how you feel, then that's your choice, Marsh," Krysta said. "Of course, if you were looking to become a more skilled cleric and better help the people of Oasis, there's a certain royal guard I have in mind who would make a wonderful teacher for you.

You'd be casting better, more powerful spells in no time."

Marsh fell silent, his eyes darting back and forth. "Well, I could certainly use better training." He glanced out the window. "I suppose they would not miss me if I were gone for a bit longer."

"Then I guess we're all headed to Alderdeem," Roland said.

"Yeah, after we get some sleep. I could sleep for a year and not have enough after all that crap." Kyo reached into his pouch, pulling out the cream to rub on his teeth while Roland and Rosette said good night and left the room.

Kyo turned the lights off and lay in bed next to Marsh, Krysta getting the other to herself.

This felt right, having the four of them close by. He found it amazing how his feelings for them could grow in such a short time. Kyo imagined lying in bed at home with no Alden or anyone around—he'd take his current situation any day, even if it wasn't technically home. Not all families had to be blood. He and Alden didn't share a bloodline after all. So, he supposed staying close to them for a while longer wouldn't be too bad. At least until Alden came back. It could even be fun. If he was honest with himself, he needed them right now, and like a real family, they were here for him.